Lucid

Jenna Boholij

Dreamsphere Books
Winnipeg, Canada

Copyright © 2024 by Jenna Boholij
Cover design copyright © 2024 by Story Perfect Dreamscape

Editor: Margaret Larson
Proofreaders: Sanford Larson

This is a work of fiction. Names, characters, business, places, events, and incidents are either products of the author's imagination or used in a fictitious manner. Any resemblances to actual persons, living or dead, or actual events is purely coincidental.

Published May 2024 by Dreamsphere Books, an imprint of Story Perfect Inc.

Dreamsphere Books
PO Box 51053 Tyndall Park
Winnipeg, Manitoba R2X 3B0
Canada

Visit http://www.dreamspherebooks.com to find out more.

For my Afi, J.T. Arnason.

Lucid

Chapter 1
Thursday, October 1st

It's hard to enjoy your birthday when the person you care most about is dead. Continuing to live, eating red velvet cake, seems disrespectful at best and like a betrayal at worst.

I listen to the cacophony of my friends and family singing happy birthday to me and stare mesmerized at the flames flickering on the "3" and "0" rainbow-colored candles. I concentrate on overcoming thoughts of shoving my face into the burning wax. I can feel the heat emanating off the candles. I close my eyes and pretend it's the warmth of the sun and that I'm somewhere far away from here.

I exhale deeply and blow out the flames in one spirited breath. Just like the big bad wolf.

After everyone leaves, I sit in my worn black leather office chair, power up my laptop and log into the software that True North Airlines uses to manage their flight systems. Being the Cabin Safety Manager offers some perks, which includes high level access to all the operations and reservation systems. I click into the reservation portal and search for passengers on the flight with a one-way ticket, or on the return journey of their round-trip flight. I click again and narrow it to passengers travelling alone.

I print the modified seat map and cut out the tiny seat

numbers. I flip them so that the numbers face down and shuffle them across the desk like a blackjack dealer. I close my eyes and pick up one of the squares of paper, my heart fluttering with anticipation. I turn it over, seat "15D". I smile and close the laptop.

Chapter 2
Friday, October 2nd

White.

Bright white.

I'm alone, sitting cross-legged on an uncomfortable cot in a small room. The mattress springs are pressing into my thighs. The off-white sheets and bedding are thin and cheap, the kind you might find in a budget motel. A shabby quilt is folded neatly at the end of the bed.

The sterility is nostalgic of a hospital, but there aren't any hastily scribbled charts or beeping monitors. No smells of sickness or over-cooked hospital food. No meal trays teeming with unnaturally colored luminescent gelatins, and mounds of congealed potatoes flecked with corn and cheerily referred to as "shepherd's pie".

Fluorescent lights buzz overhead. The air smells institutional, like antiseptic, and it stings my nose when I inhale. The bedside table is made from fiberboard and covered in a wood grain adhesive coating to make it look like real wood. A plastic alarm clock blinks like it's been unplugged and not yet reset. Beside the alarm clock is a photo of my family. I reach for it and run my finger in a serpentine path through the fine layer of dust coating the frame.

There's a leafy green plant in a pot on the floor in the corner of the room. It looks like it's made of rubber. At first glance there is nothing living in this room.

Without warning an ear-splitting, cringe-inducing scream fills the room. I drop the family photo and it smashes against the beige linoleum floor sending shards of glass flying like confetti. I cover my ears with my hands but the screaming seeps through my fingers and drills into my brain like a surgical screw.

Like surfacing from underwater, I regain consciousness and emerge from a hypnopompic state with my heart pounding. I know this term because it's one that my therapist has used. He casually tosses words like this into our conversations like we're teammates and he's passing me a basketball. I nod studiously with an interested expression and feign understanding. In my head I'm trying to commit the words to memory so that I can google them later.

Hypnagogia, he explained, is the transitional state between wakefulness and sleep. It's during this transitional state that people experience lucid thoughts and dreams, and hallucinations. A hypno*pompic* state occurs when waking up from sleep, a hypno*gogic* state occurs when falling asleep. In both states I often find myself in the white room, with a full range of sensory abilities and perception. My own personal limbo.

It's like the movie *Vanilla Sky* with Tom Cruise where he struggles to differentiate between reality, dreams, and nightmares. Except I'm not Tom Cruise, and this doesn't end with me jumping off a building trying to find my way back home. I wish it were that easy.

I pull the down duvet over my head and groan as I hear Jake rustling around and pulling a suit out of the closet. Too many birthday drinks have left me with a throbbing head and a mouth that tastes of regret. Drinking depression has started to set in. Had innocent ducks died for me to enjoy my luxurious duvet or did they just get their feathers plucked and sent on their way? I must investigate cruelty-free bedding options.

From inside the protective warmth of my duvet I can hear Jake moving predictably around the bedroom. He fastens his tie and clips his ornate watch on, the one his company presented to him on his fifth anniversary. Maybe an ironic gesture to remind him of all the time he's given them. The lint roller whirrs softly as he runs it up and down his suit to remove stray black hairs from my cat, Cinder.

Jake is a creature of habit, and I can tell without looking at the clock that it's the ungodly time of 6:53 a.m., because that's the exact time every morning that he kisses me goodbye and leaves for his job as a Financial Analyst in the bustling metropolis of downtown Winnipeg. Right on schedule he pulls back the covers and disrupts my hibernation and deep thoughts about ducks. "Have a good day, Charlotte, enjoy your first day of thirty." He kisses my forehead.

I pretend to be asleep and keep my eyes closed until I hear him walk downstairs and out the front door. My pupils dilate and adjust to the sunlight that is starting to filter in from beneath the blinds. I reach over to the bedside table and preemptively shut off the alarm. I arch my back like a cat and stretch from one end of the bed to the other. I've read that you're supposed to stretch when you first wake up to jumpstart your circulation and get your blood flowing.

I also read that if you dream of falling and hit the ground that in reality you actually die. I suppose no one would be able to confirm if that's true.

I've done a lot of reading into dreams and sleep. Apparently the involuntarily twitch your leg gives after falling into a deep sleep is an evolutionary tactic stemming from when we were cavemen and would sleep in trees or need to wake suddenly to check for predators. The reaction is the brain trying to keep you from falling from the branches, or into a deep sleep, oblivious to danger.

We are hard-wired to survive. Even subconsciously our brains are looking out for us, trying to keep us alive.

I tentatively lower my feet to the floor and shiver as they touch the cold hardwood. I assess my thirty-year old self in the mirror opposite my bed. My long black hair, unruly and witch-like in its natural state, tumbles down my bony, pale shoulders. Legs—still long, waist—still fairly small, boobs—still perky-ish. I yawn and rub the sleep out of my emerald-colored eyes, arguably my best feature. I'm pleased that wrinkles or middle-aged spread haven't appeared overnight.

I know that I'm good-looking in a striking way, rather than traditionally beautiful. My nose and jawline are sharp like the edge of a knife, and I've always thought that my side profile was birdlike, resembling a crane. My skin is the color and texture of cream most of the year except in summer when it takes on the slightest nutmeg pigment. I don't have tattoos, but a long, raw-looking scar runs down the side of my hip, and no amount of wonder cream or oil can seem to diminish it.

Cinder materializes and brushes against my leg, meowing frantically to expedite his breakfast. The bell on his collar jingles like one that you'd find above the entrance at a mom-and-pop convenience store. He stares at me insistently with creepy amber eyes until I relent. There's much to be done, no rest for the wicked.

The cat follows me down the creaking stairs of my hundred-year-old house in suburban Winnipeg. The dated three-story house needed love and I've spent the last few years updating it. I fell for the oak tree-lined streets, lilac bushes, and wild bunnies in a quiet neighborhood. I knew the house was going to be a project, but I believe that you get what you put in, nothing worth having comes easy, and all those kinds of inspirational quotes.

My house has character and I think of it as its own entity. The stained-glass windows sparkle like eyes and the big hearth stone fireplace is the mouth. The air moving through the ducts sounds like a senior citizen with asthma and the floorboards creak like old bones.

Despite my commitment to buying and regularly burning expensive, delicious smelling candles the air is always that of an old house. A stale cardboard smell that's a mixture of aging wood, something metallic, and the ghosts of previous owners. Plants in various stages of life and death are scattered throughout the house sucking in carbon dioxide and spitting out oxygen.

The living room has a large picture window and opens to the dining room and modestly renovated kitchen. I've restored the original hardwood floors throughout the house to their former glory save for a few water spots and scratches. The plaster walls are varying shades of grey and the ceilings feature original crown molding.

My taste is eclectic, so you'll find a refinished 1970s teak and glass coffee table sitting on an IKEA rug. The soft tawny leather couch and loveseat I splurged on from a local furniture place, but the ramshackle bookshelf with the slightly bowed top shelf is from a yard sale. They wanted fifteen dollars but I haggled them down to ten.

The kitchen cabinets are a deep navy which contrasts sharply with the white quartz counter tops. My sister Magnolia, the design guru, insisted that this was a *must*. Off the kitchen the small dining room area is crammed with a slightly too large farmhouse table, another one of Magnolia's *musts*.

I tip Cheerios into a chipped white bowl and the rings of cereal bob around in the milk like tiny life preservers. I serve a can of Fancy Feast to Cinder in a cut crystal bowl just like on the commercials. He ignores my effort and ravenously devours his breakfast, like I imagine a hyena would. I pour myself a strong cup of coffee and inhale it, also like they do on the commercials, trying to resuscitate my sleep and alcohol dulled senses.

This is my favorite time of the day, when I can revel in the silence and stillness of the house. Jake stays over often despite still owning a modern, sparsely decorated condo in trendy Osborne Village, and his presence invades every inch of the house when he's around. He's been hinting at moving in together but I'm holding out for as long as I can. Cinder and I like our space and privacy.

I'm not scared to be alone in my house, even at night. The creaking, moans and groans have become white noise to me. After all, there's nothing left to fear after the worst thing that could happen to you has already happened.

As per tradition, I spend the day after my birthday with my favorite person, my twin sister Cara. I turn onto Route 90 and drive the familiar way out of the city to a small town 150 kilometers north of Winnipeg called Sunshine. The prairies are especially beautiful this time of year. The last remnants of golden wheat shimmer in the sunlight and sway gently in farmers' fields. Puffy clouds drift lazily across the blue sky.

I pass a dilapidated barn, sunken so far into the ground that only the roof is visible. A tree has grown through the center of it and burst out of the roof. Life from death personified. I switch through the radio stations and stop when I hear Journey's *Don't Stop Believing*. I sing along loudly because I am in fact a small-town girl living in a lonely world.

"*Welcome to Sunshine*", exclaims a giant faded blue sign featuring a smiling, beaming cartoon sun with its arms extended. A personal invitation to visit the sleepy little town nestled on the shores of Lake Winnipeg. I turn into town, passing by Milky's, where they serve the best homemade salted caramel ice cream, and by Fare Foods where I would smoke cigarettes with Cara behind the dumpster. I turn right past King Pins, where I hit the gutter more times than

I can count, and where I shared my first kiss in the parking lot with Mike Wallace. It tasted like onion rings.

I bypass the street that leads to my parents' ranch style bungalow. With its perfectly maintained lawn that's become an obsession for my dad in his retirement, and a rubber dog statue with a bone shaped "*Welcome*" sign hanging around its neck. They don't actually own a dog so I've never understood the sign. There's a patch of black-eyed Susans that Magnolia planted by the big oak tree and ivy slowly creeping up the side of the house that my mom refuses to cut back. "Who am I to play God?" she exclaims, affronted whenever we bring it up.

I slow to a snail's pace to catch a glimpse of the lake between the houses, and take in the cobalt water and brilliant sky. An elderly woman slowly walks a small poodle down the crumbling breakwall and stops to let it bark at a few geese floating atop the waves. The once vibrant street signs are discolored by time and weather and the sidewalk cracks are riddled with persistent weeds. I don't have to check the houses or cars to know that everyone still leaves them unlocked.

It's better that my parents don't know that I'm in Sunshine today. I can't help but feel that my birthday serves as a reminder to them of what we've lost. I can't carry their sadness and grief today, mine weighs enough on its own. On mine and Cara's birthday, I permit myself to unrestricted, sequestered sorrow.

I drive a few minutes past Sunshine before turning down a narrow dirt road and pulling into an overgrown parking lot. I grab the small grocery store bouquet I brought off the passenger seat and walk toward the rusty iron cemetery gates. The decaying autumn leaves make a satisfying crunch underneath my shoes as I walk. There's no one else at the cemetery today.

Most people don't like cemeteries but I've always enjoyed them. I like the stillness and the quiet. I like that there are bodies and bones decomposing below me as I walk between the graves. I wonder how they died. Were they loved, are they missed?

Were they buried in a formal outfit or a favorite pair of jeans? Are their spirits and souls reincarnated into lovely and meaningful creatures like doves and butterflies? Or does it all end prosaically, in a wooden box buried six feet deep, or a silver urn tucked inside a concrete drawer? I pass the rows of headstones perfectly lined and spaced like fence posts.

Family plots are weird. Do people treat it as an everyday business transaction and casually pull out a pen and sign the paperwork while sipping on cheap funeral home coffee? Maybe they celebrate afterward with a nice lunch and applaud themselves on securing their family's unity, even in the afterlife. Do thoughts of bones, ashes and caskets linger as they chew on a dry turkey sandwich and thumb through the details that the funeral home so neatly organized for them in a professional, glossy marketing folder?

I assess the neat patch of real estate thoughtfully set aside for my family's bodies. The space is empty save for the plot with the headstone featuring a small stone angel. I'm surprised my dad didn't secure the other headstones in advance to get a better deal. He would hate to miss out on any sort of volume discount. I trace the round cherub cheeks of the stone angel. It's cold on my fingertips, I close my eyes and inhale. I swear I can still faintly smell her, strawberry chewing gum and too-sweet cheap perfume.

"Cara Marin, October 1st, 1986 to July 15th, 1999 — beloved daughter, sister, grand-daughter and friend. And stars climbing the dew-dropping sky, Live but to light your passing feet."

My mom, the English major, carefully chose the Yeats quote for the headstone. I remember watching her sit cross-legged on the living room floor poring over books and frantically searching for the right passage. Tears ran silently down her face as if finding the right words would somehow bring back her daughter.

Twins have a bond that can't be explained. They can never fully give themselves to anyone because a part of them will always belong to each other. From womb to tomb, it's true. When Cara died a part of me died with her.

I place the flowers on the grass in front of her headstone and lay down beside them with my cheek pressed against the ground. The pain is all that I have left of her now. It is what remains.

My tears fall onto the blades of grass and the droplets linger for a moment before soaking into the earth on top of the coffin where my sister lies. For a moment, we are one again.

"Hi, old friend," I say, reaching out to pet Stanley's soft velvet nose. He whinnies in pleasure and stretches his huge head over the wood fence to nuzzle my pockets in search of treats. "I have nothing," I laugh, pushing his head away.

"Charlie!" waves Carol, getting up from a chair on the porch, "I didn't know what time you'd be here, so I didn't pull his tack out yet."

"No problem," I smile, "I'll do it myself; I miss doing this stuff." I head toward the barn with Carol in tow.

"He misses you when you're not around," she says. "I always catch him staring at the driveway, probably hoping you're going to pull in."

"I know," I try to swallow the lump in my throat. "It's hard to get out here as often as I'd like with work and things…I thought he'd be used to it by now."

"Horses, much like humans, never forget their first love," she smiles, leading me to the tack room and pulling a worn black leather saddle down off a shelf.

I grab the bridle from the hook underneath the nameplate that reads "*Stanley*" and breathe in the musty, sweet smell of hay, manure, and animals. Carol is wearing her typical uniform of blue jeans and an old fleece sweater. Her bushy hair is pulled back into a ponytail on top of her head and her warm brown eyes are free of makeup as always. Laugh lines run deep at the corners of her mouth and her skin is deeply tanned, even in October.

They say animals can sense if someone is a good person and Carol is one of the best I know. Her warm, gentle demeanor and patient discipline draw people and animals to her. The horses love her even when she's breaking them in. No matter how hard she pushes them during lessons they still rush to the fence when they see her in the yard. They follow her around the stable, falling all over themselves to capture her attention like smitten schoolchildren.

I swing the heavy leather saddle on top of Stanley's saddle pad, tighten the girth, put my foot into the stirrup and hoist myself onto his back. I lean forward in the saddle, wrap my arms around his neck and bury my face into his coarse mane. I've missed this. I've missed him. It's too hard to see him more often, because it reminds me of her, and what happened.

I notice threads of silver hair woven into his mane and eyelashes. His chestnut coat has dulled to a muted brown. He'll be twenty-three this year.

Every girl dreams of owning a horse when they're young and Cara and I were two of the lucky ones whose dreams became a reality. We started riding lessons at Oakwood Stables the summer that we were seven. We had matching pink riding helmets with our names pasted on the inside with label maker tape. Cara was good but I was better. I took to riding like a fish to water and by the end of my first summer I was cantering around the outdoor arena like a natural.

"Dad, can we have a horse, please?" I remember my seven-year-old self whining for the fiftieth time.

"Charlie, eat your dinner," said my mom, ignoring my plea.

"Dad, c'mon, we'll use our allowance to help pay for it," Cara reasoned.

"Girls, I've told you a million times, a horse is a lot of work and a lot of money," my dad said, through a mouthful of mashed potatoes. Little bits of potatoes were stuck in his beard and there was omnipresent dirt under his fingernails that no amount of soap could ever seem to dislodge.

I don't know what my poor dad did in a previous life to deserve three daughters but despite his grumblings we were the lights of his life. Born to a working-class family that immigrated to Manitoba from Romania, dealing with the intricacies of adolescent daughters is not what he was built for. He's a huge bulk of a man, with hair covering at least eighty percent of his body. The thick dark hair on his head has receded slightly and his beard and mustache are speckled with grey.

My mom in contrast looks like a ballerina that you might find in a music box. Short, dainty and pale with bright red hair and lively green eyes. Her parents were immigrants who came over from Ireland. She still speaks with the slightest lilt of an Irish accent, more predominant when she's yelling, which is often. She reminds me of a snow globe, all her pent-up energy swirling around and contained to a small vessel.

We were taught to be grateful for what we had. Our grandparents arrived in Canada with very little, so the lower middle-class life that they had managed to achieve was nothing short of prosperous to them. Everything that we had my parents had worked hard for and nothing was to be taken for granted. They instilled in us that "*things*" are not important, and family is what is most valuable.

Christmas came and after months of pleading we broke my dad down. I woke up just after 7:00 a.m. on Christmas morning and reached over to Cara, who was still sound asleep in the bed next to me to shake her awake. She opened her eyes slowly and took a moment to register what day it was. When she finally did, she sprang out of bed and raced down the hallway with me to the living room.

Presents had magically appeared beneath the Christmas tree overnight and the stockings hung heavily from the fireplace mantle. The glass of milk and plate of cookies that we had left for Santa were empty except for a few stray crumbs. Beside the plate and glass was a handwritten note.

"Thanks for waking me up, you two," complained Magnolia, walking into the living room with my parents in her flannel pajamas and ratty slippers.

Ignoring them, Cara picked up the note and read it aloud. *"Dear girls, I had to leave behind a friend of mine who was filling in for one of the reindeer this year. Take good care of him for me, love Santa."*

Confused, Cara and I looked at each other and then at my dad who was grinning so hard I thought his face might break in half. My mom looked at my dad, shook her head laughing and pointed toward the front window. We scrambled to the bay window and flung open the heavy brocade drapes. There in the front yard, tied to the big oak tree was Stanley. A huge red bow wrapped around his neck, his copper coat gleaming in the sun.

I have treasured this moment like a precious gem, and I often replay it in my head, savoring every minute detail. A sliver of light, of happiness, that I save for when things get dark. I remember the shock on Cara's face and my own disbelief when I realized Stanley was ours. My dad beaming and laughing his great big belly laugh, his hairy arm wrapped around my mom's small shoulders. Even Magnolia breaking her too-cool teenage façade to pull on boots and a jacket over her pajamas and run outside in the snow with us to welcome the horse.

The memory dissipates, I gently nudge Stanley in the ribs with my heels and we start off toward the empty field behind the stable. "C'mon, Stanley, show me what you got," I cluck, encouraging him to pick up the pace.

I can feel his muscles stretching beneath me and he breaks into a canter. I loosen the reins and lean back, letting him lead the way. I close my eyes and bask in the warmth of the October sunshine, the wind against my face as we glide effortlessly across the never-ending prairie fields. I pretend that Cara's here with me, her arms wrapped tightly around my waist, laughing into the breeze.

I walk through my front door, toss my jacket on the couch and kick my shoes off. I'm emotionally drained and the heartache of missing my sister is a painful ache that I feel deep in my bones. I scoop a sleepy Cinder off the armchair by the front window and cuddle him for as long as he allows. He submits to a few minutes of nuzzling and cooing before wriggling out of my grip and stalking away. I sigh, defeated.

I retreat to the third-floor attic that I've made into my office. The slanted roof doesn't leave much head room, but the vintage oak desk, soft grey shag rug and assortment of plants that I'm slowly but surely killing, make it feel cozy. A small wooden shelving unit displays books, knick-knacks and dust that I have acquired over the years.

I glance appraisingly at my collection of hardcover and paperback books. Reading has always served as an escape from reality for me. Cara and I shared a love for reading. Our favorite books were the *Sweet Valley Twins* series. We agreed that Cara was Jessica Wakefield, the outgoing twin that loved fashion, gossip, and boys, and I was her twin sister Elizabeth, the more serious twin that preferred reading, writing and studying. I smiled at the memory of us strutting around the playground pretending we were the blonde, beautiful, teenage Wakefield twins.

After finishing my degree in Human Resources Management, I was fortunate to get hired as the Cabin Safety Manager with True North Airlines, one of the biggest Canadian airlines—offering regular, domestic, and international flights. My job is usually dull and uneventful, I spend most days going over supervisor reviews or hosting classroom-training sessions, and periodically I have in-flight crew training sessions. I have an upcoming in-flight training session booked for a flight from Winnipeg connecting through Vancouver and on to Seattle. I've scheduled to fly there Tuesday with one crew and back Friday with a second crew. Four days should be more than enough time to accomplish what I need to get done.

I pick up a hand carved wooden box from Costa Rica, "*Pura Vida*" is etched into the lid, a popular expression that means, "Live a pure life". The irony is not lost on me. I open it, pull out the boarding passes I have stored inside and fan them out across my legs. Five in total, soon to be six.

Chapter 3
Before

The first time I killed someone it was mostly an accident. Almost unintentional really.

I had just celebrated my twenty-fifth birthday and I was scheduled to do an in-flight training session on a flight to Toronto. arriving at Pearson International Airport just after 5:00 p.m. I was standing in the flight attendant's galley watching them prepare for service. I stole a bag of pretzels and absentmindedly munched on them as I pretended to be observing. They tasted like cardboard.

"Make sure the coffee is hot enough," I said to a curvy brunette flight attendant in training, as she poured freshly made coffee into a tall thermos. I methodically scanned the cart, looking for anything that might have been overlooked. The plane flew through a small pocket of turbulence and the bottles on the cart rattled together. I steadied myself against a nearby wall. As weird as it may sound despite my career choice, I don't actually like flying.

I stared out the back window at the metal wing jutting out of the plane's body and thought not for the first time, how unnatural it is that a two-ton metal bird can glide effortlessly through the sky. The flight attendants pushed the cart down the narrow aisle, talking and smiling with the passengers. A tall, dark-haired, broad-shouldered man stood up from his seat and made his way down the aisle to the back of the plane. He noticed the "*occupied*" sign on the lavatory door and turned to me, "You come here often?"

"Yeah," I laughed. "I'm lucky enough to have VIP."

"This might be an instance where I don't think being a VIP has any benefits."

"You're wrong." I motioned to the half-eaten bag of pretzels in my hand.

"Touché," he laughed. "I'm Tom," he said extending his hand.

"Charlotte," I replied, giving him the once-over. Nice smile, expensive suit, no wedding ring. Confidence radiated off him and I could tell he was successful at whatever he did for a living. "I'm heading home from a conference I had in Winnipeg this week. Are you from there?"

"Kind of. I grew up in a small town outside the city and now I live in Winnipeg." Our conversation was interrupted as the lavatory door opened and a startled middle-aged man stepped out, narrowly missing hitting Tom with the door. The man returned to his seat and Tom hesitated.

"Charlotte, I don't normally make a habit of pursuing women that I meet outside of airplane bathrooms, but if you're in town for the night do you want to grab a drink with me?"

"Well, I don't normally go out for drinks with men I meet outside airplane bathrooms, but why not?" I offered him my pretzel package where he scrawled his phone number and the name of the bar to meet him at later that night. He excused himself to the lavatory and I smiled coyly and tucked the crumpled package into my pocket.

I checked into the Toronto airport hotel and let myself into the room, collapsing on the king size bed. I allowed myself a moment to relax on top of the crisp, white sheets. I love staying in hotels alone, there's something luxurious about having the whole room to myself with no responsibilities. Room service? Why not? Run the hot water for an hour? Sure, I'm not paying the water bill. Make the bed in the morning? Hell no.

I stripped off my clothes, wrapped myself in a thick white terry cloth hotel robe, opened my suitcase and wondered what I was going to wear. I hadn't planned on being any variation of sexy and had packed little more than a change of clothes to fly home in the next day. After much deliberation and no other options, I finally decided that a sheer black undershirt paired with heels and a tight pair of navy trousers would do.

I leaned against the bathroom counter and quickly wrapped sections of my hair around the curling iron, letting it sit for a few minutes before releasing it into relaxed waves. I brushed mascara across my lashes, swept bronzer along my cheekbones and added a final touch of red lipstick. I pursed my lips around a tissue leaving behind a perfect outline of my lips. Tom wouldn't know what hit him.

"Charlotte," Tom waved from across the bar. I smiled in acknowledgment and made my way across the trendy, dark lounge. The walls were lined with shelves filled with colorfully lit bottles and sleek copper light fixtures hung from the ceiling. Overly attractive bartenders poured overly attractive drinks into complicated looking glasses. The lounge was filled with animated groups of fashionably dressed people eating, drinking and flirting.

"Hi." He leaned in to kiss me on the cheek. "I'm glad you came."

"Well, I decided that you might be more entertaining than room service and watching made-for-TV movies by myself." I smiled. "But the jury's still out."

"I'll do my best," he laughed. "What are you drinking?"

"Martini, extra dirty, please."

"I have a feeling we're going to get along just fine." He winked.

After finishing my second martini, filled with liquid courage I pointed to his bare ring finger, "Single, divorced or married and looking?" I teased.

"Divorced and wasn't looking."

"Until?"

"Until I saw you standing there like some sort of pretzel goddess at the back of the plane."

This guy was good. His short, dark hair was lightly threaded with salt and pepper and I noticed a few fine wrinkles around his chestnut brown eyes when he smiled. He had the confidence of a man who didn't *need* a woman, but rather *wanted* one. In the same way he might want a Ferrari, an Armani suit, or an expensive steak. I could tell that he was someone that was used to getting what he wants.

Several martinis later I was feeling more than festive

and had discovered quite a bit about Tom, "*Tom Cat*," as I secretly thought of him. He was thirty-seven and married for seven years before filing for divorce last year. They separated because she wanted children and ol' Tom Cat was more interested in wining, dining and making money. He admitted to liking all three, especially the latter, and his job as a trader provided him plenty of opportunity.

The liquor had loosened our muscles and lips and the conversation was thick with innuendo. Several times while telling a story he touched my arm or leg for emphasis. My skin tingled in anticipation under the warmth and weight of his hand. The more martinis I had the more appealing Tom became.

"So, Charlotte, what do you say we get out of here and head to my place for another…drink?" Tom finally said, looking at me like a lion might look at a gazelle. Whatever, I was a fan of safaris.

I nodded in agreement and excused myself to the washroom to reapply my lipstick, feeling like a kept woman but not really minding it, as he pulled out a thick billfold and took care of the check. We hailed a cab and bundled into the backseat together. I shivered and he rubbed my legs. Leaning on his shoulder in my lovely alcohol induced haze I felt exquisite. The cab stopped in Yorkville where he owned a penthouse loft in an old restored factory.

When you make a bad decision but it's already in motion, sometimes it seems easier just to go with it. That's how I was beginning to feel as the evening air threatened to sober me up and I waited for him to open the door to his building. I usually didn't go home with strangers. I'm not opposed to it, or above it, it's just out of character for me. As the haze of alcohol began to evaporate Tom's initially engaging laugh became grating and I noticed his face was red and slightly sweaty.

I tried to quiet my inner buzzkill and tell myself that there was absolutely nothing wrong with going back to a nice condo, in a nice neighborhood, with a nice man. I looked around for confirmation at the neatly trimmed hedges and manicured gardens. The streets were quiet and well lit, lined with beautifully kept historic houses and strategically placed cafés and upscale shops.

He led me through the foyer to an old freight elevator, inserted his key and pushed the penthouse button. The elevator groaned to life and slowly ferried us up to the top floor. Tom's penthouse was a bachelor's dream—elegantly masculine and outfitted in leather, glass, chrome and reclaimed brick. Open concept with huge floor to ceiling windows in all directions.

"Wow," I breathed, walking over to the window to take in the views of the city.

The penthouse was surprisingly neat and impersonal. It looked more like a display suite than a place that someone actually lived. Abstract art and black and white prints adorned the walls, but I couldn't find any personal effects—no family photos or mementos. Tom noticed me analyzing the room.

"I'm not home much, as you can tell," he said. "I spend most of my time at the office or travelling for work or fun. When I am here it's mostly to sleep. After my wife and I separated I hired a designer to come in and redecorate everything."

"I can tell," I laughed. "Everything is so…modern."

"Yeah, I'll be damned if I know what half this stuff is." He picked up a white sphere from a nearby table. "I'll give you a tour if you want, but let's get you a drink first." He picked up a crystal cut glass from the fully stocked bar area. "Scotch?" he asked, holding up a bottle. He posed it as a question but had already started to pour me a glass before I could answer.

The sound system came on and the gravelly blues of Bob Seger filled the room. He handed me the glass and our fingertips touched, generating a spark of static electricity. He smiled knowingly and turned to lead me on a tour around the penthouse. "Here's my office," he said, opening the farthest door. A huge glass and chrome desk sat in the center of the room with an expensive looking leather chair. Bookcases were lined with books that dear Tom Cat had probably never read, and that I'm sure his designer had selected solely based on the color and texture of their covers. The corner of the room had a white marble fireplace flanked by two black leather armchairs.

"Bathroom." He pulled apart two frosted panel doors to reveal a gigantic master bathroom with two sinks, a walk-in shower big enough for five, and a Jacuzzi tub big enough for ten. I could definitely get accustomed to this lifestyle.

"And best for last." He opened the door to the right of the bathroom to reveal the master bedroom. An elegant king bed with a padded headboard that extended to the ceiling overlooked the glittery city skyline. I stood beside the bed holding my Scotch and imagined for a second that I lived there. It all felt very *Sex and the City*.

He came up behind me and slipped his arms around my waist, softly kissing my neck. I set my drink down on the bedside table and turned to kiss him as he lifted my shirt over my head. I gave silent thanks that I had miraculously packed a black lace bra in decent shape. He scooped me up in his arms and set me down on the bed.

I inhaled in anticipation as he kissed his way down my neck, chest, and toward my stomach. The gentle kisses turned rough, and I felt a sharp pang as I realized he had bitten me.

"Tom!" I cried, shoving him off me. He stumbled backward into the bedside table and knocked my glass to the floor. Scotch and pieces of glass flew everywhere.

"Charlotte, do us both a favor and let's not pretend you don't like this," he snarled and grabbed hold of my pants trying to yank them down.

"Stop!" I said, more firmly this time. I grabbed the waistband of my pants back from him.

He paused briefly before swinging his arm forward with full force and slapping me across the face. I was momentarily stunned, my cheek stung and my eyes watered. Before my brain kicked in to properly assess the situation, my reflexes took charge, and I slammed my knee as hard as I could into his crotch. He yelped and doubled over in pain.

I rolled off the bed and made a beeline for the door but I wasn't quick enough and he tackled me to the living room floor.

"You like to play games, don't you?" he growled. He

attempted to grab hold of my wrists as I frantically tried to wriggle away from him. I swung my legs wildly, finally succeeding in throwing him off me and I scrambled toward the bar. My face still smarting from the slap, I stumbled to the other side of the room and desperately searched for anything sharp.

My hand closed over a granite topped corkscrew and I grabbed it just in time to see him stalking toward me, his face red with fury. I waited until he reached for me before lunging forward and plunging the corkscrew deep into the side of his neck. The metal spiral punctured through his skin and tendons, it reminded me of cutting through a thick slab of meat. His eyes bulged and he made a gurgling, gasping sound, stumbling backward, and falling onto the couch.

A bit overkill, right? My heart was pounding like a jackhammer as I cautiously approached him. A dark puddle of blood was pooling on the couch beneath his head as he futilely attempted to stem the bleeding.

"Bitch," he gasped.

I closed my eyes and there was Cara. She was so real and whole that I swear if I had reached out my fingertips would have brushed against her. She smiled at me and crackled in and out of view like static. I caught the faint scent of her particular brand of cherry blossom hand cream.

Was it being so close to imminent death that allowed me to see her again, even if only for that brief moment?

I opened my eyes and adrenaline was pulsing like nitrogen through my veins. I calmly twisted the corkscrew deeper into Tom's neck as Bob Seger played on.

Tom struggled for a few seconds before finally becoming motionless. His eyes were open and staring at me. This date hadn't really gone as planned.

I wiped tears on my arm and took a deep shaky breath. Pull yourself together Charlie. All trace of Cara had disappeared back into the atmosphere, and now it was just me and a dead body alone in a penthouse.

And just like that, I was a murderer.

I steeled myself to conjure up all of my acquired knowledge from *CSI: Crime Scene Investigation*. What would Gil Grissom do? I made a mental list of everything that could serve as evidence. I avoided searching *How to clean up a crime scene*, on my phone, rookie mistake. I needed to think critically and carefully.

I found a pair of rubber gloves and a cloth under the kitchen sink and set to work wiping down any area or object that I remembered coming into contact. I poured his cherished Scotch onto a wad of paper towels and roughly wiped my red lipstick off his lips before flushing the evidence. I studied him, waiting for confirmation that he was still dead. His eyes were vacant and his mouth hung open, reminding me of fish that would wash up on the shore in Sunshine.

I needed to make it look like a break in. I reached inside his pocket and grabbed his wallet, still half expecting him to grab me. I loosened the Patek Philippe watch from his wrist and dumped it into my purse with his wallet.

In the bedroom I bypassed the smashed glass on the floor and yanked open a chest of drawers. I found a few more expensive watches and cufflinks to add to my new collection. For good measure I grabbed a bottle of medical grade painkillers from the bathroom medicine cabinet. I noticed an unopened box of *Just for Men* hair color. Don't ever trust a man that dyes his hair.

I threw open a few kitchen cabinet doors and drawers to make the place look ransacked but I needed it to feel more…reckless. I picked up the bottle of Glenlivet XXV Single Malt Scotch Whisky again from the full bar cart and took a swig. It burned all the way down. I wiped my mouth on the back of my hand, set the bottle down grabbed the cart with both hands and pushed it over.

The glasses and bottles of booze shattered to the floor with a satisfying crash. I stood still amidst the chaos and waited a moment, listening. The liquor formed little rivers that snaked their way through the catacombs of glass shards.

Silence.

I was slipping my heels back on when a flash of paper on the cabinet near the door caught my eye. It was his boarding pass. I stuffed it along with the gloves into my purse and stepped into the elevator without looking back. I prayed that I wouldn't encounter anyone on the way down. Luck was with me and the elevator and foyer were empty. I scanned the entrance area for security cameras and, to my relief, didn't see any.

I pushed open the building entrance door and breathed in the sharp night air. I walked briskly, focusing on the click of my heels against the sidewalk.

I walked a few city blocks before I slid into the backseat of an idling cab, avoiding eye contact with the middle-aged Middle Eastern driver. I stared out the window as we made our way through the city and traced the shape of a heart in the condensation on the cab window. There were specks of dried blood under my fingernails.

The driver dropped me off at Queens Quay West and I cut across a parking lot to the marina area. I walked slowly along the boardwalk, waiting for a couple holding hands, a lone jogger, and a young woman walking a Golden Retriever to disappear into the darkness. The umbrellas lining the boardwalk quivered in the breeze and the water lapped hungrily against the retaining wall.

Once everyone was out of sight I reached into my purse and begun to drop all of the items I'd acquired from Tom into the water. The watches, pill bottles and cufflinks disappeared into the inky water with satisfying splashes. I pulled out his billfold of cash and decided against tossing it in. For my troubles.

I pulled out the boarding pass and studied it, reading the familiar airport jargon and boarding and departure times. I folded it in half and zipped it back into the interior compartment of my purse. I tossed the rubber gloves into a city garbage can already full to the brim with detritus and other secrets.

At the hotel I stepped into the bathroom to assess the damage. I had done a decent job of washing the blood spatter off my arms and face at Tom's house but now I noticed the dark stain of blood on the front of my shirt. I turned the shower on as cold as it would go, slipped my underwear off and stepped into the water with my tank top on. The stream of frigid water soaked my hair and I closed my eyes, letting it pummel my forehead like some sort of baptism. I opened them and watched the diluted bloody water run down my legs and swirl into the drain.

I lifted the edge of my tank and gently touched the spot where Tom had bit me. It was already bruised and slightly swollen. Something to remember him by. I turned the shower off, peeled off my wet shirt and wrung it out before hanging it to dry on the shower rod. Wrapped in the fluffy white hotel robe; feeling cleansed of my sins, I collapsed into bed and turned off the light.. After staring into the darkness for a long while I eventually succumbed to the exhaustion of the night and as sleep overtook me, I drifted into the bright white room and the screaming began.

Chapter 4

"Why do you always buy the low-fat ones?" I ask, my mouth full of Babybel cheese.

"Charlie, if you don't like them, don't eat them," snipes my older sister, Magnolia, "Mags", as she wipes the kitchen island clean. The luxurious marble of her kitchen counters pairs flawlessly with modern white cabinets, stainless steel appliances and a porcelain farmhouse sink. Her entire house looks like a spread in *Style at Home* magazine. I pick up a lemon from a glass bowl on the island and give it an exploratory squeeze trying to determine if it's real or fake.

"Where are the gruesome twosome?" I ask, scanning the open concept kitchen/dining room/living room area for my adorable, yet monstrous niece and nephew. I'm continuously amazed and impressed that Magnolia somehow manages to keep her very white interior décor, very white, despite having two toddlers. I collapse onto one of the overstuffed, white, of course, couches and toss a few of the artfully arranged throw pillows to the other end of it. A bouquet of soft pink roses sits on the gold framed glass coffee table. I feel unworthy.

"They're finally down for a nap after taking a fit during our pumpkin photoshoot today," she grumbles.

"Well, I'd be pissed, too, if you continuously dressed me up in stupid outfits to take blog photos," I laugh. "What do you expect, they're two-year-olds."

"Thanks, as always, for your support," she says dryly, pulling her long, red hair into a perfect messy bun. How do girls do that I wonder?

In addition to being a textbook perfect housewife and mother to twins, Mags also runs a ridiculously successful "lifestyle" blog that generates more income than even Paul, her architect husband, does. Mags is a natural beauty with the careless sort of good looks and style that makes people simultaneously love and hate her. She walks around the room picking up children's toys, bottles, and half-eaten snacks.

Her thick red hair is offset by a porcelain complexion and grey/blue eyes. She has one of those Julia Roberts smiles, like a Cheshire cat. It's disarming and immediately draws people to her. As a blogger she's a natural, people eat her up, enthralled with her idyllic family, house, and life. Her Type A personality and obsession with perfection serves her blog well.

She's three years older than me and has always acted borderline maternal toward me. After high school she moved to Toronto and graduated from Ryerson, top of her class, with a Bachelor of Interior Design. Shortly after graduating and starting work at a boutique Toronto firm, she met Paul while working on a project and within six months she had a rock on her finger the size of a grape. A few months after the fairytale wedding in Okanagan, British

Columbia, they announced they were expecting—not one, but two babies. Paul got offered a partnership at a top architecture firm in Winnipeg and they moved back just in time for Mags to pop out two perfect little human beans, Bridgette and Beckham.

In between diaper changes and bottle feedings Mags started a blog called "The Yummy Mummy", where she posts everything from design and style tips to DIY's, recipes and life hacks. It didn't take long before her blog reached B-list celebrity status with everyone from *Chatelaine* to *In Style* praising her small-town-meets-big-city charm and ingenuity. She hasn't gone back to work since moving back and spends most of her days coordinating photoshoots, blog posts and interviews with various media outlets.

Her husband, Paul, is of course as successful, charming and good looking as Mags, so it's no surprise that the twins are stunning creatures. I'm not a huge fan of children, I can't understand the whole unconditional love thing—especially when they're screaming or smelly. However, my niece and nephew are the exception. Beckham and Bridgette both have strawberry blonde hair, which is a combination of Mags' fiery red mane and Paul's dirty blonde. While Bridgette has her mom's slate blue eyes, Beckham has the same emerald green as me. For tiny little humans they already have plenty of personality. Beckham is very observant, focused, and quiet while Bridgette is loud, rowdy, and wild. I feel a pang of sadness as I wonder what Cara would have thought of them.

"I wonder what she would have been like at thirty," says

Mags, reading my expression and pausing from her clean up duties.

"Me too," I reply, blinking back sudden tears. Everyone dealt with Cara's death in their own way. Magnolia boxed her feelings up, tied them with a silk ribbon and packed them away never to be opened. After the funeral she resumed her life as it was and became intently focused on building a picture-perfect life for herself. A life so utopian that not even the tragic death of her younger sister could overshadow it.

I creep quietly into the twin's room to watch them sleep. Mags tried putting them in their own cribs but quickly realized that bedtime turns nuclear if they're not in the same crib. Bridgette is lying on her side, her cheeks flushed with sleep and tiny bum pushed into Beckham's side. He's lying flat on his back, his mouth twitching softly and his arm thrown conspiratorially across his sister. A noise machine, probably given to Mags by a hopeful company angling for a blog review, emits soft, lulling wave sounds. A mobile above the crib tinkles a soft lullaby.

I remember sneaking into Cara's bed after the lights were out and cuddling up to her bony, warm body. I was the younger twin by five minutes and I always needed her more than she needed me. She was the brave one, the adventurous one. We had the same long, dark hair and I would lie in bed and run my hands through hers as if it were my own, braiding the strands into mine. I could never tell whose hair was whose; where she started and where I began.

I run my hand along Beckham's forehead and brush his baby duck downy hair. Bridgette's eyelids flicker and she exhales a sleepy sigh. I feel a pang of envy for what they share, what I had, and what I lost.

"We almost forgot," says Jake, setting two huge pumpkins down on my dining room table. His dark blue eyes are sparkling and his normally perfectly arranged light brown hair is askew. I can tell he's been running his hands through it. Jake is thirty-two but with his boyish looks he could easily pass for twenty-two.

"Yes!" I exclaim, delighted. I wrap my arms around his neck and kiss him on the cheek, inhaling his familiar smell of designer cologne and laundry detergent. Jake knows how much I love Halloween and I'm pleased he remembered to pick up pumpkins. My favorite holiday wouldn't be complete without artfully gutting an overgrown squash.

I head to the basement to locate the pumpkin carving tools that I know I have buried somewhere in my storage room. When I return to the dining room slightly cobwebbed, Jake has opened a bottle of wine and poured us both a glass. I take a long sip and savor the rich taste of the merlot. I swirl it around in my glass like a vampire with a goblet full of blood.

Jake always seems to know what I need, sometimes even before I know it myself. He's intuitive and thoughtful in a way that I could never be. He randomly brings me small gifts and tokens of affection: a bouquet of flowers that he bought on his lunchbreak at the downtown market, or gourmet cheese from a local cheese monger.

I can tell that I'm on his mind even when I'm not with

him. I wish I reciprocated more. I find myself having to make a conscious effort to do something nice for him or show him affection.

We set to work carving the pumpkins, me on a basic howling cat design (Cinder was my inspo), and Jake on a meticulous carving of Jack Skeleton. He cuts into the pumpkin in the same careful, measured way that he does most things. His piles of pumpkin guts are contained into neat little piles while mine are strewn across the table and spilling onto the floor. How you do anything is how you do everything.

I'm feeling warm and fuzzy from the wine I've downed while in the throes of my creative process. The motion of the carving tool as it cuts into the thick flesh of the pumpkin makes my heartbeat quicken. Jake is focused intently on his pumpkin. I pick up one of the big, long carving knives and toy with the tip of it—making an indent in my index finger. I catch my reflection in the blade of the knife and see Cara in the distorted image of myself.

I walk around to his side of the table and the music playing from nearby speakers shuffles to *Crazy on You*, by Heart. I sit on the table beside Jake, smile in what I imagine to be a seductive way, and lean down to kiss him. He puts his hand on the back of my head, pulls me in closer and stands up with his chest pressed up against mine. I can feel the thud of his heart and a hardness against my leg.

I like kissing Jake. He could star in a gum commercial. His breath is fresh and minty, and his lips are soft and pouty—almost feminine. I like how his afternoon stubble brushes against my face like sandpaper and the way he kisses me like it means something to him.

He kisses me more forcefully and leans in with urgency, pushing me back against the tabletop. He wraps his hands around my waist and slides his hands under my shirt. His fingertips trace the hollows of my ribcage and deftly make their way up to my bra. He undoes it in one try with a flick of his fingers and I'm decently impressed, I didn't know he had it in him.

I remember my old friend the knife behind my back and tighten my grip on it. I carefully slide the knife between us and drag the dull side down his chest. Jake's pupils dilate and he inhales sharply. My mouth finds his lower lip and I bite down, the sharp coppery taste of his blood mixes with the wine.

"What the fuck, Charlie," he exclaims, pushing me away.

I'm entranced by the trickle of blood making its way down his chin. "I'm...sorry," I stammer. "It was an accident." He glares at me from the kitchen where he's pressing a piece of paper towel against his bleeding lip. I realize I'm still holding the carving knife and drop it on the table with a sharp clatter.

I lie awake watching Jake's chest rise and fall with the steady rhythm of sleep, like some sort of machine. In, out, in out.

He had studied me skeptically when I explained in a shameful tone that I had gotten caught up in the moment and the wine. He accepted my apology but didn't look at me when he said goodnight. Each footstep elicited a different creak as he walked up the stairs and disappeared to the second floor without glancing back at me. I sat on the couch feeling deflated, watching leaves drift in and out of the glow of the streetlights for what felt like a long time before finally heading to bed.

Jake is the kind of guy that every mother aspires for their daughter to date; he's smart, funny, considerate, and good-looking. I wish that his laundry list of ideal qualities did more to convince me that he's the right partner for me but I often have the nagging feeling that he isn't. It's human nature to want what's best for ourselves, even if we don't deserve it.

It's usually long after Jake falls asleep, and I lay awake, that these types of thoughts crawl into the room with the shadows. They sneak along the floorboards, climb up the walls and envelop me in a darkness.

Chapter 5
Saturday, October 3rd

I yawn and roll over in bed, my arm finding the empty warm spot where Jake once was. Cinder notices I'm awake and jumps from his perch on top of the dresser into the bed, snuggling up under my chin and purring profusely. I scratch his cashmere soft head and instinctively reach for my phone. Glancing at the clock I notice it's already 11:00 am. I slept fitfully; my REM pattern disrupted by playing out the chilling scenario from my reoccurring dream.

I hold the phone directly in front of my face and try to read my messages through squinting eyes. A text from my best friend, Becca, reads, *Drinks tonight*??? followed by a procession of drink related emoji.

Sure – see u later, I type back. I could use a night off from Jake to regroup. Cinder jumps around my bed like a bunny trying to catch imaginary bugs. I watch him, wishing enviously that I could find happiness that simply.

I pad barefoot into the kitchen with a half-fallen out ponytail and eyes still bleary with sleep. I'm wearing one of Jake's button-down shirts, knowing that he will find me endearing in my current state, like an adorable toddler that just woke up from a nap. It's all very strategic on my part.

Jake is hovered over the stove, pushing eggs around a

frying pan like a suburban housewife. I sidle up behind him and wrap my arms around his waist.

"Hi." He smiles, rubbing my arms. The adorable toddler look has melted his heart as predicted.

"Morning," I mumble, leaning my cheek against his back. "What's your plan for today?" I steal a piece of crispy bacon from a plate.

"I'm going to go by the office for a bit. I have a few things to catch up on, and then I might stop by my parents. I'll probably go out with the guys tonight but I can come by later if you want?" he says, flipping the eggs onto a plate. The yolks break on one of the eggs and the bright yellow oozes out of it like a casualty.

"Yeah, that sounds good." I pour myself a cup of coffee and feign nonchalance. "I'm going out with Becca so I'll catch up with you later."

"Behave yourself." He kisses the top of my head, and I roll my eyes.

"Thanks, Dad," I say dryly.

I sit down at the table with my coffee and breakfast, pick up the newspaper remnants and scan the pages for news of murders or missing people before flipping to the obituaries. Jake is very focused on the financial section and likely thinks I'm looking for the comics and celebrity gossip section.

On Cara's obituary in the local paper the notice had read, *Survived by her parents, Colleen and Alin, older sister, Magnolia, and twin sister, Charlotte.* She was *survived* by me. Somedays that's exactly what it feels like. That I'm simply surviving. And the only time I seem to feel truly alive is when I'm close to death.

My thoughts are interrupted by a loud knock at my front door. Before either of us can answer, it swings open and a huge Great Dane bounds in. Cinder arches his back, hisses, and jumps up onto the fireplace mantel. The dog gallops over to the dining room table like a deer on crack and inhales my bacon and eggs with one quick gulp.

"Thor!" I lament, smacking him on the shoulder with the paper.

"What's for breakfast?" asks my neighbor, Reese, strolling into the dining room.

"Ask your dog," I grumble, pointing at my empty plate.

"Don't complain, Charlie, he's just helping you reduce your caloric intake. Smart dog." Reese bumps fists with Jake in that obnoxious way that guys do and pulls up a seat at the table.

I met Reese the first week I moved in. He noticed me in the backyard struggling to start my lawnmower and offered his assistance. He couldn't figure out how to start it either but we commiserated over a beer afterward. Reese lives with Thor, a harlequin Great Dane, and a constantly changing cast of roommates. He's an electrician so he's handy to have around, and he's mostly good company except for his annoying habit of showing up unannounced. He's wearing his typical uniform of a band tee (preferably classic or punk rock), a plaid shirt and ripped jeans. His shoulder-length dirty blonde hair is wavy and askew and it's obviously been a few days since he last shaved.

His questionable personal hygiene and casual indifference has afforded him a steady stream of women. His nonchalant aloof attitude drives them crazy. Some may think it's an act to provoke interest, but it's actually because he really just doesn't care, and can't be bothered with most of life's minor details.

He chats to Jake while he makes himself and Thor toast. It's not hard to understand what women see in him. His eyes are the color of Lake Winnipeg on a clear day, and you can still see the faint scar in his left eyebrow from a long-removed eyebrow ring. He catches me watching him and smirks knowingly.

One drunken night the summer that I moved in something happened between us that still hangs around on the peripherals of our friendship. I came home late from a night out when I realized I had grabbed the wrong key and locked myself out. I stalked around to the back door, which I sometimes kept open, and twisted the firmly locked handle. I swore as the sky rumbled and opened up, unleashing a downpour of rain. Across the back lane I noticed the light on in Reese's garage.

I ran across the back lane and burst into the garage soaking wet, startling Thor, who after a requisite thirty seconds of pretending he's a real dog, stopped barking and sidled over to me in hopes of finding a treat. Reese was lying on a torn old flower sofa with his work boots still on, a cigarette hanging from his lips. After a few drinks, if you squinted hard enough he could pass for Kurt Cobain. I folded my arms across my chest, noticing that the flowy dress I'd worn out earlier that night was now soaking wet and sticking to me like cling wrap.

Unperturbed by my sudden entrance he deadpanned, "What's a girl like you doing in a place like this?" He inhaled the cigarette and exhaled tendrils of smoke through his nostrils as *Creep* by Radiohead played.

"I'm locked out," I said, wringing my hair out and making a puddle on the garage floor. "I need my spare key that I keep here."

"Relax, have a seat," he drawled, and motioned to the busted leather recliner next to him. The stuffing was coming out of a large hole in the armrest and I inspected it, wondering if a small rodent had burrowed inside.

He produced a Ziploc baggie full of weed and sprinkled some onto a rolling paper. His bloodshot eyes were a strong indicator that he had been in here getting high for at least the last hour. His phone vibrated noisily with a text message on the scuffed wood side table. He glanced at the screen uninterested before tossing it on the couch beside him.

"Who's the lucky girl this week?" I smirked.

"Already forgot her name," he grinned, inhaling the joint and passing it to me.

His skin was golden from the Manitoba summer and he had the slightest sunglass tan lines. I inhaled and choked for at least thirty seconds while Reese laughed. We passed it back and forth, listening to Radiohead in companionable silence, letting the ashes fall to the garage floor.

"Charlie…" started Reese, with a deep inhale of the joint, "have you ever done something that you looked back on later, and it made you wonder how you became that kind of person?"

"You have no idea," I said, shaking my head as he

passed the joint back my way. "It's too small now; I'm going to burn my fingers."

"Ah, you pussy, here I'll do it for you," he said, perching on the armrest/possible rodent nest next to me.

He pinched it between his fingers and held it out for me, my lips brushing his fingertips while I inhaled. He pulled the joint away and wiped a stray trickle of water off my cheek. He paused, our foreheads almost touching, and kissed me. I kissed him back. The whole moment lasted less than a minute before he pulled away.

"Charlie, I'm sorry I didn't mean…" he started to say, before trailing off.

"It's fine, it was nothing." I smiled awkwardly, patted his knee in what I hoped was a neighborly way, and jumped off the recliner. "I'm going to grab that key and call it a night, I'm exhausted."

I stripped my wet clothes off into a pile on the floor and crawled into my bed. The last thing I thought of before I closed my eyes was his lips, and how they had tasted not entirely unpleasant.

I pulled into the parking lot at Assiniboine Park, Winnipeg's largest park, where I had agreed to meet Magnolia and the twins. Paul is working and she wants to take photos of the kids for the blog and needs a handler. Her white Porsche Cayenne SUV pulls into the spot beside me and I open the passenger door to grab a twin out of their car seat. Behind door number one is Beckham, who reaches for me and screams something that sounds like, "Chawee."

I brush aside four pounds of goldfish crackers to undo his seatbelt and bundle his potato sack body into my arms.

Beckham inspects the long gold locket I'm wearing while Magnolia grabs a screaming Bridgette out of her car seat and pulls the double stroller out of the trunk. My parents gave Cara and me matching lockets for our ninth birthdays, instructing us that they were meant to hold a special photo; a keepsake of people that we loved.

Beckham has the end of the locket in his little claws and is trying to pry it open. I open it for him and show him the picture inside of Cara, Magnolia and me. Cara and I were nine and Magnolia was twelve.

Magnolia is standing in the middle of the photo wearing a flowery sundress, her long red hair braided over one shoulder. She's leaning her elbow on the top of Cara's head and her other arm is around my shoulders. I'm wearing denim overall shorts with one strap undone and my bikini top underneath; I swear at one point overalls were cool, and wearing them with one strap undone was even cooler. Cara had on her favorite red T-shirt with a pocket on the front, and a pair of yellow shorts. Our legs were both bruised from recent adventures and Cara had a Minnie Mouse Band-Aid over one knee. Magnolia had a bright smattering of freckles across her nose.

It was a time when life was as simple as waking up and enjoying it. The biggest decisions we had to make were whether to go to South Beach for the day and collect pebbles and swim in the lake, or head to Aspen Creek to chase after bullfrogs and swordfight with Cattails.

"That's Aunty Charlie, Mom and Aunty Cara," I point at the photo.

Beckham looks up at me wide-eyed and says, "Cawa?"

"That's right, sweetie," I kiss his forehead and inhale the smell of organic baby shampoo.

We strap the twins into the stroller and Magnolia shoves her buttery soft leather diaper bag and camera case into the bottom of it. Her wild curls are scraped into a bun and she's wearing black leggings with an oversized sweater and a pair of white sneakers. A blanket-sized scarf is wrapped around her neck, more for style than warmth. The sun is bright in the sky and we're enjoying the last bit of nice autumn weather before winter comes.

The twins are outfitted in matching cable knit sweaters, Bridgette in soft pink, Beckham in cream. They both have on miniature designer jeans and leather booties. Bridgette has a matching pink bow clipped into her wispy hair. My heart swells looking at them. I had always imagined that Cara, Magnolia and I would have our kids grow up together and treat them more like siblings than cousins. Now Cara's gone and I have no plans to procreate.

My preference right now is taking lives, not creating them.

We walk through the Leo Mol sculpture garden and the twins babble away, overstimulated by the life-size statues, water fountains and falling leaves.

"Paul is working today?"

"Of course he is, it's a beautiful Saturday, why would he spend time with his family instead of at the office?" This is one of the rare times I've seen Magnolia let her guard down, she must be decently frustrated to even consider venting to me.

"Everything okay with you guys?"

"Yeah," she sighs, "I just wish we were more of a priority than his work. Sometimes I feel like a single mom."

"Have you talked to him about it?" We pause by the reflecting pool to look at the waxy cement statues of the bathers frozen in time amongst the water lilies.

"I try to, he's never around so it's hard. And…I found texts on his phone, from one of his assistants, Liz."

"What do you mean texts? What did they say?"

"Well, there was nothing crazy in them, but they were kind of flirty, and used winky emoticons. I don't know, it just reminded me that he gets to have this whole life outside of being a dad, this whole adult life. And I'm just…a *yummy mummy*."

"Mags, you know that's not true. You're an amazing decorator, a talented blogger and an all-around babe. So many people look up to you. I think maybe you and Paul just need some grown-up time, so you can remember that you're husband and wife, not just mom and dad."

"It would be nice, to have an evening out with him without the twins," she admits.

"Jake and I will watch them for you next Wednesday. You and Paul can enjoy an evening out. We can handle the gruesome twosome; how hard can it be? We just have to keep them alive until you get home right?"

"True," she laughs. "Sure, that would be great."

We park the stroller at the garden pergola and unstrap the twins from the stroller.

"Okay," says Magnolia, pulling her camera out and adjusting the settings. "Now you have to help me keep them still long enough to take a few photos."

Bridgette has already scrambled down to the bottom step of the pergola and is dipping her hands into the murky pond water while Beckham attempts to climb up one of the statues. I began to wonder if keeping them alive while babysitting wouldn't be as easy as I originally thought.

Chapter 6

"Well, you sure clean up nice," whistled Becca as I bent to get into her car. It was more of a challenge than it sounds considering the length of my skirt and the height of my heels. I wore a tight black crop top underneath a leather jacket, faded jeans and black ankle boots. My hair hung in loose waves and I had on my signature red lipstick. I had even done a half decent job with a makeup tutorial I'd found on social media. Big night.

Becca looks great, her short blonde hair is artfully tousled and styled, which comes with the territory when you're a hair stylist. She's wearing skintight leather pants and a sheer indigo top that matches her eyes and leaves little to the imagination. I can spot at least three of the two dozen tattoos she has adorning her body.

"Where are we going?" I ask.

"To this new cocktail place that opened up downtown and then maybe we can head into the Village later."

"Sure, sounds good to me, I'm up for anything."

We slide into a booth at the trendy new cocktail place and I notice that all the requisite social groups are sufficiently represented. By the front window—the best place for selfies—are the *Influencers*. stylish outfits, perfectly made-up faces and fake eyelashes that they bat profusely every time a decent looking guy walks in the door. Across from them is a table of *Dudes,* in designer jeans with precisely faded one-to-three haircuts. They eye up the Influencer table and I wonder how long before they send a round of Obama shots their way.

Then there's the *Outliers,* comprised of people not uncool enough to stay home on a Saturday night, but definitely not cool enough to know or interact with anyone outside of their group. Huddled closely together in intense personal conversations they sip their drinks and nervously watch the crowds. My personal favorite group is by the fireplace, with their fair-trade, ecofriendly vegan leather shoes, and thrifted John Lennon style glasses, the elusive *Hipsters.* I don't have to hear their conversation to know that they're discussing worldly topics and which local coffee shop does the best pour-over.

"So," says Becca, stirring her gin and tonic, "how's things going with you and Jakey?"

"Oh good, same old, no complaints here." I take a sip of my martini and swallow my lie with the gin. "What about you? Who's your latest victim?"

"I have a few on the hook," she giggles, "I'm still seeing Cat Guy, but Nacho Guy has been texting me again too."

To keep the men in her life straight Becca avoids using their given names and instead refers to them by key differentiating factors. Cat Guy for example is a writer at a local radio station who lives alone with his two cats. He regularly sends Becca texts on behalf of the cats, *Boots is wondering when you are coming to visit us again.*

Nacho Guy is a realtor who took Becca to a sports bar

on their first date. He ordered nachos and was a particularly sloppy eater, with more of the nachos ending up on his shirt and the table than in his mouth.

Becca was one of the first friends I made when I moved to the city from Sunshine. I was standing at a coffee shop waiting to order when I felt someone grab my hair from behind. I turned around to Becca smiling at me apologetically.

"Sorry, I couldn't help myself," she said. "You have amazing hair, I had to check if it was real."

"Thanks," I laughed, unsure how to react.

"I'm a hairdresser," she explained, handing me a card. "Come see me anytime, I know just the style for you."

I waited a few weeks before taking her up on her offer and visiting the upscale salon on Academy Road.

"You came!" she exclaimed, coming to greet me. "They always come," she winked at a fellow stylist.

It's hard not to like Becca, she's energetic, bubbly and has a certain "joie de vivre" about her. After finishing a hairstyling program she attended tradeshows, flew to elite classes to train with some of the best stylists in North America, and became one of the hottest hairdressers in Canada. She opened her own place called *Mane Glory* and has been running a very successful salon for the better part of five years. I can always count on her for fun, and drinks.

Sufficiently buzzed we decide to try our luck, and more drinks, at a local haunt in Osborne Village. Becca stumbles up the stairs in her four-inch heels, looking like a baby giraffe and I double over laughing.

"I'm sorry," I laugh, "I'll go get us drinks." I edge past

the doorman and make my way across the crowded pub to the bar.

"Two martini's—extra dirty," I say to the cute bartender. He grins and turns to make our drinks.

To my left I spot a table of *Dudes* and a couple intensely making out by the bathrooms. Beside the couple is a busty blonde talking animatedly with a tall, attractive guy. It takes a second for my brain to process that the tall, attractive guy is Jake.

"Here's your drinks, love," winks the bartender, sliding them across the bar top toward me.

"Thanks," I reply, distracted, leaving a handful of bills on the bar top.

Intrigued, I sneak to the other side of the bar, so I'm just out of Jakes' sightlines but can still observe. I watch the busty blonde paw at Jake's arm when he's talking and throw her head back in an exaggerated laugh.

Okay, sweetheart, give it a break, Jake's not that funny. But then surprisingly, my mild-mannered boyfriend, leans forward and puts his hand on her shoulder.

Busty Blonde moves in closer to Jake and he leans down to say something in her ear. She steps back and nods her head in understanding. She grabs her beer off a nearby table and waves him a quick goodbye before disappearing into the crowd. I watch him trying to read his expression but he just stares for a moment, maybe having some sort of internal struggle, before heading in the opposite direction.

I'm not sure I would have cared if Jake had kissed that girl. Does that mean I don't love him? Is love something unconditional and constant, or is it a series of fleeting moments? I'm never sure if my feelings for him run deeper than the surface. I decide to save the self-analysis for another, more sober time. I toss back my drink and venture through the pub to hunt for Becca.

I find her in the corner draped across a heavily tattooed, moderately stoned guy. I slide the drink in front of her, "Hey, Becks, I'm going to head home now if you don't mind, I'm not feeling great." Seeing Jake had left me feeling uneasy and I wanted to be alone.

"Sure, Hun, text me when you're home," she slurs drunkenly. "Roger is going to make sure I get home okay anyways, aren't you, baby?" she croons at her new suitor.

Roger, dumbfounded by his good luck, nods in agreement and smiles starry-eyed at her. I'm not worried about Becca; she can take care of herself. I am worried about poor Roger.

I crawl up the stairs and fall into bed with the night's clothes, makeup and sadness. Within seconds I'm sound asleep and stir slightly a few hours later when I hear the front door close. I listen to the familiar creaks and sounds as Jake undresses and folds his clothes neatly on the armchair in the corner of the room like always. He slides in bed next to me and scoops me into his arms, burying his face in my hair. I sigh sleepily and nuzzle his arm. The last thing I remember before dozing off again is the strong, sweet smell of an unfamiliar perfume.

My sleep becomes restless and I enter into a hypnagogic state.

In the movie *Hook*, a version of the Peter Pan story, there's a scene where Tinkerbell says to Peter Pan, "You know that place between sleep and awake, that place where you still remember dreaming? That's where I'll always love you. That's where I'll be waiting."

That place is where I can always find Cara.

My dreams of her are so vivid, my subconscious remembers the nuances that I tend to forget in the light of day. The way her freckles would suddenly appear in the summer, like cinnamon sprinkled across the bridge of her nose. The way she delicately chewed on her fingernails when she was nervous. How she always knew what I was feeling without a word passing between us. Her annoying gasp of a laugh that sounded like she was trying to catch her breath.

When I wake, the sadness washes over me like a wave.

I lose her every time I open my eyes. I'll do whatever it takes to see her again.

Chapter 7
Sunday, October 4th

I wake to the incessant ringing of my phone and *Mom* flashes on the call display. I clear my throat and answer, blinking rapidly as my eyes adjust to the cruel light of day.

"Hello," I croak.

"Charlie, are you still in bed?" exclaims my mom. "It's eleven o'clock, what's the matter with you? I've washed the floors, made bread and gone to church already," she says, clearly exasperated with me.

"I had a late night," I grumble, annoyed.

"Do not get drunk on wine, which leads to debauchery. Instead, be filled with The Spirit," she quotes a passage from the Bible.

I roll my eyes upward and silently plead to The Spirit to end this call.

"Your father and I are coming into the city this week to Magnolia's and it would be nice to see you. You and Jake can come for dinner."

"Yes, Mom, whatever you like. Listen I've got to let you go." I let her chatter for a few more minutes before she finally relents and lets me hang up. I end the call and feel slightly guilty for being annoyed at her.

When my mom lost Cara, she lost something in

herself, and she turned to God to find it. Prior to Cara's death she had only attended church services a few times a year, token visits on Christmas and Easter as a show of faith. Keeping her foot in the door just in case Heaven really does exist. Or Hell.

But after Cara died church became her solace and Jesus became her savior. It was unfathomable to her to think that she had lost a child for no reason, that Cara's death was nothing more than an unfortunate event. It made much more sense that the good Lord took Cara from us because it was part of his plan, a plan that has yet to reveal itself. She takes comfort in thinking that losing her daughter was part of something much bigger than herself.

I can't compare her heartache to mine. I lost my twin, my sister, my best friend; but she lost her daughter. She created Cara. The love she had for her is more than physical or emotional, it's cellular. Sometimes I wonder if it hurts my mom more that Cara died, or that Cara died and she continued to live afterward.

Losing my sister was like losing a limb. It was a paralyzing pain that I had never experienced. White-hot like an ember and all-consuming like a fever. Over time the wound healed over, and now all that remains is a scar, a reminder of the loss that I had endured. And yet, even though the limb is gone, and the wound has closed, the pain remains. A phantom agony that haunts me, permeates my bones and runs like poison through my veins.

Sometimes it will be days, even weeks, until the pain finds me. I'll be walking down the street and a stranger's sweater will remind me of the particular red color of her favorite T-shirt. I'll be flicking through TV channels and catch a re-run of our favorite show, *Full House*. But it always tracks me down like a deranged bloodhound.

For my mom the pain is chronic. The wounded limb remains. It's a decaying, infected appendage that doesn't heal. For her it's not a jacket, or a TV show that does it. It's her existence in itself that is a reminder that the natural order of things did not progress as they should have. She buried a child and now it's become the basis of who she is. For the rest of her life, she will be a grieving mother.

I shrug off the grief that's started to creep into bed with me and scan through my text messages to distract myself. Jake messaged, *Went to the office and will probably stay at my place tonight. XO.*

Another text from Becca at 9:14 a.m. reads, *Tattoo guy just left, told me to swing by his parlor if I'd like any new ink.*

Only Becca.

I groan and slither out of bed. I decide to punish myself with cardio and woodenly pull on stretchy leggings and a zip-up sweater. I scrape my smoky, stale smelling hair into a high ponytail using my fingers. The old pipes on the white pedestal sink hum for a few seconds before relenting and spitting out cold water. I try to revive myself with a splash of water and watch in the mirror as water drips off my eyelashes like diamonds.

The cobwebs loosen as I quickly stretch and tie on a pair of well-used runners. I don't bother locking the door because who's going to rob me mid-morning in suburbia Winnipeg? I double back to lock it because, on second thought, maybe someone will. My legs ache as my feet pound against the sidewalk and I transition from a brisk walk into a jog. The fresh fall air is helping to revive me.

I jog to a path that loops around the Assiniboine River. The trail is quiet and I run interrupted, enjoying the steady rhythm of my feet against the dirt path. I breathe deeply; in with the good, out with the suck.

Leaves are falling carelessly from the tree branches.

I round a corner and the tree line opens to a view of the river. I catch my breath for a moment, watching the currents silently churn like batter in a mixing bowl. Anyone else would be admiring the scenery but I find myself wondering how many bodies there are at the bottom of the city's rivers.

The muddy, swift waters are the perfect place to dispose of a body. Underwater graveyards. People go missing in Winnipeg every year and a some presumably end up in the Assiniboine River and Red River that snake through the city. Every so often the rivers choose to reveal their secrets and regurgitate bloated and waterlogged bodies to their surfaces.

Local papers feature stories on a lady walking her dog that finds a skull on the riverbank, or a jogger who stumbles across a stray arm. A volunteer group, called *Drag the Red*, regularly scour the Red River, dragging fishhooks to snag human remains, bones or a sunken body.

The volunteers are primarily made up of the friends and family of those that are missing. They refuse to give up on their loved ones and search the river in hopes of finding bodies, answers and closure. Their tragedies unite them in a common cause and form a community born from heartache.

I wonder if the reason I can never entirely love Jake is that he doesn't, and can't, understand my suffering. His heart is intact, his childhood filled with memories of ball games, camping trips and family barbecues. Maybe I'm destined to be with someone whose heart has seen darkness—who has pulled a body from a river.

Twigs break behind me and a buck steps out of a nearby patch of trees. His face is regal, big, dark eyes framed in white. He stands confidently and holds his imposing antlers high. I stay perfectly still, trying not to scare him. It's rutting season and I don't want to startle him and end up on the receiving end of those antlers.

We lock eyes momentarily and his presence fills me with peace. With a flick of his white tail, he turns and leaps back into the bush.

There are times like this where I feel Cara trying to connect with me. Whether it be through a particularly luminous star, or manifested into something living, like the buck. Memories of a family camping trip to Riding Mountain National Park burn bright in my mind.

While we were growing up my parents didn't have the money to take us on family vacations, so they scraped together what they could and bought a Jayco Pop Top Trailer. Cara and I were thrilled at the prospect of new adventures while Magnolia wasn't impressed at having to give up weekend beach parties with her friends. Any weekend that my dad wasn't working we would pack up and head to a provincial park: Riding Mountain, Whiteshell, Falcon Lake, Asessippi.

The Jayco was second hand and tired looking, but in

our eyes, it was perfection. My parents slept in a double bed at one end and Cara and I shared a double at the other. A banquet seat beside the kitchen table folded into a bed for Magnolia. The walls were covered in wood paneling and the windows had heavy curtains patterned with yellow flowers.

The kitchen area had a small fridge built into the counter, a stove top and a single stainless-steel sink. There wasn't a bathroom but the closet had a port-a-potty in it for when we were too tired or scared to go outside during the night. We would shower at the campground restroom if it had showers or find a nearby lake.

The trailer's best feature was the awning that pulled out from the roof. When the mosquitoes got too bad, we could pull the screen panels down and sit in there enjoying the evening without getting eaten alive. We'd play cards late into the night, the mosquito coils burning and George Strait playing low on the portable radio.

Riding Mountain was my favorite spot to camp. I loved the flatness and the openness of the prairies but there was something about being tucked away in the woods that satisfied me. The park was abundant with wildlife and it was a common occurrence to see a giant lumbering moose, a wooly bison or a stoic elk. You could often spot a slippery otter diving off the rocks by the lake or a beaver working on its dam.

Cara and I woke up early, as soon as the sun hit our side of the trailer and turned our bed into a sauna. Deciding to explore before everyone else woke up, we dressed quietly and tiptoed past a delicately snoring Magnolia, a purple satin sleep mask covering her eyes.

We each grabbed a dried-out bran muffin from the small pantry and sat down in camping chairs outside to eat our breakfast. Cara used pieces of her muffin to lure a friendly chipmunk, letting it eat the crumbs right out of her hand. She giggled as its sharp tiny teeth brushed her fingers. I didn't share mine for fear of getting bitten, but I remember feeling envious of her. I wished that I could enjoy unrestricted moments like her. I've always had trouble letting myself go.

We chose the Grey Owl Trail because Cara liked the history behind it. Archie Belaney, also known as Grey Owl, was the first naturalist hired by the park in the 1930's and he lived in a cabin at the end of the trail for a period of six months. During his time at the park, he became an unofficial caretaker for the park's wild animals and drew attention to the plight of wild animals and wild spaces. He was known for housing two pet beavers, Jelly Roll and Rawhide, who visited the cabin as they pleased through custom beaver-sized openings.

The grassy dirt path was surrounded by great walls of bushes and trees. Fir, black spruce and white birch trees loomed over us; their shadows stretched across the path like tiger stripes. As we meandered down the trail I had an unsettling feeling, like we were being watched. We stopped every so often to inspect paw prints, interesting looking plants or wildflowers, or tiny frogs. The sun rose higher in the sky and I had no idea how long we'd been gone.

"Cara, how far are we going to go? Mom and dad are going to wonder where we are," I said, trailing slightly behind her.

"Charlie, you're always such a worry wart. We're not going much farther; besides I'm having fun."

We continued until the sound of cracking branches made us stop in our tracks. It was getting closer and Cara and I couldn't figure out which way to run. Before we could decide what to do a gigantic moose trudged out of the bush in front of us. She looked as surprised to see us as we were to see her, assessing us with beady eyes. Her Snoopy-like snout and bushy beard quivered before she turned and continued on her way through the woods.

A few moments passed before we heard more bush breaking and a lanky, clumsy moose calf fell out of the brush. It couldn't have been more than a couple of days old and it was making a pitiful mewling sound that reminded me of a baby kitten. It shivered, looking disoriented, before it seemed to catch its mother's scent and bounded into the bush after her.

Cara and I burst out laughing and before I realized what was happening, she jumped into the brush after it.

"What are you doing?" I yelled annoyed, scrambling after her like the baby moose to its mother.

"What does it look like, let's see where they're going."

I knew better than to try arguing with her, so we ventured further into the woods, tracking the mother and calf, far enough away that they didn't notice us, but close enough that we could watch them wander around tree trunks and stop to munch on tall grass or plants. We ended up at a clearing and lost interest in the moose. I sat down on the grass, tired from our walk. We had no idea how to get back to the main trail.

"Cara, this was a dumb idea. How are we supposed to find our way back?"

"I'll figure it out," she said, and sat down beside me to take a sip from the water bottle we had brought. I scanned the tree line trying to remember which direction we had come from when my arms broke out in goosebumps and I felt the strong sensation again that we were being watched. My blood ran cold as I finally spotted what it was that had been shadowing us.

A timber wolf.

I panicked and grabbed Cara's arm, turning her attention behind us. She clutched my hand tightly and whispered, "It's going to be okay."

The wolf was about twenty-five yards away and watching us intently with piercing yellow eyes. Its dusty grey and white coat bristled at the neck and its curled lips revealed sharp, dangerous looking teeth.

Cara stood up, making herself as tall as possible and forcefully shouted "GO!" Her voice echoed across the clearing and several birds hooted back in response.

The wolf emitted a low growl from its throat and just when I was sure it would lunge at her, it backed away and retreated toward the woods. Before disappearing into the trees, it tilted its head back and emitted a long, mournful howl.

I scrambled to my feet and embraced Cara; my cheeks wet with tears. Every muscle in her body was tensed. She relaxed and let me hug her, rubbing my back the way a mother would.

"I told you everything was going to be okay," she said knowingly.

Cara was never afraid of anything. She glided through life with such confidence and purpose that it seemed nothing could defy her.

We eventually found our way back to the main trail and arrived back at the campsite just in time to catch the end of breakfast.

"Where were you girls?" my mom scolded, scraping eggs off a cast iron pan onto paper plates. "You can't just take off like that, there's wild animals around here."

"We know, Mom," said Cara, shoveling a bite of egg into her mouth. "We were just out walking; we'll make sure to tell you next time." She caught my eye and it was unspoken that we would never tell her about the wolf. Another shared secret added to our vault.

In my hypnagogic state the timber wolf still watches me; still haunts me. I feel its presence long before it appears. Indigenous people believe the wolf to be a spirit animal, a symbol of both good and evil, of protection and destruction.

Chapter 8
Before

Since killing Tom I've changed.

I suppose killing someone does that, changes a person. There's something awake inside of me now that I didn't know was there; a looseness in my shoulders, a tingling in my throat, an itch I can't quite scratch—all at once. Taking Tom's life had made me feel more alive than I had in years.

The last memory I have of Cara is of pain, suffering and death. Being close to all of it again had strangely made me feel closer to her.

The second time I killed it wasn't an accident, but it wasn't necessarily planned.

I was on a flight to Vancouver doing an in-flight training session and I found myself thinking about Tom. How it had felt to watch him take his last breath. It unnerved me how much I had enjoyed it. I felt desperate to capture that feeling again.

I watched her get up out of her seat and stuff a backpack into the overhead bin. A small, pixie-like blonde. I guessed her to be in her early twenties or late teens. Straight white blonde hair hung like a curtain down her back, almost to her waist. Even from the back of the plane

I could see the heavy black eyeliner that rimmed her eyes; paired with pale skin and a septum piercing she looked like a Day of the Dead doll. Something about her intrigued me.

She wore a long white T-shirt, black ripped jeans and tapped her Converse sneakers in tune to the music she was listening to on her headphones. I deduced that she was probably travelling alone, based on her casual indifference to her seat partners.

"Flight attendants prepare for arrival," announced the captain's voice over the intercom.

I made my way down the aisle, pretending to do a seat check. I passed by her and noticed her seatbelt unfastened.

"Miss," I said, in my professional and perfected flight attendant voice, "can you please fasten your seatbelt and put your seat into the upright position to prepare for landing."

She looked up at me startled, slipped her headphones around her neck and quickly adjusted her seat and clipped her belt.

"Thanks." I smiled, taking note of her seat number.

At the front of the plane, I fastened myself into a jump seat. The plane decreased its altitude as we approached the runway and we landed on the tarmac with a jolt. I stood at the entrance of the plane thanking the passengers for flying True North and stole another glance at the small blonde girl as she departed. She nodded a tight smile as she passed, a black backpack slung over one shoulder.

I said goodbye to the crew, grabbed my carry-on bag and checked into the Vancouver Fairmont Airport hotel. I was due to fly back Sunday, so had two nights in. I unpacked my laptop and logged into our customer management system. I ran the flight and seat number of the girl and the name, *Savannah Richot*, popped up on the screen.

I closed the laptop and paused in reflection. Was I really going to do this, again?

After killing Tom, I had anxiously scanned Toronto news sites for weeks, jumping every time my phone rang. As time passed and nothing happened, I grew more confident that I had gotten away with it. Almost a year had passed since that night.

I opened the laptop back up and logged into my scarcely used Facebook profile. At least fifty pending requests and a dozen message notifications blinked at me. I typed *Savannah Richot*, into the search bar and the results displayed a page of profiles with the exact or similar name. I scanned the first few profiles and found a headshot of the girl from the plane looking moodily at the camera.

I clicked her profile and browsed through dozens of artfully posed pictures: a black and white photo of her in an alley staring intensely at the camera, perched on a rock gazing out at the ocean; an older photo (pre-septum days) smiling with a group of young girls—presumably high school friends.

I navigated back to her timeline and saw a recent post from an hour ago. She had shared a post from a bar called *The Silver Spoon*, promoting live music tomorrow alongside a photo of Savannah with three gloomy guys. *Featuring Midnight Madness,* it proclaimed.

I ran my fingers through my hair and examined my

teeth in the bathroom mirror. Grabbing the hotel floss, I threaded it roughly in-between my teeth. I spit into the sink and watched bright red drops of blood mingle with my saliva. From my suitcase I pulled on a pair of jeans, a sweatshirt and a toque. I rubbed my eyes purposefully, smudging the mascara underneath them.

Searching the nightstand drawers for something sharp I found only a Bible. That would not help. On top of the desk next to the writing pad I spied a letter opener. Good old Fairmont, with their antiquated business charm. I slipped it into the waistband of my jeans and shivered in anticipation.

"Here's good," I said to the driver, pointing to the curb in front of a London Drugs. He looked at me doubtfully.

"Are you sure lady? This isn't a safe neighborhood."

"I'll be fine," I reassured him, "I'm meeting a friend." He looked at me skeptically but accepted the handful of cash for the fare before speeding away.

Downtown Eastside, Vancouver's notorious underbelly, riddled with crime, drug dealers, prostitutes and other unsavory types. Sirens blared in the distance. It wasn't particularly covert to be dropped off here, but I knew I would find what I was looking for.

"Spare some change?" croaked a haggard man in a wheelchair parked outside of the drug store. I dug in my pocket and dumped a handful of change into the dirty plastic coffee cup on his lap. I pulled my hood up and kept my head down as I passed a tired-looking woman smoking what was likely crack in the doorway of a building. Matted greasy hair hung in strings around her gaunt scabbed face. She could have been twenty or sixty.

Another woman leaned suggestively into the window of an idling car. Her rail-thin, pale, bare legs were wedged into cheap high heeled boots. A filthy fur trimmed parka barely covered her ass, which was outfitted in a too-short, dark lycra miniskirt. Posters were plastered to telephone posts urging drug users to *shoot up safely*, at *Insite*, a legal supervised drug injection site.

Beginning to regret my decision, I sidestepped over an array of broken bottles and drug paraphernalia before stopping in front of a dingy building with a neon sign *H_TEL*. The *O* was burnt out. I looked around nervously for one of the patrol cars doing frequent drive-bys. Leaning against the stucco wall under the overhang I tried to play it cool. The grimy windows of the hotel were encased in steel bars and it reminded me of a prison cell.

It didn't take very long before a shady character casually sidled up beside me. His black hair was slicked against his skull and he wore heavy chains with a crucifix around his neck. He shoved one hand into the pocket of his leather jacket and flicked ash off his cigarette with the other before taking a long drag.

"How much?" He exhaled smoke from his cigarette.

"I'm not looking to sell anything," I said quietly. "I'm looking to buy."

He glanced around and leaned in close to me, the smell of nicotine, sweat and cheap cologne emanated off him. "You a fucking cop?" he growled.

"No," I stammered, clearing my throat. He stared hard at me. I could see the pores on his face.

"What do you want?" he demanded. I watched a nearby junkie shoot a syringe into his forearm. What the hell was I doing here. What was I thinking.

"Heroin." The junkie's eyes rolled back in his head and he slumped to the sidewalk in ecstasy. Beside him a shirtless man rocked back and forth, his hollow eyes staring blankly, oblivious to the chilled night air. Shady Character named a price, which was probably more than anyone on this street had ever paid for a baggie, and I folded a wad of cash into this palm. My skin crawled as our hands briefly touched. Who was I to barter for drugs?

He reached into the pocket of his jacket and leaned toward me, deftly slipping his hand into the front pocket of my sweater. I could feel the cold metal of the letter opener against my hip bone as I clenched my fists, trying to keep my breathing even.

He paused longer than needed and smirked, "You sure you ain't for sale, sweetheart?"

It took everything I had not to plunge the letter opener into his chest. I fixed him with a steely glare and he retreated into the night, chuckling to himself. I slipped my hand into my pocket and my fingers closed around the baggie. I transferred it for safekeeping into the corner of my bra and walked briskly back down the street.

I sat cross-legged on the edge of the bed, eating an order of room-service French toast. I sipped bitter black coffee and stared at Savannah's Facebook profile. Her show was supposed to start at 8:00 p.m. so I planned to show up at least an hour in advance. From my social media lurking I had deduced that she was twenty, her hair was naturally white blonde (childhood photos), she's vegan, and she aspires to be a famous punk rocker, and inevitably the next Courtney Love. I listened to a few songs on her Sound-Cloud and discovered that she's quite talented.

In lieu of killing people, I decided to kill time and swim laps at the hotel pool. With any luck there would be minimal screaming children. I wiggled into a black one-piece swimsuit and wound my hair like a rope into a tight bun. I opened the nightstand drawer and flipped open the Bible. The small hole I had carved into it last night still safely held the baggie. If this wasn't blasphemy, I don't know what was.

I found an unoccupied chair by the pool and slid my robe off; noticing a few of the dads supervising their kids by the kiddie pool take notice. I smiled to myself, catching a glimpse of my long, toned legs and slim torso in the reflection of the poolside glass patio doors. I padded over to the deep end, brought my arms to a point and gracefully dove into the chlorinated water.

Surfacing with a gasp, I wiped the water from my face. I pirouetted and dove into a swift front crawl across the length of the pool. Swimming always reminded me of Sunshine. Summers were spent swimming endlessly in the cold, cloudy waters of Lake Winnipeg. I embraced the weightlessness and the thrilling slightly terrifying feeling of not being able to see the bottom. I was lost in memories and thought when I heard someone call my name.

"Charlotte, I thought it was you," said Rick Wolfe, a pilot for True North, as he crouched down on the side of the pool.

"Oh, hey," I gasped, slightly out of breath. Rick was mid-thirties with a deeply tanned face and husky-dog bright blue eyes. His teeth were unnaturally white and perfect. Veneers, I wondered. I didn't know him very well, but I had worked with him on a few flights and knew he had a reputation for being a flirt.

"What are you doing for dinner later, do you want to grab a bite with me?"

My mind betrayed me and failed to offer up any reasonable excuse to avoid meeting him. "Yeah, sure, do you want to meet at the restaurant here around five?"

"Sounds great," he said, extending a hand toward me. "Let me help you out." I took his hand and his well-muscled forearm bulged as he pulled me out of the pool and onto the tile surround.

I came up to his shoulder level. He gave me the once-over in my swimsuit as I reached for my nearby towel, wrapping it tightly around me. Although tempting, I wasn't about to violate the strict *no employee relationship* policy that True North had. I'd leave that up to the flight attendants who were forever chasing pilots after too many drinks. "Cool, well, I better go get ready, I'll see you in a bit." I grabbed my robe and waved goodbye.

"You look great!" Rick smiled, as I sat down opposite him at the hotel restaurant. My hair, still wet from the pool was slicked back into a high ponytail. My eyes were lined in smoky liner, and I was wearing a black T-shirt dress and tall boots.

"Thanks." I opened up the menu. "You do too." He did look nice, dressed in a crisp white short-sleeved shirt and navy pants that complimented his tan.

"So," he said after the server had taken our orders, "do you like working for True North?"

"Yeah, it's good; I meet a lot of people and get to travel. Being a pilot must be so interesting."

"Ever since I was a kid, I wanted to be a pilot, so this is kind of like a dream come true."

"It's pretty crazy to think that you're responsible for so many lives on a daily basis."

"Yeah," he smiled at me oddly, "I guess I never thought about it like that."

Good move, Charlie. "You must get to travel to so many cool places," I said, trying to sound less morbid. I was struggling to maintain my composure as thoughts of Savannah invaded my head space. A mixture of nervousness, anxiety and excitement bubbled up inside of me like champagne.

"I do. Makes it kind of hard to meet someone when I'm never home though. What about you, are you seeing anyone?"

"No, not especially," I said trying to picture Savannah's face from memory, as the server slid starter salads in front of us.

"That's surprising, a pretty girl like you." He chewed on a forkful of salad.

"Well, you know, just waiting for the right person." Could I get any more pathetic?

The rest of the dinner was surprisingly nice and I felt guilty for turning down his offer of after dinner drinks. "I actually think I'm coming down with something so I'm just going to go to bed early," I coughed weakly, trying to look sick. My watch read 6:13 p.m., the show started soon and I needed to get to the Silver Spoon.

"Do you want me to get you anything?" he asked concerned.

"I'm sure I'll be fine after I get some rest." I thanked him for dinner and hugged him goodbye.

"Just call me later if there's anything you need," he said, holding the embrace a few moments longer than necessary.

Sure, I could use help staging a murder later, if you're not busy.

I sat at the Silver Spoon bar top and sipped Jack Daniels on the rocks. This didn't seem like the kind of place known for their martinis. Hidden in a basement suite, the shadowy, seedy bar attracted a rough crowd. There seemed to be a competition for who could exhibit the most black clothing, piercings and tattoos. The bartender wore a black mesh shirt with a neon pink bra underneath and served me with an apathetic shrug. It complimented her shaved head and black lipstick.

The dilapidated walls were plastered with artfully placed graffiti and worn posters for bands like *The Sex Pistols* and *The Clash*. The ceiling was so low that anyone over six feet tall standing on the small stage would risk grazing it with their head. I spotted Savannah as the band entered and climbed onto the stage to setup.

She had on a long, faded *Guns N' Roses* T-shirt, cinched at the waist with a heavy studded belt. Thigh high stockings, several pounds of heavy bracelets and a dog-collar choker completed the look. Thick black eyeliner illuminated her grey eyes against her deathly pale skin. She picked up a beat-up electric guitar, plugged it into a large amplifier and started adjusting the levels.

Savannah grabbed the mic off the stand, and in a surprisingly raspy, low voice announced, "Hey, everybody, I'm Sav, and this is Joey, Clutch and Luke, and we're Midnight Madness."

A few guests hooted and clapped as she launched into a cover of *Celebrity Skin*. She jumped around the small stage like a hot kernel of corn, screaming into the mic with raw energy. She radiated youth and exuded talent.

For a moment I almost wanted to let her live.

She ended their first set with her white blonde hair plastered to her forehead with sweat, her face glowing. I turned in my seat when she approached the bar, pretending to be absorbed in my drink.

"Tequila," she said to the sulky bartender who deftly poured her a shot. She tossed a dash of salt into the crook of her hand, licked it, threw the shot down her throat, and bit down on a lime before slamming the empty shot glass down on the bar top. I wondered if the tequila contributed to her rasp?

I took the opportunity to feign coincidence. "Hey, don't I know you from somewhere?" I asked, taking a sip of my drink.

She looked at me for a few moments before connecting the dots. "Right, I remember, you're a flight attendant. Crazy. What are you doing here?"

"I'm a huge punk rock fan and this place is something of a legend. I try to come whenever I'm in town. I saw *The Vandals* here a few years ago." I had the internet to thank for my newly acquired punk rock knowledge.

"That's awesome; I wouldn't have thought you were the type."

"I have to keep it toned down for work, but I'm totally into the whole scene," I said, hoping I didn't sound like I was trying too hard. "Do you have a light?" I asked, knowing the answer as I remembered seeing a cigarette behind her ear on the plane.

"Yeah, I'm heading out for a smoke before my next set if you want to join?" she offered.

"Sure." I slid off the bar stool and followed her through the door at the back of the bar that led out into an alley. "I'm Charlie by the way." The alley was dark and echoes of drunk laughter and conversation filtered out through the building's back vent. I kicked at a used cigarette butt with my boot.

"Sav," she replied as she lit her cigarette and passed me the lighter.

I pulled a cigarette out of the pack I had purchased earlier at the bar. Holding the flame to the tip of my smoke I tried to inhale smoothly and not look like an amateur.

"You did a killer job of *Celebrity Skin*. Hole is one of my favorite bands." I flicked the ash off my cigarette for effect.

"Seriously, that's so rad! Thanks, me too, I'm like obsessed with Courtney."

"Do you do any of your own stuff, or mostly covers?"

"I write a little bit of my own, I'll end the next set with one I wrote, *Perfect Poison*. There are a few A/R guys in the audience tonight, so hopefully one of them is impressed."

"Well, good luck," I smiled, as we stubbed out our cigarettes and filed back into the bar.

Savannah prepared for her next set, and I visited the bar's rundown bathroom. I shut the door firmly behind me and slid the deadbolt through the uneven hole whittled into the door frame. The walls were painted what could only be described as a boudoir red. No one would paint anything this color in the light of day. The graffiti scrawled all over the walls was so condensed that if you squinted it looked like wallpaper.

I sat down on the toilet seat and the vibrations from the sound of the band starting up again reverberated through my legs. I carefully unrolled and rolled a cigarette back up, spilling flakes of tobacco on my knees. I looked heavenward waiting for a sign of some sort. On the ceiling someone had printed in neat, block letters, *Catch flights, not feelings*.

I ordered a single whiskey and a glass of water. Now was not the time to dull my senses. Savannah jumped around the stage with energy radiating from her. Her hair danced in a silky platinum wave as she bounced up and down. I surveyed the crowd to check if anyone was as enthralled with her as I was. It was the time of the night where everyone was more interested in their drinks and who they were going home with than in the band.

For the last song the stage lights dimmed except for a solo spotlight focused on Savannah. In the bright, harsh light she looked almost ethereal. "This one is called, *Perfect Poison*."

The belligerent crowd finally remembered there was live music and hollered and clapped as she belted out an emotional, gritty ballad. When she finished, she took a bow, threw the crowd a parting kiss and stepped off stage. I waited a few minutes for the crowd to subside before approaching her.

"Great show, you were amazing, I'm so glad I came," I said honestly.

"Thanks so much," she beamed. Her face was flushed and her eyes bright.

"Celebratory smoke on me?"

"Why not, I haven't had any better offers," she laughed.

"Let's go behind the dumpster over there, out of the wind." I held a cigarette out for her. We huddled against the big green bin and I wondered idly if any bodies had been tossed in it.

"That last song was my favorite. It was the one you wrote right?"

"Yeah, I wrote it about my mom mostly, she was an addict," she took a drag of the cigarette.

"Was?"

"She's been clean now for five years. When she was using things were bad. My old man left us when I was young so it was always just the two of us. She would leave me alone a lot, while she went out to score drugs and get high."

"That must have been tough."

"It was. But that's behind us now, and things are going to take off with my music, I can feel it."

Her pale skin glistened in the moonlight and the cherry on her cigarette sizzled like a campfire as she inhaled. She reminded me of Cara. She believed that she was capable of anything.

"As soon as I scrape together enough cash, I'm going to finish producing my first album and then hopefully hit the road and tour."

"Do you have a boyfriend?" I asked, trying to stall her as she neared the end of her smoke.

"No, I need to focus on my music. Guys tend to get in the way of that. Are you with someone?"

"No, I guess I still haven't found what I'm looking for."

"Isn't that a *U2* lyric?" she laughed. "And do we ever really find what we're looking for?"

Her voice was starting to slur and her eyelids fluttered heavily. I checked my watch. Ten minutes.

"Hey, I'm not feeling so..." she trailed off, her pupils dilated. I grabbed her shoulders and lowered her to the ground, propping her against the dumpster. The alley was deserted except for a feral looking cat chasing mice and shadows.

Music drifted through the building's vent and it was *Celebrity Skin,* ironically.

I untied one of her shoelaces and pulled it out of her sneaker. I yanked up the sleeve of her shirt and tied the shoelace tightly around her upper arm.

Savannah's breath was coming out in ragged gasps and her mouth had started to froth. I swallowed down the panic and bile that was rising in my throat. I had to keep moving forward with the plan; there was no going back now.

If the 50mg of heroin rolled into the cigarette I'd given her didn't kill her, the 50mg I was about to shoot into her arm would.

From inside Courtney Love's screams reached a fevered crescendo.

I smoothed Savannah's hair out of her face and pulled out the syringe I'd bought at London Drugs. Cooking heroin is not as easy as it sounds by the way. I pulled back the plunger on the syringe and slid the sharp tip of the needle into her thin arm. She moaned and tried to say something.

"Shhh, it will all be over soon, I promise."

I closed my eyes and Cara was waiting for me, smiling as pretty as ever. I knew that this is what she wanted me to do. She could reach me best in moments of suffering.

Savannah's eyes rolled back in her head, her rosebud mouth went slack and her arm grew limp in my lap.

Her purse had fallen open onto the ground beside her and guitar picks, lipsticks and papers spilled onto the ground. I noticed a crumpled boarding pass among the scattered contents and tucked it into my purse. I wiped the syringe down with my dress and placed it beside her.

She looked peaceful, like an angel. Cara would have liked her.

I was sitting at the hotel restaurant, chewing on a dry piece of toast when Rick approached my table.

"Charlie, I was worried about you. Is everything okay?"

"Umm, yeah, I mean why wouldn't it be?" I asked, confused.

"Well, after you said you weren't feeling well last night, I called your room. Repeatedly actually. And when you didn't answer I had the front desk give me your room number and I came by to check on you. I must have pounded on the door for a good ten minutes."

Fuck. "Oh really? That's weird, I guess I took too much nighttime cold medicine and passed out," I said, trying to maintain my composure.

His expression softened and he looked relieved. "I was just worried that something bad happened to you when you didn't answer."

"Everything is okay," I smiled brightly.

Chapter 9

What does a killer look like?

Visions of a sinister looking middle-aged man with greasy hair and dark circles under his eyes maybe come to mind. His teeth are stained with nicotine and he's evil and darkness personified. Maybe it's a creepy old lady in the neighborhood that stares too long at passerbys. Her eyes are twitchy and she has a hardened look about her that suggests she'd take the life of anyone trampling her flowerbeds.

Whatever ideas that are invoked, I can guarantee that they're not of a successful, moderately attractive, mostly charming young woman with straight teeth.

Here I am breaking down barriers and stereotypes.

After Savannah is when, by definition, I became a *serial killer*. When I think of other serial killers I wonder if they are a result of nature or nurture. If the instinct to kill is innate or a result of circumstance?

I believe that everyone has the capacity to kill, but only certain people feel an actual desire to. Serial killers tend to kill for attention, infamy, revenge or justice; but that's not me. I don't do it because any of my victims deserve it. I do it because inflicting pain on them allows me a brief respite from mine.

I couldn't let my new hobby control or consume me. Like with anything enjoyable in life, I needed moderation.

Each year I would choose a victim from a training flight, picked at random using the seat selection lottery I'd developed. While I would prefer to kill people that deserve it, I'm not Dexter, or a Robin Hood of serial killers, killing only the bad, and saving the good. Through extensive research watching *CSI: Crime Scene Investigation* I learned to avoid patterns or consistencies as it almost always led to one's undoing.

Tuesday, October 6th

"Pass the rice, please," says my dad, his mouth full of food.

"Dad, I told you its quinoa, not rice. It's a super food, it's very good for you." Magnolia rolls her eyes in frustration as she tries to stop the twins from starting a food fight. She fails and I watch amused as Beckham dumps his entire plate of "super food" on Bridgette's head. The table is set perfectly, complete with a crisp white tablecloth, linen napkins, white plates and fresh lilies. A cornucopia of food that's all organic, non-GMO and locally sourced covers the entire surface of the table. I pick up a gold fork and stab at an asparagus spear on my plate.

"Paul, sweetie," Magnolia says through gritted teeth. "Maybe it's time for the twins to go to the playroom."

Paul, who was chatting with Jake as the food fight unfolded, finally tunes in and grabs the twins out of their highchairs, tucking one under each arm. Both toddlers begin to scream and their wails echo down the hallway and through the closed door of the playroom.

"Poor things," clucks my mom. "They're probably not getting enough calcium Magnolia, that's why they're so fussy."

"They're fine, Mom, they're two, and they're permanently fussy right now. I wish you'd quit reading those archaic parenting magazines."

"Well, I don't remember Cara and Charlotte fussing like that."

We all sit in silence for a few moments and push food around our plates. Cara is always on the periphery of our conversations. Her ghost continues to haunt our family, especially when we're together.

"So, Jake, when are you and Charlie going to get engaged?" asks my mom, moving her sights from Magnolia to me.

"Mom!" I gasp, choking on quinoa. Magnolia thumps me hard on the back.

"It's not an unreasonable question; you know how I feel about you two living in sin together."

"We don't even live together yet, and besides we're not ready."

Jake, who had initially turned a shade of crimson, chimes in. "We're not? I was actually going to talk to you later tonight. Someone is interested in renting my place, and we spend most nights together anyways."

"Jake, this isn't a family discussion; we'll talk about it later. Can we please go back to talking about the shitty quinoa or something?" I say annoyed. I push my chair back and retreat to the bathroom.

I sit on the side of the bathtub and put my head

between my knees. Just breathe Charlie. This family dinner is almost over and it can't get worse than your mom attempting to guilt your boyfriend into proposing to you. Your boyfriend that you don't even know if you *want* to propose to you.

Magnolia's bathroom is a terrible place to be miserable in. The spacious, luxurious room is nicer and likely cleaner than my kitchen. There's a huge soaker tub in front of a large window overlooking the lush, landscaped backyard. On the white granite vanity is an array of expensive soaps, lotions and fresh flowers. Framed black and white childhood photos of Magnolia, Cara and I, Paul and his brothers, and the twins decorate the walls.

There's a knock at the door and Mag asks if she can come in.

I unlock the knob and let her in.

"You're a shitty girlfriend and I'm a shitty mom, what else is new?" She perches on the edge of the tub beside me.

"I can't believe mom said that. Actually, I can believe she said that, I can't believe Jake brought up moving in together in front of her though. He knows how I feel about it. For him to put me on the spot in front of everyone was out of line."

Mags goes quiet for a few seconds. "I know he shouldn't have brought it up like that, but I mean you guys have been together for almost two years now Charlie. If you're not ready to move in with him yet, do you think you're ever going to be ready?"

"I don't know," I reply honestly. "Are we ever really ready for anything?"

I study one of the framed photos on the wall of Magnolia, Cara and I bundled up in neon snowsuits, our eyes barely peeking out from under our toques. Even in the black and white photo you can tell our cheeks were bright from the cold. My dad was mid-laugh and rested a hand affectionately on Magnolia's shoulder. I next to a beaming Cara who was proudly holding up a fish.

Living on the prairies the cold weather is an unavoidable part of life. We pay for our beautiful, long, summer days with subzero temperatures and mountains of snow. The cold never hindered us much as kids and when my dad suggested an ice fishing trip, we were excited. Sometimes I wonder if he ever wished for a son, he tried his best to make honest men out of us girls. He was always teaching us things like how to change a tire, fix a leaky faucet or clean a fish.

Stuffed into our winter gear we headed out to his friend's ice fishing shack. I knew that the ice was several feet thick but I rolled my window all the way down just in case a quick escape was needed. We drove across the frozen lake in our truck until a small red shed appeared, the only spark of color for miles on the blank, white slate of Lake Winnipeg.

My sisters and I piled out of the vehicle and into the shack, snuggling up against each other like kittens while my dad lit the woodstove. He scooped ice out of the newly drilled holes and handed us each a fishing rod to hold onto. We sat in silence until Cara asked where the snacks were and dug around in the backpack we had brought.

"How long until a fish comes?" Magnolia complained, staring forlornly at the icy hole.

"Sometimes they bite, and sometimes they don't. It could take a few minutes, it could take a few hours," my dad patiently explained.

A sharp noise rang out like a gun shot.

"What was that?" I jumped up.

"It's just the ice cracking," my dad said nonchalantly.

"What do you mean *just* the ice cracking!" Magnolia cried.

"The ice expands and contracts with the temperature changes. It could also just be the water moving around below us. Nothing to worry about girls."

We exchanged glances with each other but my dad seemed unconcerned and fiddled with the bait on the end of his hook. Cara's rod which had been balancing between her knees lurched toward the hole. She grabbed it just in time before it disappeared, her line was taut with tension.

"That's a fish!" exclaimed my dad, rushing to her side and helping her reel it in. A large pickerel emerged from the depths of the hole and started flapping around on the wood plank flooring. We all screamed and jumped to the edge of the shack farthest away from it. My dad laughed his big grumbly belly laugh and pulled the fish off the line, tossing it into a nearby bucket.

Later that night he told my mom that Cara had caught it all by herself and winked at us over her shoulder. She fussed over us briefly and then focused her attention back on the fish, which she expertly cleaned, de-boned and fried for dinner. We sat around the kitchen table and laughed animatedly as we told a much-embellished story of how Cara had bravely caught her first fish. I wished more than anything I could relive the warm feelings of that evening.

The car ride home is filled with awkward silence and tension. I lean my cheek against the cool glass of the passenger side window and watch the streetlights pass in a blur.

"I didn't mean to bring it up that way, about the rental," he finally says.

I count three street signs before I answer. "You know things aren't easy between her and me, and you just made it more difficult. All she does is nag me about *living in sin*."

"I know; it was the wrong time to mention it. I'm sorry. It's just that we've been having this same conversation for the better part of six months. Either you want to live with me, or you don't. I'm not going to wait around forever for you to decide."

It wasn't love at first sight with Jake, but there was something about him that intrigued me. I wasn't even sure I'd know love to see it, at first sight or otherwise. I'd hadn't formed a meaningful connection with anyone since Cara. I'd dated people, but they were mostly warm bodies or someone to keep me company. There wasn't anyone that I'd given a second thought to.

I first saw Jake at a meeting with the financial team at the True North Airlines head office. I walked past the conference room with the floor to ceiling glass panels and noticed a handsome guy in the middle of a presentation.

Ever the predator I casually waited until I heard the meeting break before rushing down the hallway to get a closer look at him. He retreated to the staff kitchen and I followed him under the guise of getting coffee. Like a lion stalking an antelope.

He was holding up a coffee pod trying to figure out how to insert it into the coffee maker. He had a Clark Kent vibe going on; with black framed glasses and a crisp white shirt tucked into tailored pants. His hair was neatly combed back and his face freshly shaved. He looked clean and honest.

"You just push this," I offered, reaching over him to open the machine.

"Thanks," he smiled, flashing perfectly white straight teeth at me. "You saved my life; I could really use some caffeine after that marathon meeting."

"You know there's a proverb that says when you save someone's life, you're responsible for them forever." I smirked and looked up coyly from under my eyelashes.

"Oh yeah?" he raised an eyebrow. "Well, that seems like kind of a raw deal, you save my life and then you have to keep an eye on me forever. Why don't I try balance it outby taking you out for dinner or a drink?"

Smooth. "Deal," I winked.

On our first date he picked me up and actually came to the front door. He opened the car door for me and pulled out my chair. Gentlemen are an endangered species nowadays. I was impressed. At dinner he seemed genuinely interested in me and he didn't flinch when I turned up my nose at the calamari he ordered for us.

I studied his brilliant white teeth, like a miniature picket fence.

It was the first time in a long time that I didn't think about Cara. My heart felt light, like it was filled with helium, and my cheeks were sore from smiling and laughing.

It wasn't until we walked to his car that I looked up and noticed an exceptionally bright star in the sky. I thought of Cara then for the first time that night. I'm not sure that I believe in heaven, an afterlife, or even a God, but I do believe that if there is life after death that we might find it in the night sky. I imagine Cara as a twinkling ball of light up there in the darkness, watching over me.

In *A Universe from Nothing*, Lawrence M. Krauss explains;

You are all stardust. You couldn't be here if stars hadn't exploded, because the elements—the carbon, nitrogen, oxygen, iron, all the things that matter for evolution and for life—weren't created at the beginning of time. They were created in the nuclear furnaces of stars, and the only way for them to get into your body is if those stars were kind enough to explode. So, forget Jesus. The stars died so that you could be here today.

Following Cara's death, I developed a brief obsession with constellations and the lunar calendar. I'd spend sleepless nights outside staring at the sky, looking for answers and a sign that my sister continues to live on. Searching for stardust.

"Everything good?" Jake asks, touching my arm and following my gaze upward.

"Everything is perfect, Jake," I said, slipping my hand into his.

He escorted me to the front door and kissed me gently on the lips. He asked if we could see each other again, "Don't forget, according to that proverb I'm yours forever now."

His car disappeared down the street and I leaned up against my front door for a long time, staring at the stars.

I fold another pair of pants into my suitcase and scold Cinder as he jumps into it leaving black hair on my clean clothes. Thankfully his fur matches the majority of my wardrobe. Jake is staying at his place tonight. My *sweet dreams* and *XO* good night texts were met with a passive *Nite* reply. I don't have the head space to deal with this situation right now; I need to pack for my flight and prepare.

Talk when I'm back OK <3, I text to Jake.

The three circles appear that indicate someone is typing and little typing dots move across my iPhone screen like a centipede.

K.

Frustrated I throw my phone on the bed and resume packing. It's always difficult deciding what I should bring. Pants or skirts, heels or flats, knives, or poison?

I tuck a zip-ties into the hidden compartment of my suitcase, as well as a thin credit card shaped utility knife, a black bandana (more for effect than purpose), and a bottle of prescription sleeping pills. I grab a book of poetry by Charles Bukowski and it falls open to a bookmarked page.

We don't even ask happiness, just a little less pain.

I run my fingers on top of the words like it could help me to better absorb them. I use a cloth to carefully grab the bunch of dried, flattened flowers I've hidden inside the book.

Oleander.

I grow it myself in a small black enamel pot that lives outside in the summer and in my office when it's colder. I learned about Oleander in a high school biology class, intrigued by the delicate, innocent looking flower that is highly toxic, and can be fatal if ingested in high enough amounts. I delicately prune it myself with gloves on, and I'm careful to keep it away from Cinder's curious paws. I'm drawn to it because I can relate—a pretty exterior that's hiding something poisonous.

Chapter 10
Tuesday, October 6th

I try to focus on the flight attendants preparing the cabin for takeoff but my anticipation is gnawing at me. I've been watching the plane bound for Seattle, Washington, fill up with passengers for the last half hour but seat 15D has remained empty. The majority of people have taken their seats and the crew is busy walking down the aisles and shutting the overhead compartments. I finger the tiny slip of paper in my pocket, I'm beginning to wonder if the passenger is going to show.

Just as we prepare to shut the cabin doors the flight attendant at the front of the plane ushers on one last passenger. I can tell by the way he ducks his head as he walks briskly down the aisle, apologizing to fellow passengers for bumping their elbows, that he's over six feet tall. His wavy dark hair is tucked into a black toque and slightly grazes his shoulders. His facial hair is well past a five o'clock shadow and bordering on a seven o'clock. He's wearing well-worn jeans, a fitted T-shirt and a beat-up black leather jacket. He shoves his duffel bag into the overhead and sits down in seat 15D.

My heart catches in my throat, and I wonder if medical intervention would be needed to push it back into my chest.

He reminded me of something tarnished and raw, like strong whiskey or a chain link fence. There was a hint of something wild, like a dog that's been bred with wolves.

The French have a term, *coup de foudre*, which translates literally to a bolt of lightning or a thunderbolt. It refers to experiencing love at first sight, and how the shock of it hits you unexpectedly. I can understand why they chose to associate falling in love with something that can kill you. I imagine the sensation is similar to a defibrillator, pulsing energy into your heart to keep it beating.

For the remainder of the flight I create every opportunity possible to walk past him and steal sideways glances. My nerves are catching up with me and as I help pour the coffee and hot water into carafes, I notice that I'm shaking. I finish up and excuse myself to the washroom.

Get it together Charlie.

I splash cold water on my face, take a deep breath and remind myself to stick to the plan. I'll spend time tonight at the hotel doing my research before I make my next move. I return to the flight attendant's galley and take my seat to prepare for landing.

The passengers deplane, I say goodbye to the crew and I'm heading toward the airport hotel when someone walks up beside me.

"Hey."

It's him.

"Uhh, hello," I say, taken by surprise.

"I noticed you looking at me on the flight, and at first I thought my seatbelt wasn't on, or maybe my seat wasn't in an upright position, but both were fine and I realized it must be something else."

"I'm so sorry," I feel my face getting red. "I definitely did not mean to stare. I just…"

"It's okay," he cuts me off. "I liked it."

Standing this close to him I notice how beautiful his face is under all that facial hair. He has a strong jawline, a wide nose and a faint scar that runs across his lower lip and stands out when he smiles. His left eye has a streak of iridescent blue running through it. Heterochromia it's called; when eyes are two different colors or have different colors within them.

This is when everything began to unravel.

I agree to meet Abel—call me Abe—Moretti for a drink later that night. Instead of refusing and going back to my hotel room to gather my bearings, I go back to my hotel room to change into something tight. Instead of spending my night formulating a plan and doing my research, I decide to do it in person.

My hands are sweating and I wipe them on my dress as I look around the lounge for him. He picked it; I've never been to Seattle. Cobain and Starbucks are the only Seattle exports that I'm familiar with. He sees me walk in and gets up to greet me, kissing me on both cheeks. How European. He smells of cigarettes and cedarwood aftershave.

We order drinks and he leans back in the booth with his hands linked behind his head, like he's settling in for the long haul.

"So, Charlie, tell me everything."

And so, I do.

For reasons unknown to me, I simply spill my guts on the table. Everything comes pouring out like a rain cloud that has been gathering moisture and can't bear the weight of it any longer.

I tell him how I hate the sound of thunder but love the electric smell of storms. How I can't stand mushrooms and the color orange. How I grew up in a small town and didn't encounter a stoplight until I first drove into the city when I was seventeen. I brag about Beckham and Bridgette claiming they're the cutest kids in the world and pull out my phone to show him pictures as proof. I tell him about my parents and that they gave me the best possible. I even tell him about Cara. The only person that I don't tell him about is Jake.

In turn he also tells me everything. That he's thirty-five, never been married, no kids (that he knows of). That he works by day as a carpenter and by night as a painter. That he grew up in Seattle and his parents are still together, and he has two sisters. Monica, who is married and lives in Vancouver with his two-year-old niece, who apparently is a serious contender for the cutest kid title. And Sarah, his younger sister who lives in Seattle, attends University and works part time at a Starbucks, surprise. He has a dog named Raptor, a three-legged mutt that he picked up at the local humane society, or rather he says, Raptor picked him.

Three hours, six drinks and two cigarettes later I think I'm in love. Or at the very least I'm drunk. Or it could be the rush of nicotine to my head as we stand outside sharing a cigarette. I tell him things that some of my best friends don't know about me. Things that my family and Jake don't know about me.

It's last call, the servers are clearing the tables and the bartenders are putting away the glasses. I don't want this night to end, so he says it doesn't have to. He knows a place that's open late if I'm not too tired. How could I be tired? This is the most alive I've felt in years. The most connected to someone that I've felt since Cara. I almost forget why I agreed to meet him in the first place.

Almost.

He takes me to another bar; this one is dark and filled with fluorescent flashing lights and I let the vibrations of the music course through my body like electric currents. He orders drinks and I can feel his eyes on me from across the crowded dance floor. Like I'm the only person in there and everyone else is just background noise. We do tequila shots and dance to house music until my hair is soaked and my feet hurt so bad I have to take my heels off.

He tells me that I've burned enough calories dancing to warrant a midnight snack, it's 3:30 a.m. at this point but who am I to argue? We stumble to an old-fashioned diner called *The 5 Point Café* and a flashing light in the window exclaims, *We cheat tourists and drunks since 1929*. We order burgers and share fries. Food has never tasted so good.

"Abe," I finally say. "I think I'm going to have to call it a night. I'm about to faceplant in the rest of these fries."

He grins and chews on the end of a fry. "My place is only a couple of blocks from here. You can crash there if you want. You can have the bed; I'll sleep on the couch, gentleman's honor," he says, crossing his fingers.

"Okay," I agree, surprising myself.

We leave the diner and he piggybacks me the three blocks back to his place and I carry my heels. He hauls me up the dilapidated stairs of his building to a one-bedroom loft and sets me down gently on his bed. I vaguely recall him covering me with a blanket. I feel the scratch of his facial hair as he kisses my forehead.

Wednesday, October 7th

The morning sunlight shines persistently on my eyelids like an interrogation light. It takes me a few seconds before I remember where I am and what I'm doing. I rub my hand across my pounding forehead. I'm alive. This is good news. Thankfully, Abe didn't turn out to be a freak serial killer, although he'd be in good company. I'm still wearing my outfit from the night before and I notice my mascara and lipstick smeared onto the pillowcase.

The bedroom is simple and calm and light is flooding in through the huge industrial window. I look out and press my palm against the glass, taking in the grey neighborhood of historical and brick buildings. The bed is low and soft and reminds me of a cloud.

On one side of the bed is a wobbly mahogany nightstand with a glass of water, a lamp, a half dead succulent and a stack of books. I thumb through them and find biographies and books on artists like Van Gogh, Picasso and Klimt.

His wallet is on the dresser underneath the window next to framed photos. I open the worn leather bi-fold and thumb through his license, bank card and credit cards.

Tucked behind a twenty-dollar bill is a wrinkled boarding pass from his flight. I slide it out of his wallet and into my purse. I'm studying the photographs when something leaps at me from behind knocking me into the dresser.

I yelp and am soon drowning in kisses from whom I assume Raptor. He's a medium-sized dog, if you could call him a dog, with grey wiry hair and a big bushy beard. Abe rushes in after him and pulls him off me.

"Sorry about that, he has a thing for brunettes." A lovestruck Raptor struggles to free himself from Abe's grip and I notice that he's shirtless, barefoot and wearing only a pair of jeans, Abe, not the dog.

I'm suddenly conscious of my hair, which smells like a regretful mixture of cigarettes and cheeseburgers. Abe is tall and lean and his ab muscles flex as he scoops Raptor up into his arms like he's a puppy. An enormous tattoo starts at his neck, circles around the right side of his chest, and continues down his side, disappearing into the waistband of his jeans. I pick out a familiar sky from Van Gogh's *Starry Night*, and a dripping timepiece from Salvador Dali's *The Persistence of Memory*. I recognize lily pads in the style of Claude Monet's *Water Lilies*, and a bowl of apples from Cezanne's *Still Life with Apples*.

He notices me staring. "A work in progress. Me and the tattoo that is." He winks. "I made you coffee. You can borrow something of mine if you want to take a shower. Bathroom's over there." He points to a door just outside of the bedroom.

I close myself in the bathroom and shed last night's clothes like a snake's skin. I turn the water on in the sleek, tiled, glassed-in shower and while I'm waiting for it to warm up, I take the opportunity to snoop. The medicine cabinet holds a normal variety of man paraphernalia and the counter has an old-fashioned shaving set with brushes and a straight razor. I pick up the straight razor and examine the blade with my fingertip. Sharp, very sharp.

I reluctantly place the razor back in its holder and step into the steaming hot water. I scrub my face and hair trying to wash away the remnants of last night with Irish Spring soap.

What am I doing?

I sigh, lean against the shower tiles and let the water stream down my chest, willing it to enlighten met. I sink to the floor and rest my forehead against my knees in the standard hangover shower pose. I sit until I've overstayed my welcome and the water starts to run cold. I cocoon myself like a caterpillar in a big fluffy towel and walk out of the bathroom and into what serves as the kitchen/living/dining room area in the very open concept loft.

Raptor rushes over to lick the beads of water off my legs. Abel is sitting at the table drinking coffee and I can feel his eyes taking in every inch of me. I clutch the towel tighter against my chest.

"I left you a variety of hoodies and T-shirts on the bed to choose from. I personally suggest the grey RVCA hoodie, it will complement your eyes best." He smirks.

I firmly shut the door to his bedroom and slip on last night's dress under a zip-up hoodie. Unsure what to do with my underwear I shove it in my purse. No underwear is better than dirty underwear, I guess? I remember that I have a phone and search my purse for it before finding it in my jacket pocket. My screen is lit up with missed text messages, three are from Jake. I shut the phone off.

I join Abel in the bright, open living area. The walls are a rough red brick and the exposed beams look original to the building. There's a fireplace hearth at the far end of the room with a well-worn leather couch and an oriental rug in front of it. Dozens of paintings are hung along the walls, propped on the floor, and perched on easels. The colors are vivid and vibrant and the textures make them jump off the canvases. They're mostly modern and abstract but I can pick out vague shapes and suggestions of elements like sunsets, oceans and trees.

"These are beautiful," I breathe.

"Thanks. Wish they paid the bills, but not quite yet." He pours me a cup of coffee and sets it down on the artfully crafted oak table.

I gratefully accept and take a sip. I can feel him watching me again.

"I'm not sure you know just how beautiful you are," he says softly.

My wet hair has begun to dry and curl in loose waves around my face. The sunshine is illuminating my eyes and making my tired skin look better than I deserve after a late night and sleeping in my makeup.

"I'd tell you the same, but I have a feeling you know exactly how beautiful you are."

He reaches for my hand and runs his callused thumb across mine. "Let's go to your hotel and collect your things.

We only have two more days together before you fly home." I marvel at his confidence and presumptuousness.

"What if I have plans?" I laugh.

"Let's not kid ourselves; this is as good as Seattle is going to get for you. And if you're lucky, I just might take you under my wing. The good news is that I can take you to grab a few things but I only have room for essentials, because the bad news is that we're driving there via my primary form of transportation; my motorcycle."

"More bad news," he continues, "you're wearing a dress, which isn't ideal. Good news, or possibly still just more bad news, I have my younger sister's boots and chaps here that she wears when we ride. You look to be about her size."

"People actually wear these?" I question, as he hands me a pair of leather chaps. It's better than bare legs I suppose, maybe.

"Not when we're riding in the city, they're more for the highway. In an accident they can save your legs from road rash, and they protect them from the elements."

I slip them over my legs and attempt to slide them up, feeling jealous of his obviously thinner sister as I struggle to get them over my thighs.

"Let me help you, mama," he says, grabbing the waistband and pulling them up my legs. My dress hikes up in the process and I am reminded of my decision to go commando. His hands pause on my bare hips for a second and he raises an eyebrow. My face burns and I quickly smooth my dress down around my waist.

"Forgot something," I say, and retreat to the bedroom to pry the chaps off and slip my underwear back on.

Correction to my prior statement; no underwear is better than dirty underwear only when not facing an impromptu motorcycle ride.

"I look absolutely ridiculous," I laugh, and gesture to my hoodie, chaps, dress and boots.

"You look absolutely perfect." He hands me a helmet.

We whip through the city on his motorcycle and the rush of wind and the speed is exhilarating. I hug him tightly and lean my cheek against his back. The tall, striking buildings contrast the mountains, trees and Puget Sound. The sky has turned a gloomy grey but slivers of sunshine are peeking through the cloud cover.

At the hotel I head upstairs to fill the backpack that he's given me. I can't risk anyone seeing us together. I rifle through my suitcase pulling out clothes and toiletries. From the hidden compartment I take the sleeping pills and oleander and zip them into my makeup case. I change into a more functional outfit of jeans, sneakers and a zip-up athletic sweater.

"Where are we going?" I ask, hopping back on the bike and fastening the helmet strap under my chin.

"You'll see when we get there," he revs his bike.

We ride to Washington Park and take Lake Washington Boulevard East to the southern end of the Washington Park Arboretum. A small wooden arrow indicates *Japanese Garden* ahead.

He pulls into a small parking lot and we take off our helmets. I shake my hair out in what I hope is a biker chic way and he leads me toward the gardens. "This is one of my favorite places in Seattle, maybe even the world." We pass under the wooden entrance and as we enter the urban oasis of the Arboretum my mouth drops open in awe. Graceful Japanese trees and shrubs surround a calm, sparkling pond alive with water lilies. Fat Koi fish swim languidly, their greedy mouths surfacing every few minutes in search of food. The park is full of life and a tapestry of rich fall colors.

We walk beside each other easily and quietly, as if we're at that stage in a serious relationship where you don't feel the need to fill the silence with conversation. We pause on a small stone bridge overlooking the water, each of us lost in our own reveries. The blazing fire red leaves of the Japanese maple and the elegant drooping branches of a weeping willow are so exquisite they could be a poem. The air hums with the sounds of birds and insects, and I swear even the flapping of butterfly wings.

An elderly couple sits on a bench beside the bridge. The woman has taken care to dress well for their excursion, and wearing a wool coat and a brightly colored scarf. Her lipstick is a shade of bright pink reserved for women of her age. The man is in a jacket and a bowler cap, he holds a cane in one hand and her hand in the other. I wonder what their secret is.

"You should see it in the spring when everything's in bloom, the cherry blossoms are out of this world. I come here often to find inspiration for my paintings. All the different colors and hues," Abe says.

"Thank you for bringing me here." I squeeze his hand.

"Well, hopefully, I've met and exceeded your expectation so far." He bends and gives a slight bow. "That's what I'm about by the way, in case you haven't noticed. Next stop, coffee—a trip to Seattle isn't complete without it, and I don't mean Starbucks."

Abe orders us two drip coffees at a cute café called Cherry Street Coffee House and the barista works his magic while I take in the patterned mirrored wall and bright murals. Abe sets our coffee down with a flourish and as I grab my cup to take a sip, he stops me.

"Mama, this ain't no Tim Horton's, this is the type of coffee that has to be savored. I'll teach you. First, you hold the cup in both of your hands and let it warm them up. Then you put your face right over the cup and inhale deep," he demonstrates.

"Then, and only then, can you take a sip. But take it slowly, and close your eyes while you do it, focusing only on the taste."

I follow his lead and relish the rich, smooth, dark taste of the coffee. "Mmm," I tease as I open my eyes. "It's almost as good as Tim Horton's."

He swats my hand and feigns offense. "Are you caffeinated? Because the Seattle tourist tour continues."

We park the bike and hop on the public water taxi that takes us across Elliott Bay to West Seattle. I lean against the railing of the upper deck with his arm around my shoulders and he points out landmarks like the Space Needle and the Seattle Great Wheel. The Seattle skyline in all its unobstructed glory is radiant. He rests his chin on the top of my head and my heart somersaults in my chest. We hop off the boat and onto a shuttle that takes us to the West Seattle Junction.

At the West Seattle Farmers Market, we fill the rest of

the backpack up with leafy green romaine and crisp vegetables still covered in dirt from the garden: cucumbers, carrots, onions and tomatoes. I select a freshly baked loaf of artisan bread and chunks of locally produced cheese: brie, stilton and smoked cheddar. The backpack is bursting at the seams when he stops at a fresh fish stall and orders a dozen oysters.

"I hear they're an aphrodisiac," he winks. "Wait here for the oysters, there's one last thing I need to grab," he says, disappearing into the fray of people.

He returns a few minutes later with his hand behind his back. "There are always flowers for those who want to see them," he quotes Matisse, with a terrible impersonation of a French accent. He produces a single white lily from behind his back and tucks it into the elastic of my messy bun.

We stroll leisurely in and out of trendy boutiques, trying on vintage hats and cowboy boots and admiring art and jewelry from local artists. We pass street murals and endless coffee shops, making our way along the water to Beach Drive and stopping to sit on a bench just as the sun is beginning to sink into the horizon. The sky has cleared and is streaked with neon orange, fuchsia and violet over the Puget Sound.

He unpacks the groceries and I excuse myself, retreating to the bedroom to check my phone. Several missed calls and texts have accumulated, the most recent from Jake asking, *Where the hell are you?*

There's another from Becca reminding me about her annual Halloween. I completely forgot. I'll have to figure out my costume when I get home. For now, I'm going to enjoy the radio silence and pretend that my phone was out of service.

Abe is chopping vegetables with a large chef's knife and making neat little piles with quick slices of the blade. The knife glides through the vegetables with a satisfying crunch. I'm reminded of my objective.

"Need help?" I ask.

"Absolutely, the wine isn't going to open itself. Why don't you work on that." He digs a knife into the oysters and expertly pries off the top shells.

I grab a corkscrew, willing away memories, and pop the cork out of a bottle of wine and pouring us both generous glasses. He sets the freshly tossed salad and bread on the table with the cheeses and a bowl of olive oil mixed with balsamic vinegar. I'm already on my second glass of wine by the time he places the icy bowl full of oysters in front of us. His face is flushed and his forehead is slightly damp from running around the kitchen like Bobbie Flay possessed.

We eat the salad with gusto, starved from our adventure, and devour the bread and cheese with little grace. We tip the oysters into our mouths, letting the cool, briny flesh slide down our throats. I'm full and borderline drunk. I stretch, leaning back into the dining room chair.

The Foo Fighters have been playing softly in the background, Seattle's own I'm told, and as it switches to *Everlong*, Abe stands up and asks, "May I have this dance?"

He twirls me around the living room, clumsily spinning and dipping.

We're both laughing as he pulls me close. I stand on his feet and we sway back and forth to the music.

His face is dangerously close to mine and I'm inhaling his exhale. I'm pressed so close against him that I can feel his heart beating as fast as mine.

He leans in and kisses me.

I've never wanted anyone or needed anyone like this. I kiss him back breathlessly, and he slips my shirt off as I unbutton his. The adrenaline is racing through me and making me feel lightheaded. He picks me up and I wrap my legs around his waist. There's no time to make it to the bedroom, there's not even time to clear the table. He pushes the dishes out of the way and sends plates and cutlery smashing to the floor. It's a beautiful disaster.

I pull my jeans off; the oyster bowl has overturned and the ice underneath my back is so cold it's burning. He grabs a fistful of my hair and pulls my head backward, kissing my exposed neck. I pull him on top of me and rake my nails down his shoulder. A trail of blood begins to form, and I can feel it warm and wet beneath my fingers.

He presses his forehead to mine and whispers into my mouth, "I think I might love you."

Chapter 11
Thursday, October 7th

Abe is asleep next to me with his mouth slightly open. I study the curve of his lips, and the sharp angles of his jawline remind me of the edge of a protractor. His hair is wild, tangled and has a musty unwashed smell that I forever associate with little boys on the playground. I'm terrified that I might love him back.

I close my eyes and try to remember the instances where I've felt something akin to love. My first kiss with Mike Wallace in the parking lot of King Pin's is where it started. He told me I had nice eyes and kissed me, for twenty-one seconds I counted. On the walk home afterward, the pavement may as well have been clouds and I had a tingling in my chest as if I had swallowed a package of Pop Rocks.

There was not a repeat encounter and a week later I saw him in the hallway at school holding hands with Lenore Grabbison. Who names their kid Lenore? It reminded me of that dark Edgar Allan Poe poem, *The Raven*, that we were forced to recite in English class.

After Mike there was Joe Rossi, an Italian boy that I dated near the end of high school. He wore his hair slicked close to his head and he had a nice laugh and warm hands.

He grew up with the traditional Italian belief that women should stay home while men provide for them, so, when the subject of me going to college came up, the relationship quickly fell apart. I still think of him every time I eat Chicken Parmigiana.

While in college I dated a classmate, Cole Andicott. He had bright blue eyes, wavy blonde hair and a politician's smile. He lent me a pen in class and when I returned it, he said the least I could do to repay my debt was meet him for coffee. He was elected president of the student union a few months into our relationship and I began to feel like he addressed me in the same diplomatic, superficial way that he talked to other students.

Then of course there's Jake. Try as I may to forget him, especially right now, he is in the back of my mind..

Abe's eyelids flicker open and he reaches for me.

"Hey," he smiles sleepily.

"I wish we could stay like this forever," I say softly.

"We can."

So, we do, for the next twenty-four anyways. He strokes my hair. I trace the lines and curves of his tattoos with my fingertips. I lie against his chest and listen to the thud of his heartbeat in my ear. It reminds me of holding a seashell to my ear when I was young and listening for the ocean.

We eat leftover cheese in bed and open another bottle of wine. I worry we'll spill the red wine on the light duvet but Abe reminds me that duvets don't matter, that nothing really matters, except enjoying moments like these until they pass.

He asks about my family, about Sunshine, about my friends. He asks what happened to Cara. I blank; and everything flickers, bright white. We don't talk about it.

At some point we find the motivation to get out of bed and he takes me to his studio a few minutes from his loft. We pull up to an old building and park his bike against the curb. The neighborhood isn't anything to look at, mostly industrial and concrete. We take a sketchy elevator up to the fourth floor and walk down a narrow hallway until we reach a nondescript pine door with a small wooden sign inscribed with, *A.M.*

The warehouse space is wide open with painted white wood floors and twelve-foot ceilings. Light floods in through tall, aluminum framed windows. In one corner of the room are woodworking tools, piles of sawdust and half-finished pieces of furniture. The other corner has canvases in various stages of completion and a table covered in a rainbow of paints and well-used paintbrushes.

"Welcome to my world," Abel gestures grandly at his creations.

"Your paintings are amazing and so is the furniture you're building." I walk around the room taking everything in.

"Thanks, babe, it's something to do in-between the boring nine to five stuff." He unzips his backpack and produces a bottle of wine and two plastic glasses. "Only the finest for my queen."

I take a glass, running my fingers along the rough surface of an end table he's building out of salvaged wood.

He sets a large canvas on an easel and pulls a cracked, black leather stool up to it.

"We're going to do some art therapy," he begins, grabbing a paintbrush and pallet. "I know you don't like talking about what happened to your sister, but I think it would help you to open up."

He looks at me meaningfully, "I know I don't know you that well, but as an artist I like to study people, and I'm fairly perceptive. I can sense a very strong energy…a darkness, about you."

I set my glass of wine down, my hands trembling.

"If you don't let it go, it's going to consume you," he says, more like a fact than a warning.

"Abel, this isn't a good idea."

"It is, mama. Don't worry." He takes my face in his hands. "Look at me." The blue streak in his eye cuts through the hazel like a river through a valley. His hands smell of turpentine.

"Nothing you say is going to scare me off, I promise. I just want to make you feel better. Close your eyes and tell me the colors you see when you think of Cara."

Hearing him say her name is a strange sensation but I like the way it spills off his tongue like ribbons. I sit on a metal fold-out chair and close my eyes.

"White. I see white."

"Why white?"

"White because it's good and pure, like she was. White like the first snowfall. She was always so excited to wake up to a fresh blanket of snow. White like clouds. White like heaven."

"What other colors do you see?"

"Grey. Grey like storm clouds. Like rain. Grey like the smooth, round stones we'd skip out onto the lake. Grey like gravestones. And I see black like her hair. Like our hair. Black like emptiness. Black like death."

My voice is shattering and I can feel tears hot on my cheeks. Images of her flash through my mind like slides in a toy View-Master reel. Thinking of everything that she's missed makes me miss her even more.

"And red. Red like the color of her favorite T-shirt. Red like pain. Red like blood."

I bury my face in my hands, trying to escape my emotions, sadness washing over me like a wave. Abel wraps me up in his arms and I cry until I'm empty.

On the canvas Abel has painted a gradation of color from black to grey to white. Deep red angry brushstrokes dominate the bottom of the canvas. The colors transition from light to dark and jump off the canvas like emotions. I inhale the oily chemical smell of the paint. I touch my fingers to the top of the canvas and run them all the way down leaving a trail behind them.

We arrive back at his loft just as the sun is setting. We sit in comfortable silence and watch it disappear behind the mountains. I pretend that this is my life and that I belong here.

We can't be bothered to go out to eat so Abe calls in an order for sushi. He swears it's the freshest I'll find, probably plucked out of the ocean this morning. A shy, pizza-faced delivery boy knocks on the door and hands over plastic bags filled with our feast. I pull out chopsticks, snapping them apart with a satisfying crack. Abe pours the salty soy sauce packets into a bowl and I dunk a piece of tuna sashimi into it with relish. The cool, buttery fish melts on my tongue.

Abe bites into raw octopus covered in wasabi and offers Raptor a piece, almost losing his fingers in the process. His hair hangs over his eyes as he leans over and I notice the slight indentation of dimples in his cheeks as he grins.

We cuddle up on the leather couch, wrapping ourselves in blankets and Raptor curls up at our feet. The fire flickers softly and we watch *What Dreams May Come*, starring Robin Williams as a pediatrician who dies in a car crash following the death of his children. He watches from afar as his wife grieves, mourns, and adjusts to his afterlife in heaven. His wife commits suicide and he ventures to the depths of hell to save her.

His character shines in an exquisite heaven he's imagined for himself. I know with certainty that Cara is in such a place; filled with color, beauty and warmth. My stomach turns when the character travels to the dark, grisly depths of an unforgiving hell, because I know that's where I'm going to end up.

In bed with Abel's arms wrapped around me, I can feel the steady rhythm of his breathing against my back. I stare into the darkness, committing every detail of him to memory. For the first time in a very long time, I feel happy.

Friday, October 8th

We arrive back at my hotel early Sunday morning and I

hand Abel his helmet. As is typical of Seattle weather it's raining and it's hard to separate tears from raindrops.

"This isn't goodbye, mama, it's just until next time." He pulls me close and we stand intertwined for what seems like hours before finally parting ways.

Chapter 12

Back home and back to reality.

Part of me wishes I could rewind the last few days like a tape and record over it, erasing the weekend with Abel. The other part of me wishes that I could rewind it only to replay it over and over again.

I'm sitting in my front room staring into the fireplace. Lana Del Ray is playing and amplifying my melancholy. I've wrapped a robe tightly around me like a security blanket. The Fiddle-leaf fig tree in the corner is wilting from neglect. My relationship is probably as well.

My thoughts are interrupted by a knock at the door. Jake is standing on my porch.

"You don't have to knock." I leave the door open as an unspoken invitation to enter. I use the wrought iron fireplace poker to nudge one of the fireplace logs. He takes off his shoes but doesn't sit down.

"Why didn't you answer me while you were away?" he questions.

"I told you; I didn't have service; something was up with my phone. I also thought it was a good idea for me to decompress and have time to myself to think about things."

He studies me. "Something is different about you."

I shrug noncommittally and pick up Cinder. I stroke

his head and look out the window. His purring vibrates against my chest.

"Charlotte, we've been dating for two years. We're in our thirties. What are we doing here? What's the end game? I can't even get a straight answer from you about living with me."

He has dark circles under his eyes and a few days' worth of growth on his face. He looks slightly unkempt, not for a normal human, just for Jake.

"Can you put Cinder down and participate in this conversation please?" he asks, frustrated.

Cinder picks up on the tension and takes it as his cue to leave, wriggling out of my arms. Traitor.

Jake puts his hands on my shoulders and forces me to look at him.

"Charlie, I fucking love you." His voice breaks as the Lana Del Ray playlist shuffles to *Ride*.

Instinctively, I want to stop his suffering. I pull him to me and kiss him. I taste the saltiness of tears but I can't tell if they're mine or his. I unbutton his shirt and kiss my way down his chest, breathing in his familiar fresh smell. I loosen the sash of my robe and let it fall to the floor.

We're laying naked on the polar bear fur rug in front of my fireplace. My head is on his chest, and he's stroking my hair. The fire crackles and spits. We couldn't be more of a cliché if we tried.

The rug is my grandparents. It's from a time when shooting and skinning a polar bear wasn't frowned upon; it was practically in fashion. The polar bear's empty stare and gaping mouth full of jagged teeth used to frighten me but now I find it comforting. Every child in my family has had at least one naked baby photo taken on the rug. I guess I've come full circle.

I analyze cracks in my ceiling that are forming in the plaster.

"I'll clean out the closet in the spare room and you can have two drawers. That's my hard stop—two drawers. And my office is off limits, you can't fill it full of your files and paperwork."

I keep my gaze fixed on the ceiling but out of the corner of my eye I can see his face break into a grin. He pulls me back on top of him and my hair hangs in wild loose tendrils that graze his chin. He puts his hands on my hips. The fire sparks and tiny embers land on my bare back. I barely flinch. It's better to feel pain than nothing at all.

I wait until Jake is sound asleep to sneak downstairs to the basement and shove my laundry from Seattle into the washing machine. I pick up the grey RVCA hoodie I took from Abe and bury my face into it, inhaling the smell of gasoline and his cologne mixed with sweat. I throw the hoodie into the machine and close the door, letting the hum of the washing machine drown out the sound of me crying.

Chapter 13
Saturday, October 17th

I pull into my parent's driveway and mentally prepare myself before entering the house. I haven't talked to my mom since the disastrous dinner and I feel guilty about avoiding her phone calls and texts. My phone buzzes with a text message from Abel, *Missing you*.

There's a cool breeze coming off the lake and I tuck my hands into my jacket pockets. Bright red and yellow leaves float off the big oak in the front yard and dance briefly in the wind before landing gracefully on the lawn. The petals on the Black-eyed Susans are wilting and their bulbous black centers are drying out, making them look like gaping mouths.

"Hello," I call and walk into the front door. It's always open.. The living room looks the same, a museum of my childhood. The velvet flower-patterned sofas, the china cabinet full of my great grandmother's china, the family photos in heavy brass frames. There's a picture of my parents on their wedding day; my dad with wild dark hair and a heavy mustache and beard, resplendent in a black suit and bowtie, towering over my mom. She looked like a porcelain doll with glossy red hair and lips and big green eyes. Her milky skin was almost the same color as the delicate lace wedding dress she wore.

A photo of Magnolia beaming, holding a scroll; a cap on her head, in her graduation photo. A picture of Cara and I aged eleven, wearing identical pink bathing suits with green flowers, holding hands on the beach. I can barely tell who's who. That's the last photo my mom put up of me.

In the kitchen of faded oak cabinets and ancient appliances, I open the fridge and help myself to a leftover piece of shepherd's pie. It always smells like potatoes in here regardless if any are being cooked. Through the kitchen window that overlooks the backyard I see my dad stacking logs into a pile. I finish the pie, wipe my hands on my jeans and walk out the screen door onto the deck.

I cup my hands around my mouth and whistle, mimicking a chickadee sound. My dad looks up and grins. On hikes he would point out different species of birds to me, he could identify them by only their songs. He used a chickadee call to summon us in from outside. No matter where we were in the neighborhood, we would hear it echoing down the street.

"Where's mom?" I ask, sitting down on a nearby stump.

"At some church thing, she should be home soon."

He grabs a piece of wood and steadies it before swinging the axe down. The wood splits perfectly with a satisfying *thwack*. He's wearing a battered flannel jacket and a pair of Levis that he's probably owned since I was a teenager. He's never been one to want for anything and every spare bit of money he's had he would spend on his family.

"Your furnace still holding up?"

This is his favorite topic of conversation, second only to conversations about my hot water tank or my car. I know when he asks me these things it's his way of showing he cares. Growing up in a Romanian family, affection was as scarce as food on the table. His parents were hard people with warm hearts and they passed their idiosyncrasies to him and his siblings.

"Yup, furnace still kicking." I draw a circle in the dirt with the toe of my sneaker.

"How's Jakey boy?" My dad has a soft spot for Jake. I think he's fascinated that Jake gets dressed in a suit every day to work at a job that relies on his brain. My dad has always relied on his brawn to make a living.

"He's good. He's moving in with me."

He splits another log with minimal effort. "Well, Charlie, I just want you to be happy. Whatever makes you happy."

For some reason this makes me sad. I bite my lip, swallow the lump in my throat and wipe my eyes on my sleeve before he notices.

"Let me try one." I reach for the axe.

I swing it over my shoulder and bring it down hard. The log splinters and cracks like bones. I chop three more until I'm sweating. The screen door squeaks and my mom walks out onto the deck.

"Hi, sweetie, when did you get here?" she asks. She's wearing her usual strand of pearls with trousers and a powder blue embroidered cardigan. She always looks like she's getting ready to board a train, and the year is 1950.

"Not too long ago." I get up to give her a hug. My chin touches the top of her head. She smells like peaches and Ponds face cream. "Let's go for a walk before it gets dark." I gesture toward the lake. She grabs a fleece jacket and we walk to the path that leads along the water.

"How was church?" I ask.

She repeatedly invites me to church but I've yet to take her up on it. I've been to church once since Cara's funeral and I'm not sure I'll ever go again. It was shortly after the funeral that my mom asked Magnolia and I to join her for a Sunday morning service. She had been invited to attend by a woman she ran into at the post office who had heard about Cara. My dad had gotten out of it; feigning atheism, indifference or ignorance. Magnolia and I were desperate to help our mom get her mind off Cara so we agreed.

We woke up early to catch the 9:00 a.m. service and dressed carefully in pastel-colored blouses and skirts. Our faces were washed, our teeth brushed and our hair pulled back into neat French braids. We could have passed for characters from *Little House on the Prairie*. We drove in silence to the small white church just outside of town. In the past we had attended services at the bigger church in Sunshine, where Cara's funeral was held. We pulled onto the side of the road to park and my mom turned off the car. We waited for her to get out but instead she sat silently in the driver's seat, her hands clutching the steering wheel as if she was drowning and it was her life preserver. Her normally, naturally, rosy cheeks were pale and her eyes were dull and had blueish circles under them.

"Mom, are we going in?" asked Magnolia after a few minutes.

It took her a moment before responding, "I don't know what it is I'm looking for but I don't know if I'm going to find it here."

Magnolia and I exchanged glances and she encouraged my mom, "Well, we're here anyways, we might as well go in."

She finally got out of the car, her unruly, red hair already beginning to free itself from a carefully slicked back bun. We crossed a small wooden bridge built over a creek and walked the short dirt path to the church entrance. I was struck by the amount of light and space inside the seemingly small church. Light streamed in through the stained-glass windows, illuminating the faded wooden floors in a kaleidoscope of colors. It smelled like a library; wood, aging books and dust.

A round lady in a deep purple pantsuit greeted us at the door. A string of pearls was strung tightly around her neck and her mother of pearl earrings looked like clip-ons. She had dark blonde, tightly permed hair and her lips were a slash of burgundy. My mom introduced her as the lady from the post office that had invited her.

She smiled at us, clasped both of my mom's hands and looked into her eyes. "He heals the brokenhearted and binds up their wounds."

My mom warmed, like a flower to the sun, and even as silent tears crept down her cheeks, I saw the first semblance of a smile in weeks. The lady, who I later came to know as Joan, was a member of the congregation. I know that it was

Joan's warmth and kindness that gave my mom the strength to continue. She reminded her that while she was destined to suffer, she did not have to suffer alone.

I sat on a hard wooden pew listening to the pastor preach and read scripture, wishing that some part of me could find comfort in his words. Flecks of dust flitted in the beams of sunlight and yet I still felt the darkness creeping back in.

I knew logically that I wouldn't find Cara in a church, or sunbeams, or the gentle ripples of the lake. I'd find her slowly decomposing five miles north in the Sunshine cemetery.

After attending the service something in my mom changed. The color slightly returned to her cheeks and the ghost of a smile played in the corners of her mouth. She had found something that she had lost that day, even if it wasn't her daughter. For that reason, I'll always be grateful to God, and Joan. Whether I truly believe in either of them or not.

As we walk along the lake my mom tells me about the latest church drama; how May Evanson didn't contribute to the bake sale because she's miffed that she was ousted as church secretary by Elizabeth Peters. I feign shock and listen to her rattle on for a few minutes. She asks how things are with me and I tell her that Jake is moving in. I can tell she's pleased but she knows better than to bring up marriage again.

We stop in front of a small section of beach and walk down to the damp sand to skip stones out onto the glassy surface of the lake.

"This was your favorite place to swim with Cara, we

would have to drag you girls out of here when the sun started to go down. You used to tell me that you were going to be mermaids when you grew up."

In the afternoon sunlight she looks every bit her fifty-eight years. Age spots are starting to appear on her otherwise clear complexion and worry lines run into deep rivulets on her forehead and at the corners of her eyes. Her once vibrant red hair has dulled to the color of an old copper penny.

I don't like to think about my parents getting older. I like to pretend that they will perpetually stay as they are. My dad puttering around in the backyard or the garage, my mom in the kitchen making Irish stew or tending to the flower beds.

As children we would visit my grandma Brennan regularly at the nursing home she lived in. We would play with the miniature crystal cut animals decorating her dresser and shove Werther's caramel candies into our mouths while our parents made small talk. When we tired of fighting over the crystal animals, we all wanted the horse, we would race up and down the sterile linoleum halls, our footsteps echoing.

Cara and I were fascinated with the nursing home residents. The elderly man with the pointed chin and coke bottle glasses who wheeled himself up and down the hallways with no final destination. The nice blue-haired lady who offered us stale cookies and dainties she kept in her room. The pale, frail man who sat outside the lunchroom, his head lolling back into the headrest of his wheelchair. We smiled at him when we passed and while his head didn't budge an inch, his milky eyes would follow us.

I hazily remember the woman that my grandma was. It comes to me in fragments. Kneeling in the garden with her straw sun hat shading her face, teaching Cara and I to plant flowers. Walking down the pier in Sunshine with her and my sisters licking ice cream cones. Her tinkly laugh that sounded like a piano.

As she grew older our grandma started to confuse Cara and I, and sometimes ask why there were two of us. We would tell her about school or Stanley and she would stare blankly, nodding and chewing an imaginary piece of gum. Her watery eyes not quite looking at us, but through us. We would give her a requisite kiss goodbye on her tissue paper cheek.

Our minds become murky as we age, like the Lake Winnipeg water. Our senses dull until eventually we're a ghost, a shell, of the person we once were. Do the things and people that bring us happiness and make us feel alive fade into memories? Are we destined to spend our final days sitting by a window watching people pass, listening to the clock tick, waiting and hoping for a dreamless endless sleep?

"I want you to get better, honey," my mom interrupts my thoughts. Her eyes are filled with tears.

"Mom, what are you talking about?" I wrap my arms around her tiny shoulders. "I'm fine. Everything is going to be fine." Even as I say the words out loud, I wish I believed them.

I decide to stay the night in Sunshine. I let myself into the bedroom that I used to share with Cara while my mom makes dinner. The two twin beds are exactly as they were, made up with handmade quilts from my grandma Brennan. I lie down on my bed and the old metal springs squeak and groan under my weight.

If I moved all the way to the edge of my bed, and Cara moved to the edge of hers, we could reach out and touch each other's fingertips. It was part of our goodnight ritual. That and talking and giggling in the dark until our parents would pound on the door and threaten us with punishments.

The walls are still plastered with pictures of horses and Hunks of the Week, from *Teen Beat* magazine. After Cara died, my mom didn't want to change anything, she wanted it all to stay exactly as it was. Our bedroom stayed preserved in time while the rest of the world moved on around it. I'm still half expecting Cara to walk in the door and sit down on the bed across from me.

"Dinner's ready," my mom calls from the kitchen.

She's cooked her usual fare of pot roast, boiled potatoes, green beans and dinner rolls. My dad piles his plate high. He likes eating her meals almost as much as she likes making them.

In grade school my dad promised to attend a school open house to see mine and Cara's science project. It was on constellations, and he'd helped us outfit our display board in blinking white Christmas lights, to look like stars. He came straight from the steel mill where he worked to make it in time. He still had on his work coveralls, covered in black dirt, and he carried his hard hat in his hands.

"It looks great," he beamed, studying our presentation board.

"Thanks, Dad." Cara and I smiled in unison.

I left the gym to grab a drink from the water fountain and passed by two teachers talking in the hallway.

"Did you see what Alin showed up here looking like?"

"I saw, not surprising, he's a meat and potatoes type of guy," said the other.

I remember thinking, of course, he loves meat and potatoes—they're his favorite. When I reported back to Cara about the odd conversation, she looked upset and I didn't understand why.

"Meat and potatoes is another way of saying dad is simple. They were making fun of him."

My throat grew tight and my ears burned hot with shame. We left the school that night with both of our hands slipped into his. We were always proud to call him our dad.

We enjoy a surprisingly nice, uneventful dinner and after we congregate on the living room couches to watch *The Shawshank Redemption*. Tim Robbins plays Andy Dufresne, a banker sentenced to life in prison. "Remember, Red, hope is a good thing, maybe the best of things, and no good thing ever dies," his character says stoically.

Bullshit, I think as I chew on a handful of microwave popcorn. Hope is a dangerous thing. It gives people reason to believe their circumstances can change purely by divine intervention. It's like that last ember in the fire that flickers and makes you think it could ignite again, only to die out anyways.

After the movie we all retreat to bed and I lay awake in

my old room staring at the glow-in-the-dark star stickers lighting up the ceiling. If I squint, I can see the little dipper, big dipper and Orion's belt. I hear my dad snoring from across the hallway. I've been tossing and turning for the last couple of hours and can't seem to fall asleep. I get out of bed and throw on a pair of pants and a sweater.

I slip quietly out of my bedroom, pad barefoot down the hallway and let myself out the back door. The night is deathly quiet except for the cicadas singing in shrill, sweet, cacophony. I slide my feet into a pair of communal sandals left on the deck and walk the short block to the lake.

I sit on the shore and stick my toes into the cold sand. A pair of ducks quack softly as they bob up and down with the waves. I pull my hood up over my head and lie back, using the sand as a pillow. The night sky is alive with auroras and a blanket of stars. I hear a sudden crack and footsteps behind me.

As the big, looming shape gets closer, I realize with relief that it's my dad.

"Couldn't sleep?" he asks, sitting down beside me in the sand.

"Never really can in that room," I admit.

"I knew I'd find you here, down by the water. Was always yours and Cara's favorite place to be."

We sit in silence watching the northern lights dance across the sky in waves of indigo, violet and green.

"The Cree people believe the northern lights are spirits of the dead who live in the sky, and that they're trying to communicate with the loved ones that they left behind here on earth. Sometimes I sit out here watching them and I think of your sister. That's where I like to think she is."

This is the most my dad has said about Cara since her death. My mom talks about her enough for the both of them and it seems he'd rather not dredge up painful memories.

The moonlight illuminates the few stray tears that roll down his cheek and disappear into his beard. I slip my hand into his and we stare out at the northern lights trying to decipher whatever message it is that Cara might be trying to send us.

Chapter 14
Monday, October 19th

I love Halloween, it's my favorite holiday. When else are you encouraged to dress up in costume, eat all the candy you want, and celebrate evil? My costumes are usually elaborate and planned out months in advance, so I'm definitely behind schedule this year. Jake is going as Indiana Jones. While not overly impressed with his creativity I'm relieved that he didn't propose a lame couple's costume like a plug and socket.

Jake was eager to move in, "Finally," he emphasized, and he moved most of his things in while I was in Sunshine. I step around his boxes in the entrance way and notice his favorite *Rocky III* movie poster propped against the wall, waiting to be hung. I bring it down to the basement and hide it behind some clutter. Hopefully, Jake will forget about it as a half-naked Sylvester Stallone doesn't fit with my current décor.

It's going to take getting used to sharing my space. I like my privacy. I feel like a double agent trying to keep up my facades with both Jake and Abel. I don't want either of them to find out about the other before I have the chance to tell them.

While I'm down in the basement I dig through my

storage room for costumes and find the black spandex bodysuit I've been looking for buried under wigs, cowboy hats and tubes of fake blood. I shake the literal and metaphorical cobwebs out of the bodysuit and bring it to the kitchen table workstation that I've set up with newspaper, paintbrushes, and glow in the dark paint. I'm going to attempt to paint an anatomically correct human skeleton onto the bodysuit using glow in the dark paint. I'm delicately painting the left tibia when my phone rings.

"Hey, mama, what're you up to?" Abel asks in his sexy, gravelly voice.

"Don't even ask. I wish you were here though; I could really use someone with artistic talent to help."

"Well, that's actually why I'm calling. I just finished booking a flight."

"That's cool, where are you going?" I ask distractedly and screw up painting the collarbone.

"Well, Winnipeg actually."

I drop the paintbrush to the floor. "Oh…really?" I'm on my knees now trying to rub the paint off the floor with the back of my hand before it dries.

"I hope that's cool. I wanted to surprise you. I miss you already."

"Yeah, no, that's amazing. When are you coming?"

"I get in Saturday, November 1st, late morning, I remembered you have that Halloween party on Friday."

I don't know how to even begin to deal with this situation right now. "Sounds great. Listen, let me figure out a few details and I'll give you a call a bit later. I'm just finishing my costume and I'm up to my eyeballs in glow in the dark paint."

"No problem, babe. Talk later, love ya."

"Love you back."

"Who was that?" asks Jake, walking into the kitchen. I didn't hear him come in.

"My mom." The lie slides off my tongue like a serpent.

"Good, it's nice to see you getting along with her again." He grabs an apple out of the fridge and bites into it with an annoying crunch. Was he always this annoying of an apple eater? I grit my teeth and try not to swat the apple out of his hand.

"Working on your costume?" He leans over the table to study my handiwork.

My phone buzzes and a text message from Abel lights up the screen. I grab for it hoping Jake didn't catch the name.

I need space from Jake so I let myself out the back door and through Reese's side gate which he always forgets to lock. I pound on the back door and wait a few seconds listening to Thor's ballistic barking before letting myself in.

"Hello," I call, patting a frantic Thor on the head as he slobbers all over my pants.

"In the living room," yells Reese over the sound of Metallica.

The kitchen is full of empty beer bottles and pizza boxes piled on the table. I find him sprawled out on the couch in his boxers.

I can't help but admire the cut of his undeserved abs as I pick up a Winnipeg Jets shirt off the floor and throw it to him. He sits up with what appears to be great effort and slips it over his head, making no attempt to put on pants. I eye the dying palm tree in the corner of the room beside a Thor-sized dog bed and Thor-sized rawhide bone. The curtains are pulled shut, allowing only the tiniest sliver of light to stretch across the floor. I'm sure the light intensifies the level of Reese's obvious hangover.

He runs his hands through his disheveled hair and cracks open a lonesome beer sitting on the coffee table. I notice a leopard print lace bra on the floor beside the couch and roll my eyes. Who wears leopard print bras?

"What`s up?" he asks weakly.

"Big night?"

"Every night is a big night, sweetheart. Some of the guys came over here after the hockey game and things got a little out of hand."

"Mmmhmm."

"What's with you. How was Seattle?"

"It was good."

"Yeah, did you fall for some punk musician while you were out there?"

"Something like that," I laugh. "I asked Jake to move in with me."

"No shit." He takes another swig from his beer. "He must be thrilled."

"I think so."

"Well, what are you doing over here already? Shouldn't

you be making him a sandwich while wearing only an apron or something?"

"You're such a pig." I chuck a grimy throw pillow at him.

He deflects it with this arm and it bounces to the floor, startling a sleepy Thor.

"I just needed to get out of the house for a bit."

"Ooo, I smell trouble in paradise already."

"Shut up and put it on something good for us to watch." I curl my legs up on the couch.

"If you're cold over there you can always come sit here with me." He grins wolfishly, patting the couch beside him.

I shake my head in feigned disgust as he switches it to *Law and Order*.

Chapter 15
Thursday, October 22nd

I flip open my laptop and nurse a Starbucks coffee while I wait for it, and me, to wake up. Work is pretty flexible but I do have to make periodic appearances at the office and today is one of those days. I spin around in my chair and look out the floor to ceiling window at the Winnipeg skyline. We're located on the thirtieth floor and I get dizzy thinking about how high up we are.

My office is nondescript; there's the token "inspirational quotes" calendar on my desk, a half-alive/mostly dead African Violet, and a few pictures pinned to my bulletin board. There's one of Jake and me at his Christmas party two years ago. He's handsome in a dark suit, and I'm wearing a cocktail dress. My eyes are slightly glazed and my smile is forced but I remember being happy.

Jake left a sticky note stuck on my coffee cup this morning, "*Have a good day xo.*" I crumpled it up and tossed it on the counter before reading through text conversations with Abel from the night before. I'm intoxicated by him. He's the last thing I think of before I fall asleep and the first thing I think of when I wake up.

I think back to the junkie on Hastings Street and wonder if this is what addiction feels like? A raw, gnawing ache in the pit of your stomach. The obsession. The ecstasy, the delirium of getting exactly what you want. I've only ever felt this way killing. Maybe that's why Abel is still alive; he simply replaced one addiction with another.

I've been feeling on edge since I got back from Seattle. Unsettled. A claustrophobic, uneasy feeling is building again—like a fever. Could I move on and kill someone else? I click open my calendar on the computer and see that I'm not scheduled for another in-flight training session until after Christmas. That feels like a long time.

"Charlie!" exclaims Kelly St. Martin, the Manager of Flight Operations, as she pops her head into my office. "Do you have time to meet now?" It's not a question, she's asking out of courtesy, but I can tell it's not optional.

I do like Kelly; she's classy, funny and fair. She has on a tailored suit that accents her trim figure and her shiny brown hair is tucked back into a neat chignon at the back of her head. Her makeup is tasteful and neutral. I've known Kelly to get a bit rowdy after a few drinks at the pub up the street but in the office she's all business.

"Sure." I fake smile. "Give me five minutes and I'll be right there." I hear her heels clicking down the hallway and I groan, collapsing back into my chair. Unexpected meetings with Kelly were never a good thing. I will myself to get up and head to the washroom.

I study myself in the mirror while I wash my hands and am not pleased with the results. I pinch my cheeks in an effort to bring some color back into my face and run a tinted lip-gloss over my lips. I smooth down my pinstriped button-down shirt, and do up another button for good measure.

"So, how was your trip to Seattle?" Kelly asks as I sit down in her office in the seat across the desk from her.

I'm taken aback for a second and unsure if this is a trick question. "It was great, I'm glad I decided to stay a few days and check out a few parks and markets."

"Yeah, it's a neat city. I'm a huge Seahawks fan so I've been to a few games there." She ruffles through a stack of papers on her desk. "Okay, so you're probably wondering why I wanted to meet with you. I'm going to be straight. We're going through a bit of restructuring now as the company is growing, and we've decided to split your position." She pauses, taking a sip of coffee from a mug on her desk with a big cartoonish smiley face exclaiming, *Have a Nice Day!*

She continues, "From now on we'd like you to handle all of the training program development and classroom training but we're going to hire someone full-time to take care of the in-flight training sessions."

I'm confused. "You mean I won't be doing any more flights?"

"That's right. No more red-eyes to Saskatoon and cleaning out air sickness bags."

I take a second to digest this information and attempt to respond accordingly. "Umm…that sounds nice."

"I thought you'd be pleased with the changes. You're doing a great job with the training programs, Charlie, keep it up."

"Thanks, Kelly." I smile brightly, trying to quell the panic rising in my throat.

I walk out of her office and head straight for the stairwell. I race down all thirty flights of stairs, my heart hammering against my chest, my sensible heels clacking against the steps. I burst out the exit door into the alley behind our building and the cool air hits my face like a much-needed slap. I bend over, my hands on my knees, desperately trying to catch my breath.

"Charlotte?" asks a man's voice from beside me.

I lift my head to find Rick Wolfe staring down at me. "Are you okay? We have to quit running into each like this." He ashes the cigarette he's holding and exhales a cloud of smoke away from me.

"I'm fine," I gasp, trying to regulate my breathing. "Just doing a little bit of cardio on my break."

He looks at me strangely and smiles his brilliant white smile, shaking his head. "Well, you certainly don't look like you need it."

"What are you doing downtown?" I stand up, nonchalantly attempting to tuck my shirt back into my pants.

"Just came by to meet with the bosses about some new schedules."

"Can I have a drag of that?" I nod toward his cigarette.

"Sure, I didn't know you smoked?"

"I don't." I breathe in the acrid taste of tobacco and exhale deeply. My head feels light and I start to relax. "Are you done your meeting?"

"Just finished."

"You have plans now?"

"Free as a bird."

"Is it too late to take you up on that drink offer?"

I'm on my third martini and the hand on the vodka brand bar clock has just crept past five o'clock. I'm having a surprisingly good time with Rick, gossiping about co-workers, talking about places we've travelled to, and indulging in harmless flirting. Rick knows I'm with Jake, he's met him a few times at company functions, but it doesn't seem to stop him from mildly pursuing me. The liquor has relaxed my mind and my tongue and I'm almost inclined to tell him about Abel and my dilemma. I've never been one to confide in others. I hold my cards close to my chest.

I'm smiling and laughing and going through the motions but my head is going through a tailspin about my job. The changes are going to affect my life in more ways than one.

"You look like you've got a world of trouble on your mind, Charlie," Rick takes a sip of his beer.

"Sounds like the beginning to a bad country song."

"I mean it, if there's something you need to get off your chest you can tell me. No judgment here."

I hesitate. The words are on the tip of my tongue. "I just…how do you know when someone is the one? The person that you're going to spend the rest of your life with."

He looks thoughtful and calls the server over to order two whiskeys. "This kind of conversation is best suited to hard liquor," he explains.

"Well, I think that people have to make the choice whether they want to love just one person for the rest of their life, or if they want to love more than one. As I grow older I continue to reinvent myself, and the things that were once important to me become not so important, and my priorities change. And as I change, the things I look for in love change.

"In my twenties, I loved a girl who was beautiful, fun, and adventurous. In my thirties I wanted a girl that was easy-going and ambitious. In my forties, so far anyways, I find myself wanting someone that is confident and independent. It's not easy to pick someone that will grow in the same ways that you do."

Our whiskey arrives and we both take a sip. It burns my throat, warms my chest, and makes my fingertips tingle.

"So, you don't believe in 'the one'?" I ask.

"I think there are those rare breeds of people that find someone that they never want to let go. Like swans, they mate for life. For me, I doubt there will ever be just one. I think there will be many. What about you, do you believe in the one?"

"Do I believe in my ability to love one person unconditionally for the rest of my life? I do." But I'm not thinking of Jake, or even Abel, as I answer his question. I'm thinking of Cara.

"Are you sure you're okay to get home yourself?" asks Rick, holding my arm to keep me upright outside the pub.

A couple of hours and many drinks later I probably am

not, but I am sober enough to know that Rick escorting me home at this point would be a bad idea. "I'll be fine," I slur. "If you can just help me get a cab that would be great."

He hails a cab down and tucks me into the backseat, repeating my address to the driver and handing him a handful of bills with the promise that he'll get me home safely. He leans his head through the back window and reminds me to text him when I make it home safely.

"Thank you, Rick." I kiss him lightly on the side of the mouth. He winks and the cab pulls out into traffic.

I stumble in the front door and kick my heels off, narrowly missing Cinder who comes to greet me.

"Sorry, baby," I mumble, and head to the kitchen for a glass of water. The house is quiet and dark and I wonder where Jake is before remembering with relief that he has a game at the squash club tonight. I rip my hair out of the elastic, massage my scalp, and let the tap run a few minutes until the water runs cold. I grab a mason jar from the cupboard, fill it to the brim with water and gulp it down. I set the glass down on the counter with a clank and steady myself.

I run my hand along the knife block and slide the knives out, one by one, laying them out on the counter beside each other. I am a knife salesperson hawking my wares; a utility knife, a boning knife, a bread knife, a carving knife and my personal favorite, a chef's knife. I hover over the knives and adjust them into a shiny perfect row, letting my hair fall onto their glimmering blades.

I've had long hair my whole life. When I was twelve, I was obsessed with Joey from *Dawson's Creek* and I wanted to cut my hair in a shoulder length style similar to hers. When I casually mentioned it to Cara she freaked out.

"If you cut your hair, we won't look the same anymore," she accused.

Cara and I were identical twins but as we grew older slight differences revealed themselves. Cara had more prominent freckles across her nose, and I was taller than her by a half inch. If you studied us closely, you'd notice my chin to be pointed while her chin was more square. Despite the minor differences even close friends and family members sometimes had trouble telling us apart.

"Yes, we will, I'll just have shorter hair. You could always cut your hair," I suggested.

"No, Charlie, we have to stay the same as long as we can." She linked both of her hands in mine and stared at me intently.

I relented like I always did and agreed to keep my hair the same.

I gather my hair into my hand and loosely twist it into a long black braid. I pick up the chef's knife, hold the braid taut in my hand and start hacking into it. Hunks of my hair fall to the kitchen floor and I keep sawing at it until I'm left holding the decapitated braid in my hand. I drop it into the accumulated pile of hair on the floor.

I feel better already.

In the living room I look into the ornate gold mirror hanging on the wall. My hair, which had previously hung well below my breast, almost to my belly button, now lightly grazes my shoulders. The ends are completely split and uneven from my butchering.

I'll get Becca to fix it for me. For now, all I want is to go to bed.

I crawl under the covers and feel like I've just barely fallen asleep when Jake is shaking me awake.

"Charlie, what the hell is going on?" He asks angrily, standing over the bed with a handful of my hair.

"Mmm, I dunno…I cut my hair," I mumble into the pillow, closing my eyes again.

"I'm not stupid; I can see that; I'm asking you *why* you did it?"

I squint and look up at him. "I don't know, I wanted a change."

He shakes his head at me. I hear the door to the spare bedroom down the hallway slam.

I fall back asleep and I'm back in the white room again waiting for the screams to begin.

Chapter 16
Friday, October 23rd

I feel the draft from the ceiling fan on my shoulders and neck and pull the covers over my head. Pieces from the night before start to assemble into a hideous puzzle. I rake my fingers through my hair, less than half the length it used to be. Thankfully I'm not due at the office today. I grab my phone and text Becca, *911*.

I slink out of bed to get ready and press play on the music app on my phone. It shuffles to Stephen Stills, *I'm dreaming of snakes.*

According to the dream books I've read, of which there have been many, dreaming of snakes signifies that you're afraid of facing something or dealing with a difficult situation. I don't need serpents slithering through my subconscious to tell me that.

My reoccurring dream of the white room means that there is a part of myself that I'm closing off or isolating from others. I don't need the white room to tell me that either.

The hallucinations began after Cara died and have stayed with me ever since, like some sort of poltergeist determined to unbalance me. The first time I experienced a hypnogogic dream was shortly after the funeral. I woke up disoriented and terrified with tears streaming down my face and calling for my parents. They rushed to my room, my mom with night cream all over her face and a frayed purple housecoat wrapped tightly around her. My dad in flannel pajama bottoms with his hair askew and bleary eyes.

My mom sat on the edge of the bed with her arms around me and tried to soothe me. My dad was unsure how to react and instead went to the kitchen to make me a pot of tea. I didn't even like tea but I accepted it anyways, trying not to hurt his feelings. I knew it was his way of trying to make me feel better. When the dreams began occurring more frequently, my mom brought me to our family doctor and explained my "sleeping issues" as she nervously twisted her fingers in her lap.

Dr. Morris listened carefully. He had been our doctor since birth and had a long bony nose, a sharp chin and kind eyes. His once full head of hair was now mostly gone and the overhead fluorescent light bounced off the top of his bald head. He scribbled notes in his notebook and asked me a few questions about my bedtime habits and sleep routines. After several minutes of head nodding and scribbling he referred me to the Sleep Disorder Clinic at a hospital in Winnipeg.

I protested, insisting that they were nothing more than bad dreams.

"Charlotte, hypnagogic hallucinations are something to be taken seriously," said Dr. Morris, not unkindly. "Stress or anxiety is often an underlying cause. Some patients with this condition accidentally harm themselves during episodes because they are unable to distinguish between the dreams and reality."

On the car ride home from the doctor's office my mom was silent and I remember wondering if she thought I was going crazy. I remember wondering if I was going crazy. The dreams and hallucinations happen less often than they used to when I was younger but I notice their frequency increases when I'm anxious, stressed or upset.

I walk into Mane Glory with a baseball hat of Jake's pulled down low on my head. Becca stalks over to me, her heels clicking furiously against the floor tiled floor.

"What the hell did you do?" she hisses, yanking off the baseball hat.

"I...it's a long story," I say, sheepishly, self-consciously patting down my hair.

"Come, sit," she orders and marches to the back of the salon leaving me trailing behind her like a peasant.

I sulk past the black marble reception desk with *Mane Glory* written out in gold cursive on the dark grey wall behind it. The salon marries industrial and luxury with its concrete floors, quartz workstations and black leather barber chairs. The interior walls are stark white and outfitted with modern white shelves displaying trendy and expensive hair products. The sitting area has white leather couches and black and gold end tables with huge vases of white lilies, Becca's favorite. A huge ornate crystal chandelier hangs in the center of the salon and the walls are adorned with black and white photos of beautiful men and women sporting nothing but a hairstyle.

I sit down in her chair and she throws a cape over me,

pulling at the strands and assessing the situation. She frowns and wrinkles her forehead in distaste. She bites her bright purple lips in concentration. She's wearing a tight sweater dress, a leopard print scarf is wrapped around her neck and she has on fishnet stockings with black leather knee highs. Only Becca could manage to look like a knockout in that combination.

She sighs and puts both her hands on my shoulders, talking to my reflection in the mirror.

"You're going to listen to me, and you're not going to say one word while I clean up the mess you've made. What did you hack it off with a knife?"

"Well…"

"Stop, I don't even want to know the details," she throws her hands up and leads me to the sinks.

Many curses and about an hour later she spins the chair back around so that I can see myself in the mirror. My jaw drops. The hatchet job from this morning is gone and in its place is a haircut so beautiful that I barely recognize myself. My thick black hair is waved softly around my face and cut bluntly so that the tips, all evened out now, brush against my shoulders. The result is stunning. Without an overwhelming amount of hair swallowing me, the sharp contours of my jaw and cheekbones are more obvious.

"Oh my god, Becca…I don't even know what to say, other than thank you." I spin around in the chair to give her a hug.

"Don't mention it; I couldn't have you walking around looking like Britney Spears after that incident with the hair clippers."

My phone buzzes and I glance at the screen. A message from Abel. Becca catches a glimpse of the text and looks at me suspiciously.

"You're still coming to the Halloween party, right?" She submerges her combs back into the aqua blue bottle of barbicide.

"Of course, wouldn't miss it."

"What about Jake. Is he coming too?"

"Last time we talked about it he was." I get up and unfasten the black plastic cape from my neck. "I know you're busy and you just fit me in between appointments so I won't keep you. I'll give you a call later, okay?"

"Sure, honey, call me if you need anything." She air kisses me to avoid leaving a bright purple lipstick imprint on my cheek.

I wait until I'm in the parking lot before opening the text message from Abel. *Flight gets in the Saturday at 11:30 a.m. – xx.*

Send me your flight number, I'll pick you up. I have something special in mind. That's a complete lie. I don't have something special in mind, at this point I have nothing in mind.

Can't wait, he replies.

I breathe deeply and try to center myself. I need to pull it together or Jake is going to think something's up, if he doesn't already. My stomach grumbles and I'm struck with the inspiration to cook dinner for Jake tonight. Rumor has it that the way to a man's heart is his stomach.

I grab a cart and join the other housewives, seniors and shift workers that frequent the grocery store at this time of day. I toss a fresh produce, garlic cloves and a bag of potatoes into the cart. I assess the pale pink chicken, mounds of ground beef and thick looking pork chops on display. I pick up a package of tenderloin steaks and turn it upside down, letting the rivers of blood run from one end to another like sand in an hourglass. The shelves in the seafood section are filled with ice, chilling everything from fresh fish to crabs and oysters. The oysters remind me of Abe.

In the centre of the seafood area is a large tank filled with water and half a dozen live lobsters crawling around. Their beady little eyes dart around and their antennae flex. Feeling like a prison warden overseeing death row I motion for the clerk and point to two particularly fat lobsters scuttling around aimlessly.

I add a hunk of brie and a package of soft goat cheese to my burgeoning cart. The cashier packs my groceries into bags and I feel slightly cheered at the prospect of surprising Jake. He hasn't texted me back yet today, which is probably not a good sign.

At home I unpack the groceries and place the foam box of lobsters on the counter. With a fresh cup of coffee in hand, I open my laptop and distract myself with emails and reports. My newly cropped hair keeps falling in front of my eyes and I reflexively tuck it behind my ears. An hour before Jake typically arrives home, I close the laptop and begin chopping up vegetables. The sharp knife slices through the cucumber, peppers and mushrooms with ease. "Cool it, Charlie," I say aloud to myself.

I dump the piles of chopped vegetables into a salad

bowl and toss it loosely a few times with a pair of tongs. I walk barefoot out the French doors off the kitchen onto the deck, loosen the valve on the barbecue and turn the burner on. By the time I'm done wrapping up the potatoes into neat tinfoil bundles and seasoning the steaks, the barbecue is ready for them. I place the potatoes and steak on the grill, watching with interest as the flames reach greedily for them and they begin to sizzle.

Now for the lobsters. This is the closest I've come to killing something since last year and I'm like a kid in a candy store. I dump both lobsters into the sink and they clamber around disoriented, trying valiantly to escape and crawling all over each other. I grab the bigger one around the middle and try not to drop it as it squirms. My fingers are grateful for the rubber bands binding its claws shut. Its bony, cold shell freaks me out and I quickly drop it into the pot of rapidly boiling water on the stove. The article I read on cooking lobster suggested that killing them before boiling is more humane, but I am a modern-day monster.

I toss the other lobster into the pot (till death do they part), and am slightly disappointed when they show no indication of pain or discomfort. I check the steaks and when I look at the lobster again their blue/green shells are blooming into a deep sunburnt red. I just finish setting the steak and potatoes down on the table when Jake walks in the front door. Poor Jake, he can't help being so reliable and predictable.

I've set the table properly with real linen napkins and in the center, propped up in an old glass coke bottle, is a sprig of Oleander. I'm flushed from standing over the steaming lobster pot and my hair is curled around my face. I have on an old-fashioned ruffled apron that Magnolia gave me last Christmas (it's the cutest new kitchen trend she exclaimed), giving me the aura of a 1950's housewife.

"What's all this?" He sets his laptop bag down in the living room.

"Just thought we should properly celebrate moving in together, and my new haircut."

He moves to inspect my hair closer and places an arm around my waist. He tenderly tucks my hair behind my ear.

It's moments like this that fill me with false hope. That I could be happy and lead a normal life with a great guy, and not periodically kill people.

"I love your hair. I love you." He kisses me gently on the lips. Playing the benevolent housewife I place the newly scorched lobster onto a crystal platter of my moms and set it on the table beside a bowl of hot butter.

"I have no idea what to do now," I admit.

Jake laughs and demonstrates how to twist off the claws and break it into sections. In place of a lobster cracker, he grabs a meat tenderizing mallet from the utensil drawer and cracks the shell of the claws, removing the tender white flesh. He twists off the legs and removes the meat, turning them over and dragging the sharp tip of a knife down the length of their bodies and splitting them in half. He chops off their heads with a casual brutality and disposes of the non-edible intestines. After a few minutes of slicing, cracking and scraping he sets the knife down and admires his bounty.

I'm impressed not only by his knife skills but with the

nonchalance with which he tore apart the lobster. He cuts into his steak with similar energy and I study him thoughtfully as I chew on the butter soaked lobster meat.

The post dinner table resembles a crime scene; with pieces of lobster scattered about and chunks of steak pooling in their own juices. He offers to clean up, and exhausted from my foray into domesticity, I thank him and retreat upstairs to take a bath.

I try not to think about the lobsters as I pour bath oil and salts into the steaming water. The antique claw foot tub is one of my favorite features of the house. As soon as I saw it, I envisioned lazy evenings spent reading by candlelight and enjoying a glass of wine. I also pictured how poetically I could drown someone in it.

I catch a glimpse of my naked self in the vanity mirror and try to picture myself as Abel would. I run my hands down my shoulders and breasts resting them on my hips. I try to remember what his hands feel like.

I wince as I step into the tub and the water scalds my skin. I lower myself down slowly and rest my back against the porcelain edge. I relax and sprawl out, letting my toes linger by the drain.

I grab a bar of soap from the windowsill that overlooks the backyard and lather it onto my arms, neck and chest, enjoying the slippery texture. I sink deeper into the tub submerging up to my nostrils. It would only take one more centimeter for the water to flood my airways and seep into my lungs. It's a delicate line between life and death.

I decide to continue living for now and resurface. The door creaks open and Jake looks in.

"Sorry, I didn't mean to interrupt, I was just wondering if you wanted dessert. I think we have butterscotch ice cream in the freezer..." he trails off, and I can feel his eyes taking me in. I bend a leg upward letting the water run down it.

"Come here," I command, in a voice I don't recognize as mine.

He does as he's told and crouches beside the tub. His tie is loose and his starched white shirt is slightly unbuttoned with the sleeves rolled up his forearms. I remove his glasses and place them safely on the windowsill.

I run a dripping wet finger across his lips and he watches me expectantly, not daring to move a muscle. He's hypnotized by me; like I'm a snake charmer, manipulating his movements, leading his head back and forth in a rhythm.

I wrap my hands around his head, kissing him and pulling him closer. I pull him over the edge and into the tub with me. His pants are drenched, his shirt is soaked through, and his tie hangs limply on my chest. He doesn't object as I reach for his belt and unbuckle it. I close my eyes, bite my lip, and try not to scream out the wrong name.

Chapter 17
Before

The third time I killed someone was a turning point.

I became harder, calloused; I could cauterize my emotions. Each time I killed I began to feel a little bit more whole.

In her prime, Viola Harris would have been a stunner. Her wavy, smoky grey hair once brilliant charcoal. Her chocolate skin once vibrant and smooth. Even now in a boxy angora sweater you could still see the suggestion of her hourglass shape. She smiled at me and I recognized it as a smile that had broken hearts.

"Thank you, dear," she said, as I pushed her wheelchair through the San Diego airport.

I pocketed the tiny little of slip of paper I had been clutching, Seat 17F couldn't have worked out better for me. At ninety-two years young, Viola could walk slowly with the help of a cane but preferred to use a wheelchair to navigate the airport. Enter Charlotte; the ever so helpful Cabin Safety Manager. I graciously offered to assist with her luggage and find a taxi. I pushed her past the endless stream of people toward the baggage area and formulated a plan. I chatted sweetly while we waited for her suitcase to make its way onto the baggage carousel.

"There it is." She pointed to a large navy suitcase.

I grabbed it off the turnstile and wheeled it beside her.

"Are you sure you're fine to walk to the taxi on your own without the wheelchair?"

"I should be fine dear; if you just help me to the entrance here, I'll be okay."

She rose shakily from the chair and I offered her my arm while she steadied herself with the cane.

"Ms. Davis, listen, I hope this isn't too forward, but I hate to send you in a cab all the way to Coronado by yourself. It doesn't feel proper. I have a rental car while I'm here—why don't you let me take you home?" Fingers crossed.

"Well, I really wouldn't want to inconvenience you..." she said.

"No, really, it's my pleasure, honestly. I'd love to take a drive over to Coronado and maybe I'll check out some of the sights while I'm there."

"If you're sure you don't mind." It was settled.

I left her at the baggage area while I quickly filled out paperwork at the car rental desk. After securing the keys I tucked Viola and her baggage into a Ford Focus. I punched the address into the GPS and the map loaded onto the screen with a cartoon car representing us. Coronado is a resort city just over the bridge from San Diego.

We turned onto North Harbor Drive and I admired the towering palm trees with their great billowy fronds swaying in the breeze. I cracked the window slightly and let the warm, dry air fill the car.

Living in Manitoba it's easy to forget the sensation of

sunshine on your skin. In the dead of a Western Canadian winter your frozen brain can barely recall what warmth even feels like. The air hurts your skin and lungs; tiny crystals of frost form on your eyelashes within minutes of being outdoors. The prairies become a brilliant, blank, white canvas and the wind whips the snow across the roads in mesmerizing swirls. I often daydream about moving somewhere hot, like San Diego. But a daydream is all it will ever be. I could never leave Cara.

We pulled onto the Coronado Bridge and I was dazzled by the expanse of blue. The cloudless sky and brilliant turquoise water stretched as far as the eye could see, it was hard to tell which was reflecting the other. Every few meters signs were pinned to the lampposts with information about a suicide hotline. Dozens of people have attempted to or succeeded in ending their lives by jumping off the Coronado Bridge. The speed and force with which they hit the water breaks their bones, and if they're fortunate, their necks. If the impact fails to kill them, they suffer a prolonged death from drowning.

Viola noticed me noticing the signs and mistook my interest for empathy.

"Poor souls. Hundreds of people have jumped off this bridge, and keep doing it every few months, like sheep. Last month a lady jumped on her four-year wedding anniversary. Her husband followed a couple of weeks later."

I shook my head in what I hoped was an acceptably sad way.

"Have you got a husband dear?" she asked, shifting her focus to my bare ring finger on the steering wheel.

"No, not yet, Ms. Davis, I'm focused on my career for right now." Among other things.

"Young people today," she chuckled. "Take this old lady's advice; catch your fish before you run out of bait. Don't wait until you're my age before you start looking for love."

We turned onto Alameda Blvd. and I parked in front of a small, dated, white bungalow, partially hidden behind a giant Sugar Gum Eucalyptus tree. A broken grey stone path led to a weathered storm door and the compact yard was enclosed by a peeling white fence. Next to the door hung an American flag that waved listlessly in the arid afternoon breeze.

I grabbed her suitcase out of the trunk as she hobbled to the door to unlock it.

"Please tell me you'll stay for tea, dear. It's the least I can do for you after you drove me all the way home."

"Oh, I wouldn't want to impose, I'm sure you have things to do," I said, feigning indifference.

"Absolutely not. It's not every day I get to spend time with a smart young woman like yourself. Do me one more favor and keep me company while I enjoy a glass of lemonade out in the backyard."

"Well, if you insist." Twist my arm, Viola. "Is your husband home?"

She laughed a throaty chuckle. "Of course, I'll introduce y'all."

I try to mask my disappointment. It was a miracle that Viola was still breathing, let alone that she had an equally decrepit counterpart.

I walked into the entrance and was overwhelmed by a smell which can only be described as "old". Old furniture, old drapes, old skin and bones. Was it a smell that manifested over time? A combination of varnished coffee tables, Clairol hairspray, homemade jam and Polident. Or was it a naturally occurring smell, that seeps from your skin as it darkens with age spots and wrinkles like tissue paper.

"Sit, sit." She motioned toward the living room.

I took a seat on an overstuffed, flower print armchair while she shuffled to the kitchen to prepare whatever "tea" consisted of. I wondered why her husband hadn't appeared yet. A giant wood shelving unit took up one of the walls displaying fragile dishes, tchotchkes, books, and photos. Many of the photos appeared to be of Viola's children and grandchildren.

Her wedding photo was encased in an ornate silver frame. Viola was resplendent in a lace, high-necked, long-sleeved wedding dress, with a crystal tiara sparkling atop her black, silky hair. Her veil billowed around her face making her look celestial. Her long lashes looked downward, focused on cutting the three-tiered wedding cake. The man beside her had radiant skin, the color of coffee beans, and shortly cropped, dark hair. His simple dark suit hung nicely off his broad shoulders and his attention was focused on his beautiful bride.

He looked at her with a kind of devotion rarely witnessed in real life.

Has true love gone out of style? Did the last of the great romances die out with Johnny and June, and JFK and Jackie O.? Has love become more convoluted, with the introduction of online dating, texting and social media all but eradicating phone calls and hand-written love letters.

Absorbed in my own observations I let out a surprised yelp when something huge and orange suddenly jumped onto the side of my chair.

"Oh, that'll be Arthur," Viola said, peeking her head out of the kitchen. "Don't worry he's friendly."

Arthur looked anything but friendly as he sized me up with his milky, cataract eyes. Did I hold potential for his next meal? It wasn't out of the question; I'd hedge bets that Arthur could take down a small giraffe if he wanted to. I ignored his penetrating stare until he gave up and stalked away.

"Okay," Viola clapped her hands together. "Let's go out back; it's much nicer to sit in the sunshine."

"Sure, will your husband be joining us?"

She laughed and slapped her hand against her knee. "Oh, right, I was going to introduce you to William, where are my manners." She pulled a small brass urn off a shelf on the wall unit. "Charlotte, meet my husband, William."

"Oh…I'm so sorry I…"

"Don't worry your pretty head, William passed on a few years back but he still manages to keep me company. He doesn't talk as much as he used to though," she gazed at the urn affectionately.

She set William back in his place and led me through a screen door in the narrow, dated kitchen and to the backyard. It was a small, well-kept space with a shaded porch swing and a patio set that faced tidy gardens of colorful shrubs, grasses and desert flowers.

She set down a wooden tray with a plate of biscuits and a tall sweating pitcher of lemonade. Lemon slices and pulp floated around in the crystal pitcher. Old people were too damn precious. The time they invest in things we think don't matter, make you realize that maybe those things do still matter.

"What a nice way to spend the afternoon," Viola said beaming. Her dark brown eyes sparkled in the sunlight. She radiated warmth and kindness and for a moment I almost forgot why I was there.

She plugged in a small cassette player and popped the hatch open to accept and swallow a tape. The player crackled in protest and sprung to life spitting out slow, soulful blues.

"So, how did you end up on Coronado Island?" I asked, nibbling on a stale wafer biscuit sprinkled with chocolate.

"I was born in Kansas, but my mama convinced my daddy to move my brothers, sisters and me out here when I was six. My mama loved the ocean. She had a job working as a maid at the Coronado del Hotel, the most beautiful hotel I've ever seen—even still to this day. I would sneak to visit her at work and my jaw would drop staring at the high ceilings and twinkling chandeliers. The tables were always set perfectly, and you should have seen the gowns the ladies would wear.

"I loved the hotel, and I loved the peacefulness of Coronado, compared to the city. I liked the feeling of being surrounded by water. It felt safe. I followed in my mama's footsteps and got a job at the hotel and that's where I worked for many years, even after I met William.

"I would clean the rooms and when no one was around I'd pretend I was a guest. A well-traveled rich lady with nothing to do but enjoy the crisp, white, European linens and sweeping views of the ocean." She stared into the garden and looked like she was miles away.

"How did you meet William?" I took a sip of the icy, tart lemonade and caught the taste of vodka.

"During World War II he got a job at the North Island Naval Air Station working in the aircraft factory. He had dreams of becoming a pilot, like those Tuskegee Airmen, but on Coronado in those days his best opportunity as a black man was working in that factory. My friend, Clara, and I had a day off so we went to Glorietta Bay Park to lie in the sand and give our aching feet a rest. We were lying on our towels, enjoying the sound of the ocean when a football landed in the sand about a foot away from my head.

"I scrambled to my feet and grabbed that stupid football, ready to toss it into the ocean. Then William jogged toward me, and Lord, he was a vision. He smiled that perfect smile of his and apologized, offering to buy both Clara and me an ice cream for our troubles, and I was enamored.

"We were inseparable from that day on. Later he admitted to me that the football had been a ploy all along to catch my attention. He was persistent like that, never gave up on what he wanted. After the wedding, we had our first child, Autumn, and he began his pilot's training. He finished the training and flew planes well into his late fifties. He loved the sky as much as I loved the ocean. I expect that's where he is now," she said, her eyes shining with tears that she quickly blinked away. "Up there somewhere in the sky, having the time of his life, looking down on me."

I reached across the patio table and put my hand on her arm. I remembered reading that old people; especially those who live alone don't receive enough human contact. Touch is an essential part of the human experience and people who receive regular physical contact are happier and healthier.

She gave me a watery smile and took a sip of her lemonade.

"Are all those pictures of your children and grandchildren?"

"Yes," she said cheering up. She gathered a handful of photo frames from the living room to use as points of reference. "Autumn is my first born, she's some sort of celebrity dentist and lives in LA with her husband, AJ. They have two children, Ashleigh and Kyle."

Autumn could pass for Vanessa Williams and had inherited her parents' perfect smile. In the photo she stood next to a tall, handsome blonde man and two well-dressed children with striking similarities to their parents and the same perfect smile as their mom.

"Next came the twins, Daphne and Dahlia. They both live in San Diego with their ever-expanding families. I can barely keep track of how many kids they have now between the two of them. They own a spa together called, *Wild Rose*."

I studied the picture of two identical girls laughing at the camera with their arms around each other's shoulders. They both had silky dark hair and long legs and were obviously close. I felt a pang of jealously.

"Cliff is my baby, and a perpetual thorn in my side. I'm

surprised I have any hair left after raising him. Cliff is still a bachelor and a self-proclaimed 'free spirit' and 'artist'. He's in LA right now as well, still trying to make it as an actor or musician—not sure which one it is this week."

She handed me Cliff's headshot, he had a leather jacket slung over one shoulder and was wearing a tight white T-shirt and jeans. He was staring intensely at the camera.

"Do you get to see your family quite a bit?" I asked, handing back the photo.

"Well, the kids are all busy with their own lives, they don't have time for an old relic like me. I see the twins maybe once or twice a month and I was just in LA visiting Autumn and Cliff. That's where I flew back from today. They're good kids, I'm proud to be their mama. They still take turns calling me to say goodnight."

"It sounds like you are well loved." I need to make more of an effort to visit my parents.

"Well, dear, I truly have enjoyed our visit, but I'm having trouble keeping my eyes open. Would you mind helping me to my bed so that I can lie down? Travelling has me feeling a bit woozy." Her head bobbed slightly and her eyes had started to droop.

"Absolutely, and maybe if you're up for it tomorrow I'll pop by for another visit."

"I would love that." She leaned forward to give me a dry peck on the cheek.

I held her arm and helped her to the bedroom. In the center of the room was an antique four-poster bed with a rose patterned bedspread. Above the bed was a brass cross with a pink beaded rosary hanging from it. Framed photos of Viola and William were on display on the walls and on the vanity in front of the mirror. The sun shone through the open window onto the pillow. Viola laid down and I pulled the lace curtains shut.

Her arms were folded across her chest and her breathing steadied. She looked so peaceful. It was the serenity afforded to someone that had lived a happy, full life. Or the look of someone who had just inadvertently taken several high dose sleeping pills in their lemonade.

A meow from Arthur startled me and I picked all thirty pounds of him up and set him down on the bed next to his owner. He began to purr and settled down beside her, eyeing me suspiciously. I took a throw pillow off the bed and gently placed it over Viola's face. I held it there for a few minutes until the rise and fall of her chest slowed and finally stood still. I took her soft, weathered hand in mine and checked for a pulse.

I removed the pillow and her eyes were still closed peacefully, her mouth relaxed into a faint grin. She was with William now. I wondered if she would see Cara.

I closed my eyes and Cara was there smiling, waiting for me. She knew I would always return to her.

I left Viola with Arthur and returned to the patio to clean up the remainders of our tea party and any evidence of my presence. After I finished, I sat in a patio chair in the backyard, staring into the distance, watching the sun disappear and listening to the chirp of the cicadas and the low croon of Otis Redding singing *(Sittin' On) The Dock of the Bay*.

The sun dipped further into the horizon and the

shadows stretched across the lawn. A monarch butterfly fluttered toward me. It landed gracefully on top of the cassette player, delicately shaking its wings before gliding back into the hot, dry night. Cara loved Monarch butterflies.

She admired their tenacity and persistence. They take flight every fall in search of warmer weather than what the frigid prairies have to offer. They travel over 2,500 miles to Mexico and Southern California to find refuge in the Eucalyptus and Oyamel Fir trees. They migrate in masses to the same trees each year, as if they understand the concept of "home".

The phone began ringing, echoing through the still house. It stopped for a few moments before beginning its frantic ring again. I reached my hand inside my and ran my fingers along the outline of Viola's boarding pass.

Chapter 18
Wednesday, October 28th

I'm thankful for the routine and monotony of work. It provides me with stability in a time when I'm feeling anything but. I'm sitting upstairs in my office with my feet stretched onto the top of my desk while I type up a training report from Seattle. Cinder provides moral support and positions his furry body in a sunbeam on the floor.

I had never planned on owning a cat. I had Stanley and that was enough for me. I didn't want to fall victim to the dangers of becoming a crazy cat lady, I already had the crazy part covered. But Cinder fell into my life in a way that I couldn't refuse him.

Just like Abel.

I was at the office headed to the photocopier when I noticed a commotion in the lunch room. I joined the crowd hoping for donuts from the bakery down the street but as I pushed closer, I heard tiny mewling sounds, like a squeaky door. On the lunchroom table was an empty photocopy paper box with a pile of kittens in place of copy paper.

"Oh!" I exclaimed, slightly disappointed in the absence of donuts, although the kittens were similar in size.

"Terrible right?" clucked my co-worker, Melanie.

"Lucy found them outside in the dumpster while she was having a smoke. Someone just chucked them out like garbage."

"Awful," I mumbled, noticing the smell of garbage resonating from the kittens. "What's going to happen to them?"

"Well, I think Blair is going to bring the bigger striped one home with him, his little girls will love it, and Lucy is going to take the other striped one."

"What about that little black one?"

"Lucy is going to drop him off at the Humane Society after work."

I stared at the small, black, matted bundle of fur writhing around with his siblings. Poor creature. I knew that superstitions made black cats a hard sell. I picked it up despite its odor and it fit neatly into my palm. Its bones were still soft and malleable like a baby's, and it conformed to the shape of my hand.

It began to purr and the vibrations rattled up my arm. I allowed it to comfort itself, and me, to a certain degree, before putting it back in the box with the others.

Back at my desk I tried to focus on reports but my mind kept wandering back to the black kitten. I knew what it was like to feel unwanted, and certainly what it was like to feel second best to your siblings. I drummed my fingers on the desk and typed, *Humane Society Statistics*, into my computer, reassuring myself that the kitten was destined for a great home full of kids to play with and furniture to destroy. I swallowed hard and read through reports citing that almost one third of cats surrendered to shelters are eventually euthanized. But they wouldn't euthanize a kitten, would they?

I speed walked to Lucy's desk and caught her putting on her jacket, the box with the remaining kitten sat on her desk.

"I'll take the black one." I reached for the smelly ball of fur and tucked it into the crook of my arm. "The one that no one wanted."

I've barely made a dent in the report when my phone buzzes with a text message from Magnolia, *Be here for 5:30?*

I groan inwardly. I completely forgot I had promised to watch the twins tonight. I couldn't bail on her, I know that she and Paul really needed time alone together.

My minimal attention span, now broken, I click onto the local news website. Stabbing, cold weather, stabbing. Much of the same. One of the article headlines exclaims, *Manitoba Needs More Organ Donors*. I read with great interest how many lives can be saved or improved by just one donor. I click on the hyperlink in the article that brings me to the organ donation website.

I type in the required registration information and am feeling quite pleased with myself. I may be able to save just as many lives as I've taken. A selection menu asks me to choose which organs I'm willing to donate. I check off the basics: liver, kidney, pancreas, lungs and heart. I pause when it comes to bones, tendons and cartilage. Why the hell not? I check all three, feeling benevolent.

I add stomach and small bowel, feeling euphoric. I draw the line at corneas and skin,

Feeling satisfied and philanthropic I stand up and stretch my legs. Through the window I watch a red squirrel run across the telephone wire like an acrobat. I look longingly at my wooden box full of secrets and boarding passes. I roll my neck from side to side and walk down the stairs to my bedroom.

Light streams in from the open window making the white duvet look like a cloud. I pull open the nightstand drawer on Jake's side of the bed revealing reading glasses, a cell phone charger and a watch. Nothing interesting here. I turn my attention to the dresser where I had grudgingly sanctioned him two drawers. I open the first drawer and thumb through a variety of plain colored shirts before losing interest.

I open the second drawer where he keeps his socks and underwear. I'm not quite sure what it is I'm looking for. My fingers brush up against something hard at the back of the drawer. I push aside his jockey shorts and pull out a small black velvet box.

I feel sick.

I can't un-see it now. Inside the box is a delicate gold ring with a large oval diamond, flanked at each side by a cluster of smaller diamonds. Its facets catch the light from the window, casting dozens of tiny rainbows across the wall and ceiling.

What is Jake thinking? Our relationship hasn't exactly been perfect lately and we only just moved in together. I tuck the box back into the drawer and cover it with a pile of underwear. My phone vibrates in my back pocket.

Can't wait to see you, says a message from Abel.

I sigh and head to the kitchen to make myself a coffee. And Baileys. With more Baileys than coffee. Living a double life is stressful.

I'm not even sure that I want to get married. The few times I'd considered it I'd imagined something small, simple and intimate. By the lake, or in a clearing in the woods. I'd wear something light and lacy and let my hair hang in loose curls. I'd hold a handful of wild flowers and a my family and a few friends would watch as I lovingly recited heartfelt vows to my soulmate.

We would dance under the stars and drink champagne and cocktails until our eyes grew heavy and our feet became tired. I had imagined the details, the minutiae of the day, but there was one part of the fantasy that remained blank, incomplete. The groom.

I pictured Cara there with me, bending to straighten the train of my dress or brushing stray bits of sand or pine needles off it. Signing the wedding certificate, listening as I promised "till death do us part", and knowing that caveat would never apply to us, because even after death her and I would still be together.

I glance at my watch and regret getting into my emotions and Baileys when I had to be at Magnolia's soon. Jake had agreed to meet me there and I tried to push thoughts of the ring out of my mind for now.

I open the stately front door of Magnolia's house and immediately enter a war zone. The kitchen is covered with child feeding apparatuses and toys coating the floor. I can hear both of the twins screaming at the top of their developing lungs.

A frazzled looking Magnolia greets me. Outwardly she looks perfect, but inside I can tell she's close to a meltdown. Her hair hangs in perfect red waves across one shoulder and her makeup emphasizes her blue eyes. She's wearing a simple knit navy dress that hugs her curves and make it hard to believe she had given birth to twins.

"You look beautiful ,Mags." I give her a quick hug and feel something wet stuck to my cheek. A spaghetti noodle? I hold it out in front of me questionably and Magnolia explains that she was trying out a new organic spaghetti squash recipe.

"Didn't go over so well, hey?" I pull another few pieces of what I believe to be squash out of her hair.

"It went well enough to get a few photos before they decided to fling it all over the walls and each other."

"Where's Paul?"

"Where do you think?" she says frustrated. "He's working late, so I'm meeting him at the restaurant. Listen, thank you so much for doing this, I really appreciate it. Are you sure you'll be, okay?"

"Umm…yes? Don't worry about it, Jake is going to be here soon, and I mean how much damage can two toddlers do…" I trail off looking at the kitchen.

"Okay, thank you again, we won't be too late. They're in the playroom covered in tomato sauce. I didn't have time to clean them up, you're going to need to throw them in the bath." She kisses me on the cheek, slips on a pair of heels and ducks out the door, presumably before I can change my mind.

I head to the playroom to see what the twin terrors are up to. As soon as they notice me, they rush over, wide drooling grins on their sauce-covered faces.

"Cha-wee," they cry in unison.

"Hi, babies!" I scoop them into a group hug. They're so cute I'm not even mad that I'm now also covered in sauce.

"Aunty Charlie is going to give you a bath, doesn't that sound fun?" I ask, trying to make it sound as enticing as possible, like a bath could provide the same level of enjoyment as a bag of candy. I grab their hands before they can protest and lead them to the bathroom. I have no idea how to bath them, I've helped Reese bathe Thor, it must be similar.

I pull their clothes off and lift them both into the slowly filling bath. They stare at me expectantly. I look in the bathroom vanity and find a box of bath appropriate toys, unsure which ones to give, I dump the entire box in with them, much to their delight.

They're splashing around like fish and I pour in organic, all-natural lavender bubble bath. Lavender means sleepy, sleepy is good. I'm shampooing Bridgette's hair when I hear Jake come in and I yell to him from the bathroom.

"Whoa, what's going on here?" He rolls up his shirt sleeves and ruffles Beckham's wet hair. Beckham giggles with delight and claps both his arms down into the water, drenching both Jake and me. I smooth my wet hair back off my face and Jake rubs his glasses on a nearby towel. The twins think this is hilarious and continue splashing until half the bathwater is on the floor of the bathroom.

"Okay, that's enough bath time for now." I hand Jake the fluffy towel embroidered with *Beckham* and scoop Bridgette into hers. After what seems like hours, they are both clean and sleeping peacefully in their bamboo pajamas. Jake and I stand over their cribs exhausted, admiring our handiwork.

We retreat to the living room to watch TV and kill time before Mags and Paul get home.

"Doesn't it make you want one?" Jake pulls me onto the couch with him. "I mean when they're sleeping anyway." He stretches out on top of me and strokes my hair.

I flip through the channels. "Kind of, I guess. I don't think I'm ready to be a mom, or know if I'll ever be ready. I'm quite happy being cool Aunty Charlie."

"You're not sure you ever want kids?"

"Well, I'm not quite sure yet."

Jake goes silent and sits up, leaning away from me on the arm of the couch. We focus our attention on the episode of *House Hunters*. A couple is moving from Texas to London and is disappointed in what they can buy for their budget and is annoyingly focused on paint colors.

"Is that a problem?" I question him.

He doesn't meet my gaze and continues to stare at the annoying house hunting couple on TV. "It's whatever, I guess I just always pictured myself having a family."

"You do have a family." I snuggle up against him. "Cinder and I are your family."

He can't resist me and puts his arm around my

shoulders allowing me to nestle into the crook of his arm. My phone buzzes on the coffee table and notifies me that I have two new text messages from *A*.

"Who's 'A'?" Jake asks.

"Someone from work," I say unconvincingly, shoving my phone into my pocket.

He seems to accept this answer and turns his attention back to the show.

I can't picture myself with children. I've been waiting for some sort of maternal urge to arise and wonder if it will just appear suddenly as my biological clock ticks louder. I consider that the void in life that most people fill with children I've filled with something else. Instead of creating life, I'm taking it.

We must have dozed off on the couch because the next thing I remember is Magnolia and Paul stumbling half-drunk through the front door. Mags trips out of her heels in the entrance.

"Hey, what time is it?" I ask, disoriented, shaking Jake to wake him.

"I have no clue." Mags giggles, her face flushed and her eyes bright.

Paul's tie is loosened around his neck and his eyes are hazy. "Thanks so much for looking after the kids, guys, I hope they weren't too much trouble."

"Never." I grin wryly. I pat him on the shoulder as I slip my runners on and Jake fumbles in his pockets for his car keys.

"Good night," I whisper to Mags on my way out.

"Great night." She winks. I'm not sure I want to know

what she's alluding to or why her perfectly waved hair is now a matted mess. I'm fairly sure I noticed lipstick on Paul's collar.

Jake collapses into bed at home while I go outside to call Cinder. He has never grasped the concept of a curfew and will stay out all night if I let him.

"Cinnnnderrr," I call blindly into the night. After a few minutes my persistence pays off and a set of amber eyes, followed by the thick black body of Cinder materializes from behind the garage. I reward his obedience with a spoonful of stinky cat food.

In the bedroom Jake is snoring softly and I creep quietly to the dresser and pull open his sock drawer. I slide my hand in, feeling for the velvet box, but I find nothing. I shut the drawer and climb into bed, unsure whether I feel concerned or relieved.

Chapter 19
Friday, October 30th

It's the day before Becca's Halloween party and I woke up feeling uneasy and filled with apprehension. Similar to the way the air becomes thick and charged prior to a storm.

Abel has been texting me off the hook and I'm beginning to worry that Jake suspects something. I still don't know how I'm going to pull this all off. I do know that by the end of the weekend I'll need to decide, Jake or Abel. I can't continue this charade forever; It's only a matter of time before it blows up in my face.

I know that I'm preening for Abel, but I tell myself that I was planning on shaving my legs regardless. I prop my leg up on the edge of the bathtub, lather it up with shaving cream and slide the razor down it in smooth, even strokes.

When I'm done my deforestation process, I rub lotion on my legs until they gleam. I contemplate painting my toenails but I don't want it to seem like I'm trying too hard. I feel like I'm a teenager again. I can't seem to shake the sick, anxious feelings and haven't decided if it's guilt or butterflies fluttering around in my stomach.

I braid a small section of my hair so I can deter it from falling in my eyes. I first learned to braid on Stanley. I would spend hours at the stables grooming him until his coat shone and picking knots out of his coarse mane. In the spring I'd braid his tail so he didn't get it full of burrs when we rode down the trails.

An idea suddenly comes to me. Carol has a small cabin at Little Limestone Lake. The lake is about five hours north of Winnipeg, nestled in the Canadian Shield. She rarely goes there anymore but she used to bring horses and spend time riding in the wilderness. She says she liked the solitude.

I call Carol and inquire about the cabin, which of course is vacant, especially at this time of year. She's more than thrilled that I'm offering to take Stanley on a road trip and says it's no problem to borrow a horse trailer. I hang up feeling quite pleased with myself. Now I just have to figure out how to tell Abe about the half-ton third wheel that will be joining us this weekend.

With one weight lifted off my shoulders, I decide to work on reports for a few hours and grudgingly trudge up the stairs to my office. While I'm waiting for my laptop to wake up, I open my *Pura Vida* box and take out the collection of boarding passes.

Marty "the Party" was definitely the most interesting person I've killed. The details would make for a decent straight-to-video movie, with Marty, himself, in the starring role.

Chapter 20
Before

I met Marty on a flight to Miami. As soon as he took his seat in 11D I smiled. He stuck out like a sore thumb, with his wide-brimmed hat decorated with what looked like animal teeth, and a bright orange Hawaiian shirt. Marty was a big guy, both horizontally and vertically, and his wide, toothy smile reminded me of an alligator. A long, dirty-blonde braid hung down his back and he had an eye-patch over one eye.

At my hotel room in Miami, I wasn't surprised to learn through my extensive internet searching and social media lurking that Marty resided in nearby Everglades City where he operated a tour company. I had three days in Florida before my return trip to Winnipeg, and a rental car booked for tomorrow. It looked like I would be driving out to the Everglades to arrange a chance meeting with Marty.

I typed *Everglades City, Florida,* into my browser search bar to find out exactly what it was that I was getting myself into. Wikipedia informed me that this small town (population 352, according to the 2020 census), was a city in Collier County Florida, situated at the Gulf coast gateway to the everglades. Sandwiched between Everglades

National Park, Big Cypress National Preserve, the 10,000 islands and the Fakahatchee Strand Preserve State Park. Visit Florida's website proclaimed Everglades City as *the gateway to ten thousand islands*. I clicked through photo galleries full of swamps, gators and more swamps and made note to stock up on bug spray.

The next morning, I woke with a spring in my step and visions of crocodiles dancing in my head. I picked up my rental car and headed to the nearest Walmart to stock up on necessary items. Walmart is lower class America at its finest. I wandered past the gun counter where a frazzled looking woman with a baby on her hip was arguing with the salesperson. She wore sweat shorts and a too tight pink tank top with *bullets make me happy,* emblazoned across the chest. Her baby stared at me and drooled, its blonde, curly hair comically askew. The store smelled like rotting fish although I had yet to see seafood.

I tossed binoculars, bug spray with the highest amount of deet allowed, sunscreen, and a baseball hat into my basket. I thumbed through items in the women's clothing section before finally deciding on a pair of jean shorts, a camo tank top and a nondescript zip-up sweater. I needed to blend in.

Without having a plan established yet, I decided that buying a bundle of rope, a waterproof bag, a cheap wetsuit and a Gerber light-weight, all-purpose knife certainly wouldn't hurt. After leaving Walmart I hit the road and began the quick one-hour drive to Everglades City. The fast-food chains, box stores, and personal injury lawyer billboards slowly disappeared and were replaced on either side with trees and water.

As I passed the fluorescent orange and pink *Welcome to Everglades City* sign featuring a leaping fish and pensive looking bird, maybe a heron, it felt like I was travelling back in time. I drove past sun-faded signs advertising airboat rides and promising *all you can eat stone crabs.* Past dated, crumbling trailer parks littered with vehicles in various states of disrepair and decomposition.

I pulled off the road into the parking lot for Captain Ron's Motel. The outside looked simple and well-kept, which I hoped was an indication of what I could expect on the inside. I entered the office and was greeted by a large, jolly looking, sunburnt man with a thick, white moustache. "Hello, ma'am, how can I help you?" he said in a Southern drawl.

"I was hoping I could get a room for a night or two?"

"Well, just let me see about that." He pulled on a pair of reading glasses and consulted a thick, tattered book on the counter in front of him.

"You're in luck. Room 17 is free."

"I'll take it, do you accept cash?"

"That's my favorite kind of payment," he bellowed, and let loose a belly laugh as he handed me the keyring for room 17. The room key dangled from a large blue plastic anchor. How nautical.

The air was thick with humidity and the swampy smell of decaying plants and insects. Room 17 was small and simple with cheery yellow walls and cold, white-tiled floors.

The cheap duvet cover was a mardi gras of colors and large photos of crocodiles hung on the wall. I put my bags down on the bed, threaded my ponytail through my new baseball cap and doused myself liberally in bug spray.

I sat in the driver's seat of my rental vehicle and tapped Marty's home address into the navigation system, obtained with the help of True North Airlines customer directory. A few minutes later I pulled into a parking lot across the street from a two-story building wrapped in a large yellow and red banner emblazoned with *Marty's Everglade Tours*. A cartoon crocodile wearing a hat like the one Marty wore on the plane, grinned toothily and leaned casually against the cartoon block lettering. His skinny scaly arms were crossed in front of his chest like he was the coolest crocodile on the block.

I was just about to get out and casually inquire about an air boat tour—feigning surprise and exclaiming coincidence if he recognized me from the plane, when Marty strode out of the building and hopped into his truck, a large behemoth of a vehicle with oversized wheels and shiny silver grills. The exhaust belched out a filthy looking cloud of smoke as he tore out of the parking lot. The too-cool crocodile character was decaled across the side.

I decided to follow Marty and see what he was up to. He drove a few blocks before turning into the parking lot of a church. I drove past it, watched Marty leap out of his truck, it was a long way down, and flick a cigarette aside before disappearing through the bright red door of a white steepled church. Marty did not strike me as a church going man but I could be wrong. The parking lot was mostly empty and despite my lack of church knowledge it seemed like the wrong time of day for a service.

Large wooden crucifixes stood in the ground outside the entrance as if to ward off evil. I shivered slightly but did not burst into flames. *Everyone Welcome*, the sign exclaimed. I'm sure murderers were probably the exception, but it didn't appear that anyone was going to stop me.

The chapel was empty and the mid-afternoon sunlight streamed in through the long, tall windows, warming the inside of the church to a stifling temperature. I noticed a separate stairway leading down to the church basement. *Alcoholics Anonymous*, and a black stick arrow pointing down was scrawled on a piece of paper taped to the wall. I guess Marty wasn't as much of a party as he once was.

There were a half dozen people of various ages in the room. They were listening intently to a middle-aged, tired-looking, brunette woman speak at the podium. Off to one corner was a table with stale looking donuts, store-bought cookies, and thermoses of coffee. Trade in your alcohol and drug addictions for caffeine and sugar.

A few people looked at me before turning their attention back to the speaker. I noticed Marty in the front row and took a seat in an uncomfortable folding chair closer to the back. The brunette finished her spiel and sat down to a round of polite clapping and words of encouragement.

Marty stood up and took his place in front of the podium.

"Hello, everyone, my name is Marty and I'm an alcoholic," he said, in the same tone as if he was delivering an election speech.

The crowd greeted him in unison, "Hello Marty."

"I've been sober for seven years, two months and eighteen days," he continued. "Not a day goes by that I don't think about having a drink. Alcohol has been my infatuation, my obsession and a cruel mistress since I was sixteen years old. Much of my life prior to sobriety is a blur. I always remember the drinks though. How a cold beer tasted on a hot afternoon or how a whiskey sour could make up for a bad day. The liquor and beer I always remember."

He paused, looking around at his captive audience for effect. "It was all of the other things that I didn't remember. I didn't remember to attend school, or football practice. I didn't remember the night I met my wife, now my ex-wife, hell—I barely remembered our wedding. I didn't remember the birth of my son or my daughter's first word.

"Alcohol took these things from me. These moments. And all it left me with were headaches, blood shot eyes and a self-loathing so deep I couldn't bear to look at myself in the mirror some days."

He cleared his throat and fiddled with the tip of his hat for a moment. "But one thing alcohol did not take was my will to live. And deep down I knew the path that I was on would not allow for me to live very long. So, I choose to live over alcohol. And all of you sitting here in this room can make that same choice. But it's a choice we make every day, when we wake up and choose not to have a drink."

The room was rapt to his attention and several people were conspicuously wiping at their eyes with shirtsleeves or the back of their hands. He was like some sort of evangelist preacher whose religion of choice had been Jack Daniels. Even I felt a bit emotional and my throat had begun to tighten.

Cara was the sensitive one, not me. She could let others people's sadness consume her. The elderly man at the nursing home who never had visitors, the seagull with the broken wing or the kid at school who sat alone at lunch. Their circumstances weighed heavy on her heart. I envied her ability to empathize. It was so…human. I wondered if all of the ability to empathize went into her DNA, and I was left with nothing.

"Now, before we end this session and enjoy some coffee. I'd like to invite someone else to speak. Would anyone like to come up?" he asked, scanning the room. His eyes landed on me.

"You, miss, at the back of the room. Don't be shy. I haven't seen you around here before. Why don't you come up here and share?"

"Oh…no, I couldn't, I…" I stammered.

"It's okay, we're all fighting the same demons here. A problem shared is a problem halved."

I felt the eyes of a dozen alcoholics on me. I decided I was more likely to blow my cover if I refused to speak. Marty gave me an encouraging nod and patted me on the shoulder as I took his place at the podium.

"Hi, everyone…my name is…Carley…"—very original choice for a fake name—"I haven't really done anything like this before, but I saw your meeting and thought…well, that maybe it would help for me to deal…with my addiction." My palms were sweating and I wiped them on my bare legs.

I looked at the faces in the audience and realized that none of them held judgment. They were all listening intently to me, with something akin to support and encouragement on their faces. Almost like they cared.

"I've struggled with my addiction since my sister died. I…drink because it makes me feel closer to her somehow. I drink to remember her and forget her. My drinking has hurt others, and it's something that I'm ashamed of. But it's a compulsion and an obsession that I'm not sure how to control."

I shifted my weight from one leg to another. "I'm worried that I'm in too deep, and that I'll never be able to stop." A wave of panic rose over me and I quickly thanked them for listening, grabbed my purse and ducked out of the room and up the stairs.

I burst out the exit into the bright sunlight and leaned against the railing with my head in my hands. I heard the door open behind me and looked up to see Marty standing there with a look of silent understanding on his face. He reached out and put his hand on my shoulder.

"There are three things that you should know. One, is that you were very brave to stand up in front of those people and admit that you have a problem. Two, is that you are not the first person and definitely not the last person to feel helpless. And lastly, and most importantly, I want you to know that you can, and you will, overcome your addiction."

He stared at me with such confidence and resolution that for a moment I almost believed him.

"Now," he continued, "why don't you come back inside with me and have a cup of coffee and a snack." The sun glinted off the animal teeth on the brim of his hat. It was the best offer I'd had all day.

I followed him back inside and accepted a Styrofoam cup filled with strong, black coffee. I sipped it slowly, nibbled on a spongy, sticky donut and engaged in small talk with the fellow addicts. I surreptitiously watched Marty work the room, shaking hands, listening attentively and laughing affably. He eventually made his way back over to me.

"So, Carley," he said with a mouthful of cookie, "what brings you to Everglades City?"

"Well, I was actually hoping to get out and see the everglades, maybe take an airboat tour or something?"

"Darlin' you came to the right place," he grinned.

After Marty had given me a ten-minute spiel on airboat tours, we arranged to meet the next morning for a private airboat tour. I explained that I was an ornithologist looking to observe birds in their natural habit, and I required a private tour to focus on my research. The ease and complexity of my lies continued to amaze me.

The idea had come to me from an in-flight movie I watched on the way to Florida. *The Big Year* followed bird enthusiasts as they embarked on a yearlong bird finding mission in order to break a world record.

I said goodbye to my newfound addict friends and promised Marty I'd see him tomorrow morning. The sun had started to sink in the sky as I drove slowly along the road by the water's edge hoping to find somewhere decent to eat. I'd already vetoed the local subway and a shady looking restaurant called *Buns and Guns*.

I decided on a blue shanty type building on the water called *Barnacle Bistro*, with an open-air patio. I decided that this was probably as good as it gets in the glades. A tarty looking hostess with bleached blonde hair and dark roots greeted me from behind the hostess station, which was shaped and painted to look like a boat.

"Table for one on the patio please."

"Right this way, ma'am," she said with a smack of her chewing gum. I followed her through the dark, wood paneled interior of the restaurant and out onto the patio. We passed by a glowing red vending machine called *The Lobster Zone*. The sign on the machine exclaimed, *You catch em', we cook em!*, and invited diners to use the overhead claw mechanism to select their lobster of choice for dinner from the grimy tank.

The hostess pulled out a greasy, plastic patio chair for me at a small bistro table overlooking the water. I asked her for the Wi-Fi password and connected my phone for the first time since landing in Florida. My phone buzzed like a bumblebee with several messages from Jake. We were still in the "honeymoon" stage of our relationship; he asked me how Miami was and said that he missed me. I looked around at the backwater clientele of the *Barnacle Bistro* tossing back happy hour shooters at the bar top and typed back, *It's really nice…very high end.*

The waitress returned and I politely turned down the *Taste of the Everglades* special that was advertised: gator, frog legs and conch fritters), and opted for the fresh grouper and a house drink appropriately named *The Crocodile*. I dug into the fresh, flaky grouper and watched the constellations start to appear in the evening sky.

I was sipping the last of my shockingly green and surprisingly delicious drink when a flash of light over the dark water in front of me caught my attention. It disappeared as quickly as it came but then there was another, and another. Fireflies.

Their unexpected appearance made me think of Cara and a twinge of grief shot through me. Summers in Sunshine weren't complete without fireflies. In the evenings we would find them in the brush by the lake, sparkling in the night sky as if they were put there just for us. When we were young my mom told us that they were stars that had fallen to earth. Eventually we learned that their bioluminescence is caused by a chemical reaction inside their abdomen/tail, but I always liked the star story better.

Chapter 21

Remorse.

It's one of the only things that separates us from animals. Have I felt remorse over the things I've done, or regret for the lives that I've taken? If I said I felt nothing, I suppose that would make me some type of monster.

After I kill someone, I obsessively read news sites, waiting for mention of their demise. Their obituaries eventually surface and in Tom and Savannah's case it looked like investigations into their seemingly suspicious deaths ultimately led nowhere. I don't return to the scene of the crime or attempt to watch the reactions or suffering of their friends and family members from afar. When it's done, it's over, and I believe it's all part of a scene that I'm meant to act out.

I pulled into Marty's lot at the crack of dawn and found him ready and waiting, dressed to impress in head-to-toe camo safari gear.

He rolled down the window of his pickup, "Hop in with me, gal, and we'll head to the boat launch. Best bird sightings are usually in the early morning but I'm sure you already know that."

I did know that, thanks to the internet. I had spent most of the night trying to commit as many native everglade birds as possible to memory. Cheap binoculars hung around my neck in what I hoped was an official looking way. I had brought along a small notepad for "field notes".

We arrived at a small marina which, thankfully, seemed to be deserted at this hour of the day. An American flag fluttered in the wind next to a small boat launch. The waves lapped gently at the side of the dock and the sun rose up over the water, streaking it red and orange. I tried to recall the old sailor's saying, *red sky at night, sailor's delight, red sky in the morn' sailors forewarn.* I was nothing more than a nautical disaster, so I was going to have to assume Marty the Party knew what he was doing.

Marty strode purposefully over to an aluminum airboat with his name and crocodile cartoon helpfully plastered across it. He threw his bag in, reached for mine and grabbed my hand to help me aboard the rocking boat. I had never seen an airboat in person and was surprised at how simple they were. Two benches of seats sat along the slim, flat bottom of the boat and another set was elevated and directly in front of the fan mechanism. The fan looked similar to one that I set up in my bedroom on hot summer nights. I was skeptical that this was going to propel us across the vast network of the everglades.

Marty untied the rope from the dock and the boat rocked sharply.

"Umm, Marty, do you have a life jacket for me?"

He laughed loudly like a hyena. "Darlin', you don't need a life jacket here. If you happen to fall out of the boat for some reason just stand up."

My confused expression prompted him to laugh again.

"The water is only four to five feet on average, the deepest it gets here is nine feet."

"Oh," I said, feeling embarrassed.

"The bay is cut off from the ocean by sandbars, mangroves, and the Florida Keys so there's not much water circulation. The mix of salt and fresh water make it the only place in the world where gators and crocs co-exist," he exclaimed proudly, as if the reptiles were children that he had created and was directly responsible for.

"Will we see any alligators or crocodiles today?" Marty turned on the boat and I took my seat as it rattled and whined. It wouldn't take much to topple over the side of my seat into the murky water.

"If we're lucky! I'll take you to a favorite spot of mine, great for spotting gators and birds."

He pulled back the lever and we sped out onto the waterway skipping along the surface like a stone.

"Here," he yelled, tossing me a pair of noise reducing headphones. "You'll be needing these." He slid his on over his wide brimmed hat.

"What's the difference between crocodiles and alligators?" I yelled over the shriek of the boat.

"Gators have rounded snouts, whereas crocodile snouts are pointed. Crocodiles are the larger, and meaner of the two. Crocs are the ones with a weird, toothy grin, like they're always smiling at you."

We raced along for a few minutes before he slowed down and turned into a narrow channel thick with mangroves.

"Our national park has the largest amount of protected

mangroves in the hemisphere. While other vegetation dies off in the harsh conditions here, the mangroves thrive. They prosper in the strong winds, salty water and beating hot sun. Although they might not look like much they're an important part of the ecosystem and provide shelter for birds and other marine life."

I was beginning to wonder if my initial impression of Marty the Party was wrong and I was surprised at how knowledgeable he was, and how eloquently he spoke. He turned the boat off and we drifted with the current down the waterway. I pulled out my binoculars, pretending with great interest to look for birds. A large tree branch extended out from the shoreline over the water and an adult and baby turtle suntanned lazily on it.

I reached into my bag and pulled out a bag of beef jerky, offering Marty a piece. I chewed thoughtfully on the dry, leathery meat as I contemplated my next move. I tipped the rest of the contents of the beef jerky bag into the water while Marty wasn't looking.

A flash of white to the left of the turtles caught my eye and I was excited and relieved that I recognized the species of bird.

"Look," I whispered, in my best impression of an ornithologist voice, "a great blue heron."

The heron tiptoed gracefully along the shoreline, stepping deliberately with long, delicate movements, like a ballet dancer. It extended its elongated, thin neck and plunged its head into the water. Seconds later it emerged with a flailing fish struggling between its beak. Marty and I watched the tableau in companionable silence until the boat drifted past and we lost sight.

Marty scanned the shoreline and water with his good eye, and I wasn't sure if it was a reflection or coincidence but it looked to be the same color as the everglades water, a dark muddy green.

"How did you get started in ornithology?"

"It was actually my sister that was the bird lover. She loved all creatures, big and small. I guess this is just my way of honoring her memory and carrying on her legacy."

Marty was quiet for a moment. "I'm sure she's proud of you, and looking down on us right now." He motioned overhead to the cotton candy clouds bursting with sunshine. It wasn't hard at that moment to believe that Cara really was.

He revved up the airboat again, sending the birds hiding in the mangroves into a flutter, and we sped down a maze of channels until we reached a particularly swampy area of water, dense with sawgrass and lily pads.

"This here is my sweet spot," he whistled, pointing to an exquisitely colored bird that resembled a cross between a duck and a peacock. Its glossy purple feathers, accented with mossy green, shone as slick as oil in the bright sunlight. It had a sharp, bright red beak tipped with yellow and long, spindly legs. It tiptoed from lily pad to lily pad poetically and effortlessly. My birding cram session had ill prepared me and I had no idea what this particular species of bird was.

Marty watched me hesitate, with my pen poised over my notepad before offering, "Purple Gallinule isn't it?"

"Of course," I tried to recover. "I've never seen one in person before. It's just so…enchanting."

"We'll drift here for a bit, bound to see some birds and maybe even a few gators and crocs."

I scribbled several official looking notes down as I spotted a Limpkin, Roseate Spoonbill, White Ibis and Cormorant.

"Do you mind me asking what happened to your eye?"

He laughed. "Well, it's not a very good story or a long one. I was drunk and started a fight at a bar and it ended with me getting a beer bottle to the side of the head."

"That's awful!"

"The morning after was worse. When my wife told me she was leaving me. I couldn't blame her. Those were dark days."

"What made you want to be sober?"

He stared off into the distance for a moment at the dark clouds moving our way.

"I'm not sure it was any one thing. There was no epiphany, no defining moment. I just remember waking up one day and feeling tired. Tired of disappointing and hurting the people that I loved. Tired of feeling like I was more dead than alive. I was sitting in my recliner, half-drunk, watching *The Curious Case of Benjamin Button*, when Brad Pitt came on screen and said, 'I hope you live a life you're proud of. If you find that you're not, I hope you have the strength to start all over again.' I swear it felt like he was talking right to me through the TV."

"So, I did. I started again."

He looked me directly in the eyes, well, eye. "It's never

too late to start over. You're never too far gone that you can't come back."

I wish.

He broke his gaze and turned his attention back to the rapidly darkening sky. "Looks like it could be a real boomer, we better head back to shore."

I took my seat and kept a lookout for familiar landmarks that I'd been trying to commit to memory.

Chapter 22

"Would you mind slowing down up here real quick, I thought I saw a crocodile."

He looked appraisingly at the looming clouds. "Okay, but let's make it fast, we don't want to be caught out in the glades in an airboat during a storm."

He slowed the boat down so that I could look into the water. A few pieces of my jerky were still floating around. I swallowed down a gasp as I spotted what I was looking for. Penetrating, unblinking eyes and a prehistoric looking snout skimmed through the water a few meters in front of me.

"I think I saw one over there." I pointed to the opposite end of the boat and Marty got up out of his seat to look. I grabbed hold of the tree branch that had previously held the family of turtles and swung it as hard as I could at Marty's head. The branch connected with his skull with a loud crack, and he fell forward into the water with a dramatic splash.

Silence, save for a few water bubbles. The water turned red with his blood and Marty did not resurface. It didn't take long for the crocodile to investigate where Marty had fallen and it slowly disappeared below the surface. Two other crocs slid off the banks and into the water in pursuit of poor Marty. Their tails thrashed and snouts snapped as they embarked on a feeding frenzy. I positioned myself in the middle of the boat, as far away from the crocodiles as possible. I didn't want them getting any ideas about dessert.

I closed my eyes and looked for my sister. She crackled in and out. "I'm so sorry, Marty," I whispered. I knew that he didn't deserve to die like that. But Cara hadn't deserved to die the way that she had. Prematurely, unnaturally. Marty was a tribute, a sacrifice, collateral damage.

I threw the tree branch into the water to distract the swarming crocodiles and my hands trembled as I sat down in the captain's seat of the airboat and tried to remember how Marty had maneuvered it. I pushed the steering stick forward, stepped on the accelerator and the airboat sprang to life. The sky was turning a menacing shade of grey and I felt the first raindrops hit my skin.

I stepped off the accelerator just before the end of the channel that led into the open bay and estimated I was about a fifteen-minute swim from shore. I unzipped my pack, pulled out water shoes and quickly shimmied into a wetsuit. I shoved my binoculars and notepad into the waterproof pack, tied one end of the rope around it, and the other around my waist.

Abandoning the boat would make it look like an accident. It would arouse less suspicion if the boat was found out here in the channels versus parked at the boat ramp. I was a decent swimmer but the most dangerous water predator I'd had to contend with was leeches. When I was constructing my elaborate plan, swimming to shore had seemed like a feasible idea.

After seeing the crocodiles in person; how big and powerful they were and how jagged and unforgiving their crooked teeth were, I was having second thoughts. Thunder rumbled like a growl in a Tiger's belly and a flash of lightning lit up the sky. If the crocodiles didn't get me, sitting on a large piece of metal in the middle of the swamp during a lightning storm might.

The rain had started to pelt me as I jumped into the water with my bag trailing behind me. My head was submerged for a second and I surfaced with a gasp, pushing my wet hair out of my eyes. My feet had touched bottom but just barely. I dove forward into a front crawl, remembering to pace myself. I tried not to panic or think about what might be beside me as I swam steadily through the turbulent water.

The rain was getting more intense and pounding against my head like marbles. I looked forward, gasping, and could see the lights of the shoreline within my reach. The rope with my bag tied around my waist suddenly pulled me back with a lurch. I scrambled to regain my footing and stand up, refusing to turn around. My fingers fumbled with the rope as I frantically tried to undo it from around my waist. The rope was pulling more violently and insistently when finally it undid, setting me free and leaving the bag trailing behind.

I dove underwater and swam as hard as I could, my muscles burned and my arms flailed madly. I kept waiting for the inevitable. I swear I felt hard scales brush against my leg. I didn't stop until I collided with the shore, my knees banging into the ground.

Lights flashed and I heard voices yelling before everything went dark.

My eyes flickered open to two unfamiliar faces staring down at me.

A scruffy, heavily bearded man and a clean-shaven, suntanned man were both looking at me with concern.

"Ma'am, are you all right, can you hear us?" asked Beardy.

I was lying on the floor of a small room, on a pile of sour smelling towels, next to a variety of fishing and boating equipment. The rain poured down the glass of a nearby window and rattled incessantly against the roof.

"Where am I?" I croaked, a trickle of muddy tasting water making its way down my chin.

"We pulled you out of the water by the shore there. The glades is not a place to be swimming miss, especially during a storm, you're lucky you made it out alive," scolded Suntanned Man.

"I was kayaking," I lied, "and I flipped my boat and panicked. I was trying to make it to shore and the storm hit."

Suntanned man's expression softened. "Well, we're glad we spotted you and pulled you into the storage shack here. We better get you to a hospital and make sure you're all right."

"No," I protested, sitting up. "I'll be fine, honestly. If someone could take me to my hotel room I'd appreciate it."

Suntanned man exchanged a glance with beardy,

"What tour company were you with, we'll call them and let them know you're all right."

"None. I brought my own kayak out here. I promise I'm okay. I'd just like to change out of these wet clothes." The wetsuit clung to my trembling body and my legs were covered in mud and blood.

Beardy relented, helped me off the floor and wrapped a towel around my shoulders. He held my arm as I limped to his truck and climbed inside. He was silent for the quick ride to the hotel and I was grateful he didn't pry for more information. We pulled into the hotel parking lot and I thanked him for his help.

"Are you sure you're all right?" Beardy asked again.

"I'm sure." I smiled at him in what I hoped was a healthy way.

Chapter 23

I fell through the door of my hotel room, stripping my wetsuit off on the way to the bathroom. I sat down in the small, hard tub and turned the water as hot as I could bear. The steam radiated off my cold skin and the chill in my bones started to subside. The water swirled around me and mixed with the dirt and blood. I leaned back and let my body relax.

My work was not done. I needed to clean up, wake up, finish what I started and get out of Everglades City as early as possible in the morning. I pried myself out of the bath when my skin had turned a bright pink, wrapped myself in one of the thin hotel towels and hobbled over to the in-room, one-cup coffee maker. I dumped nondescript grounds and a cup of water into it, flicked the switch and it began to sputter and gurgle. I picked up my phone to finally respond to Jake, who had been texting me all day.

I hope you're having a great time. I can't wait to see those tan lines, he had messaged.

I just got in from swimming, I can't wait to see you too, I typed back, pleased that I didn't even have to lie to him.

I pulled a pair of tights and a sweater on over my battered and bruised body, grabbed the coffee cup and headed to Marty's house.

I parked a block away behind a local bar so that no one would see my vehicle in his driveway. Thinking like a criminal had become second nature to me. That and I had been watching *Law and Order*, *48 Hours* and *Forensic Files* on repeat. I pulled up my hood as I walked up the driveway to Marty's house and used the sleeve of my sweater to try the back door. Locked, damn it.

I walked around the exterior of the house and noticed the kitchen window slightly ajar. I pulled on the black leather gloves I'd brought and grabbed a plastic lawn chair from the backyard to stand on. I pushed the window open, hoisted myself up and crawled in through the window with little grace or stealth. I flinched as my bruised legs banged against the windowsill.

I was surprised to find the kitchen tidy and orderly. The butcher block counters were wiped clean and the chairs pushed in neatly against the small card table. I picked up a stack of papers on the counter and rifled through them, finding nothing of interest. I paused to look at the photos pinned to the refrigerator.

Marty posing with a crocodile. Marty standing on his airboat giving two thumbs up. Photos of a little blonde girl laughing in his arms, Marty sunburnt and smiling down at her. Another one of the same girl, a bit older, and a tow-headed boy, posing with Marty by the water. I assumed they must be his children and felt a twinge of sadness. He looked like a good dad.

I wandered past the living room and into his bedroom. A double bed was neatly made up in a homemade quilt. Over his bed hung a framed script of the Serenity Prayer.

God grant me the serenity to accept the things
    I cannot change,
Courage to change the thing I can,
And the wisdom to know the difference.

I sat down on the bed, opened the bedside drawer on a whim and exhaled a sigh of relief. The boarding pass. I was worried that it had been in Marty's wallet. I couldn't feel like I'd finished the job without it. I slid it into my pocket and crawled back out the window, leaving the memories of Marty to echo in the empty house.

Driving to the hotel I was so tired I could barely keep my eyes open. I flicked the radio on and Neil Young's southern drawl, singing *My My, Hey Hey,* filled the vehicle.

I rolled the window down to let the air hit my face. The moon glowed brightly, unnaturally illuminated in the clear evening sky.

Chapter 24
Saturday, October 31st

I tie what is left of my hair back and liberally apply moisturizer to my face. It's a peace offering in advance of the heap of makeup I'm about to trowel onto it. I found skeleton makeup tutorials online and I'm going to attempt to paint my face to resemble a human skull. Where is Becca when I need her?

There's a sudden, sharp, jabbing pain in my mouth. I push my tongue against my teeth in an exploratory way, causing a spike of pain as I run it across my back molar. Great timing for a cavity. I'll call and book a dentist appointment for next week.

I sponge and apply white makeup evenly all over my face. Then I dip my makeup brush into the black face paint and draw dark circles around both of my eyes and on top of my nose. My eyes are a spooky vibrant green against the black. I delicately paint jagged stitches across my lips, widening my smile into a pseudo-Joker-type grin.

"Why so serious?" I mumble to myself.

I suck my cheeks in and assess myself in the mirror. Not bad. I brush out my hair and curl it into waves. Jake is downstairs watching TV and waiting for me. I hear the door open and Reese calls out, joining Jake.

"I'll be right down," I holler.

Cinder has been watching my transformation and looks at me confused. I try to pick him up and he bolts. His loss.

Now for the hard part. I grab my skintight costume and pull it over my legs, wiggling to get it past my hips and boobs. I can forget about going to the bathroom in this. I check myself out in the full-length bedroom mirror and am pleased with the final result. I've done a decent job of painting an anatomically correct skeleton and I think it might even give me the illusion of having muscles. For the finishing touch I slip on black ballet slippers, remnants from the year I went as the Black Swan.

Jake and Reese are standing in the living room drinking beer. Jake is in his Indiana Jones costume, complete with khaki pants and shirt, a brown fedora hat that he'd rescued from Value Village, and a tan leather jacket. One side of his belt loop is threaded with a long, coiled rope and the other side holds a holster and fake gun. In very un-Jake like behavior, he hasn't shaved in the last few days and has a five o'clock shadow.

Reese has a plaid shirt on over a vintage punk rock shirt and a pair of white sunglasses is holding back his long, wavy hair.

"What are you supposed to be?" I ask, confused.

"Duh…Kurt Cobain."

I laugh. "Let me guess, you made zero effort to get a costume until tonight and then realized you had nothing, so you just dug around in your closet and this is what you came up with?"

He pretends to be offended and shrugs. "Yeah, that's pretty much exactly what happened."

"You look great, babe." Jake leans to kiss me then thinks better of it after considering my face makeup. Instead, he puts his arm around my waist in a gesture of affection.

Reese shotguns the rest of his beer and slams the empty can down on the table. "Let's get this show on the road!"

We arrive at Becca's Halloween party. The decorations are incredible. The front lawn is covered in gravestones and tiny jack-o'-lanterns light the way up the path. The yard is a tableau of flamingo, cat and human skeletons painted every color of the rainbow. A red skeleton is pushing the lawnmower and a blue one appears to be watering the bushes. A yellow skeleton is laid out in a wheelbarrow full of leaves holding its bony skull in its hands.

People fill every inch of Becca's modern two-story house. We shove our way past the crowd of people and into the house. Music is reverberating off the walls and there's a DJ spinning in the living room. The open concept main floor is packed with people dancing, drinking and talking. I push and elbow my way toward the kitchen to find Becca. The dining room table is teeming with Halloween themed food made to resemble fingers, brains and eyeballs, and there's a huge bubbling vat of something labelled "Witches Brew".

The sleek, white stone fireplace mantle is veiled in cobwebs and decorated with jars of body parts, reptiles and insects suspended in green liquid. A huge glass hurricane with a glowing red light displays an amazingly real-looking plastic snake. I lean in closer to inspect and jump when the snake hisses and slithers its tongue. Of course, Becca would have a real snake here.

A nude zombie girl covered in sashimi, nigiri and sushi rolls is lying on the dining room table. I shake my head in awe and shove a Cleopatra and Superman out of my way.

"Charlieeeee!" I hear Becca's unmistakable growl calling my name.

I turn around and my jaw drops at Becca's Marie Antoinette costume. She's wearing an extravagant 18th century gown and a huge white-blond wig, piled at least a foot high on top of her head. Ribbons and flowers are intricately threaded into the elaborate hairpiece. She has a pearl cameo choker around her neck and is wearing white silk gloves. Her face is immaculately made up into a deathly white pallor. Two spots of bright pink blush on her cheeks and a precisely painted blood-red pout make for a stark contrast.

"Love your costume!" she exclaims as she spins me around.

"Are you kidding? It's nothing compared to yours. I mean you've outdone yourself Becca—this is unreal."

"Right? It took two hours and three stylists to pull this hair piece off," she laughs.

"Well, it was definitely worth it."

"Thanks ,doll, I'm going to go greet some people, help yourself to some Witches Brew," she gestures and disappears into the mass of people.

I've lost track of Jake and Reese at this point so I decide to follow through on Becca's suggestion. I grab a plastic cup and dip the ladle into the cauldron, filling my glass. I notice several empty bottles of Absinthe, aka "The Green Fairy" next to the cauldron. I take a sip of the Witches Brew and my eyes immediately water. I feel breathless, like someone is standing on my chest. I inhale sharply and break into a coughing fit. I feel a hand on my shoulder.

"You okay?" asks Jake, looking at me with concern.

"Fine," I croak. "I'm just going to use the washroom, I'll be back." I push past elaborately and barely dressed party goers to the upstairs bathroom. I close the door behind me and put my drink down on the bathroom counter. I catch myself in the mirror and startle before remembering I'm a skeleton for the night. I pull my phone out of my purse and open a new text from Abel. I had sent him a picture of my costume.

The most beautiful girl–inside and out–Ha.

I smile and type back, *Very punny, can't wait to see you tomorrow. Bad jokes and all.*

You too. Be safe tonight.

I take another swig of my drink and fill with pride as I barely cough. I open the bathroom door and walk directly into someone, spilling my drink on them.

"I'm so sorry…" I begin to say, and then look up and realize who it is. "Natalie?" I drop what's left of my drink on the floor.

Chapter 25

It's not exactly the Natalie I remember. It's an older, tired, hardened-looking version of the girl that I once knew. But I'd recognize her anywhere. She was Cara's best friend.

We met Natalie at summer camp during Cara's last year. Beginning the summer that we turned ten, our parents would ship us off each year to Pine Falls Summer Camp, located twenty minutes outside of Sunshine. The camp was situated on the shores of Lake Winnipeg and surrounded by forest. Being out there felt different than the rest of the prairies. The camp was only a few kilometers from the nearest farmer's field, but the dense woods made it feel like the middle of nowhere.

A half dozen wood cabins for the campers were scattered across the property and other cabins served as the activity and dining hall, counsellor residence and washrooms. The best part about the camp was that Stanley got to come along too. There was a corral behind the guest cabins where campers could board their horses and use them for riding lessons.

In addition to riding lessons, Pine Falls offered several other activities such as arts and crafts, windsurfing, kayaking and survival classes. Campers were divided up according to juniors and seniors. Magnolia was a senior, in her fourth year, and Cara and I were going on our third year. She chose to mostly ignore her younger sisters at the camp, sometimes blessing us with a cursory smile or nod of acknowledgment when we passed each other in the common areas.

For two years in a row Cara and I had been housed in cabin number six. Each log cabin held four sets of bunk beds and a cubby for each camper. It was an unspoken agreement between Cara and I that she would always take top bunk and I would take bottom.

When our mom dropped us off at Pine Falls that year, we barely glanced back at her as she drove away. We raced down the path to the camp notice board, our sneakers kicking up dirt into little clouds behind us. We arrived breathless at the board and scanned the posting dictating who belonged to what cabin.

We ran to cabin six and burst through the door laughing before noticing a girl sitting on one of the bottom bunks and unpacking her things.

She turned around, startled by the noise and smiled, "Hi, I'm Natalie."

Sunlight from the open window shone on her creamy olive skin and reflected on her long, wavy, glossy black hair. She could have been a haircare product model. She had bold, thick brows, unheard of in the 90's, that framed brilliant aquamarine eyes. She had a delicate rosebud mouth and I didn't have to smell her breath to know that it was probably minty-fresh. Jealously burned molten through my veins and instantly turned to dislike and disdain for this dainty, beautiful creature invading our cabin.

My bushy hair was tied back into a knotty ponytail and

I was wearing ripped jean shorts that I made myself and a plaid shirt rolled up at the elbows. Earlier in the day, what I thought had been the perfect casual outfit for my first day at camp now seemed sloppy and disheveled.

Natalie was wearing a simple black tank top and red shorts but the way they hugged against her curves made her look older and stylish. I crossed my arms self-consciously across my chest. I had started wearing a bra last summer after being urged by Cara that everyone was doing it, whether we needed them yet or not.

Cara sat on the bed beside her and introduced herself. "And this is my sister, Charlie," she motioned for me to join them.

"Hi," I gave an awkward wave and set my duffle bag on the ground beside the bottom bunk adjacent to hers.

"Oh, you guys are twins? That's so cool!" she exclaimed. "I wish I had a sister my age. My sisters are younger than me and total pains, and my older brother is always chasing girls and stealing booze from my parent's liquor cabinet."

"I don't recognize you from school," said Cara. "Are you from around here?"

"We actually just moved to Sunshine last month from Toronto. My dad got transferred to a job in Winnipeg and my mom only agreed to move if we could live in a small town and he could commute. I think she reads too many magazines. She's dead set on instilling 'small town values' in us," she said, making air quotes with her fingers.

"So, you don't know anyone here?" I asked, hoping that she knew someone we could pawn her off on.

"Nope, no one. I was hoping to meet some people at camp."

Cara ignored the glare I was giving her and said to Natalie, "That's no problem, you can hang with us."

And so began the summer of Natalie and Cara.

I learned the hard way that three really is a crowd. There was an intruder in a world that had been only mine and Cara's. The worst part was that Cara didn't see it that way. She was enraptured by Natalie and brushed away my snarky comments about her. I can't blame Cara for being drawn to Natalie. She had always been drawn to beauty, and pretty things; stopping on walks on the beach to pick up a perfectly shaped shell, a sparking piece of quartz or a sparkling piece of sea glass.

That night in the dining hall, Cara sat between Natalie and me as we listened to the camp counsellors welcome the new campers, cover available activities and review the camp rules.

"And no swimming after the sun sets," squeaked a blotchy, chubby counsellor into the microphone. There was an unspoken "because" that hung in the air, but the counsellor continued listing the dos and don'ts at Pine Falls.

Five years ago, several of the senior campers had brought some of the new junior campers to the lake in the middle of the night for "initiation". The seniors had commanded the juniors to strip and swim out to the dock and back. While the younger campers flailed and splashed through the cold, black water, the seniors took off with their clothes to force them to run back to the cabins naked.

It was a harmless prank until the shivering naked

campers on shore realized that one of them was missing. Will Jensen was nowhere to be found. Will was a weak swimmer at best and amidst the splashing and yelling of the others his struggling had gone unnoticed. His pale, bloated body was pulled from the bottom of the lake the next day by a team of divers. His short life was memorialized by a bronze plaque on one of the benches down by the shore.

I remember chewing on bland, tasteless mashed potatoes and imagining Natalie being pulled down into the belly of the lake. Her long hair billowing behind her as she sank deeper toward the bottom.

It was the first time I could remember feeling darkness overtake me. Like a cloud, passing in front of the sun, extinguishing the warmth and light.

"Charlie," said Cara; she and Natalie were looking at me questionably.

"What?" I said, snapping out of it.

"I said, we're going to go for a walk, do you want to come with?"

"No, it's fine," I replied, a little sharply. "I'm going to head back to the cabin and unpack."

Cara held my gaze for a moment and I knew she could tell I was upset. She shrugged her shoulders, grabbed her plastic tray and left the dining hall with Natalie anyways, talking animatedly.

As soon as they were out of sight, I picked up my own meal tray and dropped it by the garbage bins. I would go visit my only true friend at Pine Falls that summer.

"Hi, Stan," I crooned, standing on the bottom rung of the fence so that I could lean over and grab his neck. He whinnied gently and I snuggled my face into his coarse mane, inhaling his sweet, musty warmth. I reached into my pockets and fished out oats I'd grabbed from the stable. I held my hand flat and let him gobble them with his long, scratchy tongue.

"Stan, what am I going to do?" I questioned as I grabbed his tack and saddled him. If a ride wouldn't get my mind off things, nothing would. Cara and I rarely disagreed, let alone fought, but I had felt the tension between us all afternoon whenever Natalie was around.

I jumped on Stanley and we took off down the well-worn riding trails. We galloped for a few minutes before slowing to a steady walk. I relaxed under the rhythm of Stanley's walk and was enjoying the symphony of the forest. Birds sang overhead and squirrels chased each other up the tree trunks.

We came to a fork in the trail and one path continued down the familiar riding trail while the other looked slightly overgrown. I had never ventured off the trail before but I pointed Stanley's head left and we took the road less travelled. The farther we walked down the trail the more overgrown it became. I'd be picking brambles out of Stanley's mane for weeks to come.

I was just about to turn around when I noticed a break in the tree line and what looked like a clearing up ahead. I nudged Stan forward until the path ran out. Just outside the clearing was a wide-open field thick with prairie grass and wildflowers. In the middle of it was an old, run-down barn. We trudged through the long grass, stepping carefully in case of ruts or old animal traps. When we finally arrived at the barn, I tied Stan to a post and jumped off him to look around.

The sun was starting to set and the field was bathed in a soft orange glow. There's nothing quite like a Manitoba sunset. The endless sky stretches as far as the eye can see and transforms into a whirlpool of color. I walked the perimeter of the barn until I found an entrance. One of the big wood doors was busted and slightly ajar.

Inside the barn, piles of dead lumber were stacked against the wall and old tools lay rusting on the ground. Slivers of sunlight streamed in through holes in the roof and walls and dust lingered in it. I could see a few ramshackle stalls with decaying piles of hay. It was clear that animals hadn't been in the barn for a while.

A crooked wooden ladder leaned against one of the walls, leading up to what looked like a hayloft. I stepped on the bottom rung testing its weight, and when it didn't snap, I climbed to the next one. Rung by rung I slowly made my way up the ladder and onto the loft.

I noticed a large, metal hook contraption hanging from the ceiling. It reminded me of scorpion pincers. Four prongs hung from a pulley system with a frayed rope and ran along the barn ceiling. It looked like some sort of torture device. I brushed stray hay off my legs and carefully walked around the device, testing the sharpness of the metal points with the edge of my finger. It was a hay pulley, used to bring bales up to the loft from outside.

Shadows were beginning to overtake the barn as the last bit of light faded. I carefully climbed back down the ladder and returned to Stanley. I apologized for leaving him and he snorted, pretending to ignore me. We rode back to camp just as the moon began to rise, a golden orb in a velvet sky.

By the time I had put Stanley away and kissed his bristly muzzle goodnight it was dark and the smell of campfire hung in the air. Cabin six was empty and Cara and Natalie were nowhere to be found. I walked toward the fire pits and could hear the comforting crackle of the wood and see the glowing silhouettes of the flames. Cara's laugh cut through the smoky air and I spotted her cuddled up on a bench by the fire with Natalie. I clenched my fist and felt my face begin to burn as hot as the embers.

"Charlie, hi!" said Natalie, beaming at me as if we were friends.

"Hi," I said curtly. Cara eyed me, acknowledging my presence but not welcoming it.

"Sit down." Natalie patted the seat beside her, shoving Cara further down the bench.

I sat on the hard, wooden bench and leaned toward the fire, trying to thaw the coolness that was emanating from Cara toward me. Was she mad at me, I wondered? I wasn't sure how to bridge the chasm that opened between us in only a few hours. Then again, maybe it had always been there, waiting for an opportunity to present itself. Maybe it was inevitable.

Everyone thinks twins are a two for one deal. You're used to sharing everything because from birth what's yours is theirs—womb, blood, cells. As you grow older, it's a room, toys, clothes and friends. You're thought of in a collective sense so often that you lose your individuality.

When a semblance of independence from one another appears, you feel unnerved. Like the rough draft of a person.

"Tomorrow we're going to arts and crafts during the day if you want to come. I think it's friendship bracelets," said Natalie.

The use of "we" was not lost on me. "We" as in Cara had already agreed to attend without consulting or inviting me.

"Sure, that sounds fun." It did not sound fun. It sounded terrible. Like something Cara and I would ridicule others for doing and choosing to explore on our own instead.

"Okay, guys, back to the cabins, early start tomorrow." A camp counsellor blew her whistle and clapped her hands together as if she was rounding up cattle.

Back at the cabin, I pulled the scratchy wool blanket against my chin and stared into the darkness. I listened to the gentle shuffling as the other girls in the cabin settled into their beds and drifted asleep. There was a heaviness in my chest like Stanley was standing on it.

Chapter 26

The next morning, I woke to the sound of the camp bell and rubbed the sleep out of my eyes. Cara's bed was already neatly made and so was Natalie's. I quickly got dressed and walked to the dining hall where I found the two of them giggling over their pancakes.

"You guys got an early start," I said, and sat down across from them with a plate of pancakes.

"We didn't want to wake you up, you looked pretty deeply asleep," said Cara, her mouth full of pancake.

How thoughtful of her.

"Arts and crafts start soon and we wanted to make sure we got a spot," said Natalie, her hair shining.

At the craft table I grabbed a handful of colored thread as one of the camp counsellors explained in a bored voice how to weave them together. I felt like the third wheel of the budding relationship of Cara and Natalie. Cara kept looking at her with adoration and admiration and Natalie seemed thrilled to have found companionship.

I excused myself to the bathroom and when I returned to my almost finished "friendship" bracelet, I noticed that Natalie and Cara had completed theirs already. Cara had woven together navy, aquamarine, cerulean and turquoise blue thread that was now displayed on Natalie's wrist.

Natalie had used violet, lavender and burgundy thread to form a bracelet which was now wrapped around Cara's dainty wrist.

My bracelet had been haphazardly thrown together using mismatched colors. I shoved it into my pocket and left the arts and crafts cabin without saying goodbye. I went straight to the stable, where, at least, Stanley was delighted to see me. Or, at least, he had the decency to pretend he was happy to see me, and not the handful of oats. I buried my face in his mane and tasted the saltiness of tears on my lips.

I took the bracelet out of my pocket and braided it into a piece of his forelock.

"There," I exclaimed, and stood back to admire my handiwork. I stroked his head softly, feeling like he might be the only one left who cared about me.

Camp continued over the two weeks as it had begun. The closer Cara and Natalie grew together the more Cara and I drifted apart. I had taken to spending most of my afternoons at the abandoned barn with Stanley, daydreaming in the hayloft. Usually a discovery like the barn was something that Cara would have been thrilled with, but I had yet to mention it to her.

Back in the cabin I was trying to fall asleep but the sound of Cara and Natalie whispering was keeping me up. I pulled the pillow over my head trying to drown them out when Cara put her hand on my shoulder and shook me slightly.

"What?" I asked, annoyed.

"I said we're going swimming, it's a full moon. Do you want to come?" She had a bathing suit on and a towel wrapped around her shoulders.

I looked at Natalie who was waiting by the door watching us.

I shrugged and got up to put my bathing suit on.

We walked the dirt path to the lake in silence, careful not to alert the counsellors. The moon shone brightly enough so that we could see where we were going but the rustling of branches and shadows that crept across the path unnerved me.

The three of us stood on the edge of the shore listening to the sound of the water. I tentatively dipped in a toe, letting the cold water chill my blood. I shivered. Even in the dead of summer, Lake Winnipeg rarely warmed up much, which wasn't surprising considering it's one of the largest freshwater lakes in the world. I dug my toes into the squishy clay bottom.

Natalie looked mischievously at both of us before slipping out of her bathing suit and skipping into the water. The light of the moon highlighted her curves and created a celestial glow around her. In a few steps she was deep enough to dive in. Her long hair trailed behind her like an oil spill and disappeared below the surface. Everything became so oddly still and quiet that I was sure she was never going to reappear. Or, at least, I hoped.

She resurfaced with a gasp and called us to join her. My face grew hot with embarrassment and I crossed my arms against my flat chest. I remember reading that the full moon was thought to make people go crazy. The word "lunatic" is derived from the Latin word "lunaticus" meaning "moonstruck".

Cara giggled, slid off her suit and jumped in after her. I stood awkwardly on the shore for a moment before quickly pulling off my suit and crashing into the water behind them. The cold, black water swallowed and spit me back out again. I gasped as I rose to the surface and caught my breath.

We followed the trail of moonlight on the water and swam to the floating dock. We hoisted ourselves up on to the damp platform. I wrapped my arms around my knees and tried to cover myself while Cara and Natalie sprawled out, unashamed of their nakedness. We swayed back and forth with the rhythm of the waves.

"People say that if you go swimming during a full moon you can see the ghost of Will, the camper that drowned here," whispered Cara.

"That's not true," I scoffed. "You're just trying to freak us out."

Somewhere in the darkness the eerie cry of a bird broke the silence.

"They say that the lake turns red with his blood, and that he's destined to haunt these waters, waiting for a full moon…so that he can find more bodies to join him," Cara continued.

Suddenly something grabbed my leg and before I realized it was only Natalie, the two of them burst out laughing and I stumbled backward, losing my balance. My head cracked against the side of the dock like a gunshot and I fell into the water.

I remember the sensation of floating and looking at the

stars, unsure whether I was looking down or up at them. My head throbbed relentlessly and my arms and legs were like dead weights pulling me down into the darkness. I opened my mouth to cry out and water flooded my airways.

Just when the haziness began to envelope me entirely there were arms around me, pulling me upward. As soon as my head surfaced, I simultaneously gulped in fresh oxygen and coughed out lake water. Natalie had dragged me onto the rocky shore and I could feel the prickle of little stones rubbing against my skin.

The cold water burned my lungs like lava and I choked, rolled over, and let it spill out of my mouth like a fountain. My tears mixed with the fishy taste of lake water and I sobbed, violently expelling water from my body. Natalie rushed to wrap a towel around me while Cara watched terrified, her face ghostly pale in the moonlight. Natalie gathered my head against her chest, rocking me back and forth.

Once I felt strong enough to stand, they slowly walked me back to the cabin. I shrugged off waking a counsellor, knowing we'd all be kicked out of camp for our shenanigans.

"It was just a joke, Charlie, we didn't mean for anything bad to happen," Cara said quietly.

I didn't acknowledge her and climbed into my bed, burrowing deep into the covers to try to calm my violent shivering. I lay awake long after the others fell asleep, staring out the window at the full moon.

Chapter 27

"Charlie..." Natalie begins and pulls me into a hug. Her hair still hangs long and dark and smells like wildflowers and honey. Her arms clutch against my back in the way that a drowning person might cling to a buoy. I awkwardly put one of my hands on the side of her hip when she exceeds the appropriate amount of time to release me. She finally let go and pulls me directly in front of her. "How are you?" she asks, her eyes bright.

"I'm...good," I finally reply.

"I've never forgotten her, Charlie; I think about her all the time." She holds up her thin, tanned arm to reveal a worn, faded woven bracelet. The one that Cara gave to her at camp.

I don't know how to respond. I try awkwardly to find words, but my tongue feels like its swollen and is filling my mouth. My cavity is pulsating and I instinctively touch my hand to my face. Reese rounds the corner with his arm around the shoulders of a sexy redhead in a nurse costume. He notices my obvious discomfort and quickly brushes the nurse off to interrupt my conversation with Natalie.

"Charlie, let's go get that drink I promised you," he says, guiding me toward the stairs with a smile.

"Go ahead. We can catch up another time," says Natalie, with a defeated smile.

I open my mouth to say goodbye but then shut it. I feel like a balloon is being blown up in my throat.

"You okay? You look like you've seen a ghost," says Reese, pulling me to his chest.

"Something like that. I just need another drink."

"Your wish is my command." He leads me to the drink table, pours something black into two shot glasses and hands me one.

I tilt my head back, toss it down my throat, and slam the shot glass down on the table.

"More."

Reese smirks and pours me another.

Everything is fuzzy and warm. Every sound is amplified. I'm hyper aware of my heels clicking against the floor and the bass from the music booms in my chest like a secondary heartbeat. I glide through partygoers like Moses parting the sea. I open the back door and spill out into the cool night air.

I sit down on one of the deck chairs and my face is now throbbing. I can visualize the decaying tooth like a black, jagged rock sticking out of my gums.

The patio is set up to look like a torture chamber, complete with chains, torture devices and a skeleton tied to one of the patio chairs. I toy with a tray of tools and pick up a hooked metal rod and a pair of surgical scissors covered in fake blood. I put them down and pick up a pair of pliers, the cold metal feels delicious against my burning skin.

I slide the pliers into my mouth and clamp the pincers

down on either side of my tooth. I tug at it and the pain is blinding. I don't stop pulling until I'm holding the pliers in front of me with my tooth encapsulated between its claws. I laugh at the sight of it and hear a gurgling sound, my mouth filling with the warm aluminum taste of blood.

I spit onto the grass and notice a dark clump of blood. I shove my finger into my mouth and feel the empty socket where my tooth once was. I'm amused as I notice blood trickling down my arm.

"Charlie, what are you doing out here?" asks Reese, his smile suddenly turning into shock.

I press my sore cheek against the window of the taxi, the cool glass providing momentary relief from the pain.

Jake is in the backseat with me, looking angrily out the window. The cab smells like curry. I wish I had East Indian food right now. The thought makes me want to laugh but I swallow it, knowing it will only infuriate Jake even more.

We pull up in front of my house and he pays the driver and stalks to the front door. I slowly hoist myself out of the back seat and shut the door, balancing against the cab to try to keep my head from spinning. By the time I make it into the house Jake's coming down the staircase with a duffel bag.

"Where are we going?" I ask. My mouth feels like it's full of cotton candy.

"We are not going anywhere. I am going. I'm done with your shit, Charlie."

He stares at me with enough resentment and disdain to

fill the entrance way. I keep quiet and explore the newfound hole in my mouth with my tongue. He shakes his head and leaves, slamming the door behind him so hard that the house shakes for a second. Or maybe it's just my knees. The task of standing is too much for me right now so I crawl up the stairs to the bathroom.

I feel like a shamed animal and know that in Jake's eyes I haven't evolved much past one. I strip off my costume and stumble into the tub, leaning forward into a Child's Pose position that would make my yoga teacher proud. Colds water pounds against the back of my head and streams down my face in punishment. The black and white face makeup mixes with the dried blood and creates a swirl of colors going down the drain that reminds me of Abel's painting.

The last time I had seen Natalie before tonight was at Cara's funeral. I let the word tumble around in my head like a Tic Tac.

Funeral.

I had never been to a funeral prior to Cara's. The sun was shining; the flowers were in full bloom. I woke groggily out of a sedated, dreamless sleep to singing birds. How could they sing when my sister was dead? I turned over and looked at her empty bed. I blinked. Still empty.

I got up, robotically brushed my hair and teeth, and rifled through our closet looking for a dress we owned. Just I owned now. I looked at myself in the vanity mirror and an unfamiliar face started back at me. My skin was pale with a sickly pallor underneath my summer tan. My eyes were vivid green and bloodshot. My lips were the same color as my skin, almost translucent, and chapped with teeth marks.

I walked into the kitchen and Magnolia looked up from her cereal. She didn't say anything or acknowledge me and I sat down beside her to stare into space. We each had our unspoken assigned seating at the kitchen table. My mom sat nearest to the stove so that she could jump up and tend to anything that was cooking if necessary and Magnolia sat beside her. My dad sat at the head of the table, following the time old tradition of the man of the house. Cara and I sat opposite my mom and Magnolia, facing the back door, so we had the best view of any action in the backyard.

Who would sit in her spot now, I wondered? Would we just leave it empty? Magnolia looked at me with red, puffy eyes. Would I serve as a constant reminder to everyone of what we had lost? Sometimes even Magnolia would confuse Cara and me, calling us the wrong name or mistaking us for one another.

My dad came in and let us know that it was time to go. I wondered where my mom was until she appeared, cloaked in black, like a shadow. Her bright, red hair contrasted so sharply that it was almost comical. Her eyes were blank and red rimmed. She stared at me, but it was more like through me. She said nothing and walked silently out the door to the car.

My dad was wearing the only suit he owned, his wedding suit. It was worn and didn't fit him properly, but I guess your daughter's funeral wasn't cause to purchase a new one. He fiddled with his tie and his sleeves rode up slightly too much, showing an expanse of his hairy arms. My heart ached.

Weddings and funerals have a funny way of bringing people together. Both of our extended families were planning to attend. My dad's family—all brash, dark and round, and my mom's—small, quiet and pale. They had been in and out of the house with sympathy cards, sympathy casseroles and pitying looks. I dreaded the forced hugs and amplified emotions that the day would surely bring.

The drive to the church was only five minutes long but it might as well have been five hours. I stared out the window and listened to Stevie Nicks singing *Dream* on the radio.

We pulled onto the side of the road beside the church and even after my dad turned off the ignition no one made a move. We all just sat there, trying to delay the reality that we were burying Cara today. My mom finally got out of the car and Magnolia trailed after her. My dad waited until I opened the car door, grabbing onto it, unsure if my legs were going to hold me. He put his hand on top of mine. I searched his eyes for forgiveness but came up blank.

I sat through the service like I was a bystander. Like this tragedy did not belong to me. I remember looking at a black and white framed photo of Cara at the front of the church and thinking she wouldn't have liked it. It was taken at the beach, and the wind was blowing her hair in front of her face. She wasn't looking at the camera, and she was laughing at something I had said to her. She said her smile was too big, you could practically see her molars, she said, and her freckles were too prominent, they looked like dirt, she said.

My mom had insisted on keeping the photo, because she said that it perfectly captured the way that Cara looked when she didn't know anyone was looking at her. And that's how my mom liked to think of her.

The air was heavy with sadness and thick with tears and I was beginning to feel claustrophobic. I picked at my cuticles with broken fingernails. After the service I avoided the sympathetic stares and tear-filled eyes and went to the reception area. The folding church tables were lined with ham and cheese pinwheels, scones and other finger foods. I felt nauseous.

The first guests started to trickle in, clinging to my mother, father and sister like survivors of a natural disaster. Magnolia chewed on a pinwheel sandwich. Bodies are not meant to stay in prolonged states of shock. Eventually we normalize the abnormal so that we can continue living. Because the sadness and grief of losing someone you love is too heavy for your heart to sustain.

I slipped out the back door, gulping in the fresh air. The fucking birds were still singing.

"Stop!" I screamed at them, sitting on a low hanging tree branch, oblivious.

"Why won't you stop!" I pleaded with them hoarsely.

I felt the blood rushing to my head and collapsed into the grass. I laid there, letting the ants crawl all over me for what felt like hours. When I finally lifted my head, I noticed someone watching me from the bike rack.

It was Natalie.

Chapter 28
Sunday, November 1st

Reckless people are the scariest people.

Sure, I suppose I have more to lose. But none of it really matters now that Cara is gone.

I regain consciousness, and the white room from my dream slowly evaporates like morning mist over the lake. My face is throbbing like a kick drum. I grab my phone, no messages from Jake. It's 9:05 a.m. Abel will be here in an hour.

I groan and get up to fumble around in the medicine cabinet where I know I have over-the-counter pain medicine. I pull the bloody gauze out of my mouth with disgust and examine the hole where my tooth once was. It seems to have stopped bleeding and I'm hoping painkillers will do the trick. I open and close my mouth experimentally like some sort of demented Pac-Man.

I splash cool water on my face hoping to wash away my sins, but it doesn't seem to work. I twist my hair into a knot and quickly apply makeup. My eyes are bloodshot and I rub underneath them hoping to will away the dark circles. In short, I look like a mess. And not even a hot one.

I accept defeat, grab a backpack and fill it with clothes and toiletries. Thankfully, Sober Charlotte had the foresight to pack a cooler with food that I had hidden in the garage last night. The deeper the lies get the harder it becomes to see the surface. I kiss Cinder goodbye and text Reese asking if he'll check in on the cat while I'm gone since I have no idea when, or if, Jake is returning. He knows I'm gone out to Carol's cabin, he thinks I'm going with her.

On the way out the door I hastily scribble on a post-it note and stick it to the fridge. *I'm sorry*, it reads. And for what it's worth, I am.

I spot Abel walking down the boulevard outside of the airport, a leather duffel bag slung across his shoulder. I watch him for a moment before he sees me. The curve of his jaw could be chiseled from rock. He's even more beautiful than I remember.

He notices me watching him and grins, his intense expression fading. I hop out of the car and head toward him, ignoring the angry beeps of motorists behind me and the annoyed parking attendant motioning for me to move the vehicle. He wraps his arms around me and spins me before putting me back down and kissing me. I exhale a breath I feel like I've been holding on to since I last saw him, and my body finally relaxes.

I tell Abel that Carol thinks he's a cousin, visiting from out of town. I explain that she's wary about letting strangers use her cabin so it's best if we pretend to be related. Abel agrees to go along with it and if he finds it strange to lie to her he doesn't say anything about it to me.

We drive along the mostly deserted highway and I feel

like the big sky might swallow us up. We pass a farmhouse and there's a couple of children running around in the yard in front of the road, kicking a soccer ball. There are two girls, probably eight or nine years old and a little boy in a baseball cap, maybe six years old. The girls are passing the soccer ball back and forth and the little boy is trying to keep up, his stubby legs working overtime.

"You want kids?" asks Abel.

"Mmm, not sure, I don't know if I'd make a very good mom."

"Why do you say that?"

"I don't know if I have that maternal instinct that most women have. That urge to take care of something."

I imagine for a moment, watching Abel kick a soccer ball with a muddy little boy while I sit in a lawn chair, holding a baby girl whose smile reminds me of Cara. The moment passes and I remember that I specialize in taking lives, not creating them.

"We'd make beautiful babies." He grins. "We'd get top dollar for them on the black market."

I laugh and swat his shoulder.

My SUV kicks up a trail of dust behind us as we pull into Carol's driveway and I back up to the waiting horse trailer. Abel gets out and as we're connecting the hitch, Carol appears with Stanley in tow.

"Hi, old boy," I wrap my arms around Stanley's head and bury my face in his forelock.

"He's going to love it out there, I'm so glad you're taking him," smiles Carol. "Is this your cousin?" she motions to Abel.

"Umm yeah, one of my dad's nephews, we don't get to see each other much so I thought this was a nice...bonding trip for us. He's really into the outdoors."

Carol smiles and I can tell she's assessing Abel, who looks like he could have stepped out of an ad for men's magazine. "Well, I hope he brought some riding shoes," she says, eyeing his scuffed black leather boots.

"Thanks again, Carol, you don't know what this means to me."

"Don't mention it, sweetheart." She presses the keys into my sweaty hands and holds them there for a moment, giving me a meaningful look. "Be safe."

We used a handful of oats to coax Stanley into the trailer and shut the door behind him. He figures out pretty quickly that he's been duped and starts snorting and stomping around the trailer like an irate toddler. Back on the highway the sun beats through the window and warms my face. With the weight of Abel's hand on my knee happiness starts to seep back into my bones for the first time in maybe a long time.

Golden prairie fields give way to exposed Canadian Shield bedrock and boreal forest. Hardy trees like black spruce, pine and birch densely line the highway. The never-ending rows of hydro towers are the only reminder of civilization. It feels like we're in the middle of nowhere, and it's not far off. By the time we get to Little Limestone Lake we'll be at least sixty-five kilometers from the closest town.

My heart swells at the wild beauty of the passing landscape, and I feel irrevocably patriotic as *Wheat King* by The Tragically Hip comes on the radio and I turn it up.

A transport truck looms in the rearview mirror and the driver pulls out to pass me on an empty stretch of road. The trucks load looks to be that of unfortunate pigs, likely headed for slaughter. I catch patches of their bristly coats and sad eyes through the peepholes, but they're not fooling me. Pigs have been known to eat human remains and even devour the bones. Robert Pickton, arguably Canada's most notorious serial killer, disposed of his victims' bodies by feeding them to pigs on his farm. I push the dark thoughts out of my head and look over at Abel, who's looking out the window deep in thought.

Halfway to Little Limestone we pull into the parking lot of a beat-up rest stop called *Smokey's Diner*. Overhead bells jingle as we push open the door and seat ourselves in a booth by the window. The red vinyl is cracked and little tufts of stuffing are billowing out of it. The tabletop is mottled grey and worn down so much in places that it's turned white. A short, stubby, middle-aged waitress with baggy stockings and unnaturally blonde hair drops off yellowing menus and disappears to grab us what she promises is freshly made coffee.

There's an elderly man with a bowler cap sitting in the booth behind us. He has a cup of coffee, a sandwich and a newspaper in front of him but he's looking quietly out the window instead. Across from us a harassed looking mom is balancing a toddler on one knee and negotiating with her other child, who looks to be seven or eight, to finish his grilled cheese sandwich. A thickly bearded heavyweight of a man tucks into a cheeseburger and the ketchup drips out as he bites into it, forming little red puddles on the plate.

The whole place is transient and reflective of the area. Everybody's just passing through, on their way to somewhere else. Our waitress returns with two cups of tar black coffee and we order a turkey club for me and a cheeseburger for Abel. She disappears into the back, probably to defrost our order and heat it in a basket full of seldom changed cooking oil.

Abel reaches across the table and grabs my hands in his. "There's nowhere I'd rather be right now than in a shitty roadside diner with you."

"Save that thought until you taste the cheeseburger." I laugh and lean across the table to kiss him gently on the lips, not caring who's watching.

Chapter 29

Carol's great-grandfather bought land from the Cree people and built a small wood cabin on the property almost a hundred years ago. The nearest neighbor is almost ten kilometers away. Little Limestone Lake is a hidden Manitoba gem, and one of the largest and best examples of a marl lake in the world. Marl lakes change colors like a chameleon when the water temperatures rise. The lake turns from clear to a stunning aquamarine or milky-light blue.

Following the map that Carol has haphazardly drawn a route on with black marker, we finally find the mile marker prompting us to turn. I drive cautiously down the pothole ridden road, doing my best not to jolt poor Stan. We follow the arrow on a broken piece of barn wood nailed to a tree and turn left, pulling into the narrow driveway of the cabin.

A small cabin made entirely out of logs sits about a hundred meters away from a steep limestone cliff overlooking the lake. The grass grows tall and wild next to a worn-down dirt path and the spruce, pine and fir trees are clustered so densely around the cabin that I can only see small glimpses of the lake beyond them.

I lead an agitated Stanley out of the trailer and over to a makeshift pen that Carol has made for the horses. There's a hobbled together wood fence and a rough looking lean-to with a trough. I toss Stanley a handful of hay as a peace offering and he accepts it, his big buck teeth happily munching away.

Abel walks out to the edge of the property and whistles as he surveys the surroundings.

"This is incredible."

I walk up behind him and wrap my arms around his waist. It's sturdy and solid and reminds me of the trunk of one of the nearby trees.

He kisses my head. "You're incredible." We could be the main characters in a Nicholas Sparks novel.

The water sparkles like a sapphire and contrasts with the deep and vibrant greens of the jack pine, tamarack and trembling aspens along the shore. I breathe in the earthy, wild, outdoor smell that you can only find in the middle of nowhere. I feel like I'm in a Group of Seven painting. I hear the low honk of the Canada Geese as they fly overhead, heading south for the winter. I don't blame them.

The inside of the cabin is small but cozy. A cast iron woodstove sits in the middle of the living area and we stock it with kindling to get it going. The cabin is warm enough now with the sun beating in through the windows, but as soon as it sets it will get chilly. In addition to the open kitchen/living area the cabin has two small bedrooms and one bathroom. The walls are lined with family photos and taxidermized animals. A large buck head hangs over the woodstove and the eyes of the stuffed white owl, perched on top of the kitchen cabinets seem to follow me. The air in the cabin is damp and slightly stale, like it's been closed up for months, and it probably has been. As far as I know,

Carol is the only one in her family that really comes here and she hasn't been for a couple of months.

Abel returns from turning on the generator and I finish putting our food away in the fridge. He wraps his arms around me from behind, nuzzling his chin into my shoulder.

"I can't even tell you how much I missed you, mama."

"Why don't you show me how much?" I smile wolfishly and turn to face him.

He grabs me by the waist, hoists me up on the countertop and kisses me.

I inhale his salty smell of sweat and aftershave as he carries me to the bedroom.

I watch the rise and fall of Abel's chest and shiver despite the heavy duvet. I exhale slowly like I'm smoking an imaginary cigarette, and watch the tiny puffs of my breath hang like little clouds in the cold night air. I slide strategically out of bed, pull on Abe's sweater and a pair of jeans and creep quietly into the living room.

The basket beside the wood stove is empty and I silently curse myself for not bringing in the wood earlier. The hand of the old wooden wall clock, with each hour represented by a different bird, is sitting on the redheaded woodpecker—1:00 a.m. I grab a heavy metal flashlight off the kitchen counter and venture outside into the night.

There's something about the woods at night that has always unnerved me. The cracking branches and rustling bushes. The way the outlines of the trees seem to all blend together, and how it can feel like there's someone, or something, hiding behind them. The crickets and frogs sing melancholy lullabies and every so often, in the not too far distance, you'll hear a howl, a screech or a cry from something wild.

The moon and the stars are much brighter out here past the city limits, like they're in high definition. I train my flashlight beam on the wood pile off the side of the cottage and am grabbing logs off the pile when I hear a crack. I pause for a second, holding my breath and then I hear another. Each crack gets a little bit closer to me until whatever it is, is right behind me. I scream.

A hand grabs my shoulder and I drop the flashlight and logs on the ground with a thud, narrowly missing my feet.

"Hey! Charlie, it's just me," Abel says, picking up the flashlight.

"Jesus Christ, you scared me!" I hold my hand over my heart trying to calm myself. "Why did you sneak up on me like that?"

"I noticed you got out of bed and thought you might want help with the woodstove."

I look around nervously as my eyes try to adjust to the darkness. "Let's go back inside, it's creepy out here."

"It's fine, I got you, mama, nothing's going to happen to us. I just want to check something out."

"Check what out? I'm not following you aimlessly into the darkness," I say, still annoyed at him for creeping up on me.

"Just trust me." He grabs my hand and leads me toward the edge of the cliff.

I follow him closely and focus on the beam of the

flashlight in front of us, terrified to look beside me. We reach the edge of the property and I can hear the water lapping up against the rocks and the wind rustling through the branches of the trees.

"Look," he points upward.

The sky is alive with the northern lights. The farther north you travel in Manitoba the more intense they become, and tonight they're out in all their glory. We hold hands and watch the lights shimmer and dance like they're a living entity. A wolf's howl pierces the air and I shiver. I can feel Cara's presence, now more than ever; the lights, the wolves, she's trying to tell me something.

"We rarely see them in Seattle," he says, referring to the northern lights. "People go their whole lives without seeing them. With all of the air pollution now it's not surprising though."

We watch the light show for another twenty minutes, but it might as well have been hours. The auroras begin to dim and flicker out and my frozen fingers are too much to bear. On the walk back to the cabin I can feel my sister's presence encompassing me. We finish stoking the woodstove and I drift off to the sound of wood crackling and thoughts of her. When sleep finally comes, I'm back in the white room, playing out the familiar scenario it seems I'm destined to repeat.

Chapter 30
Before

The last time Cara reached out to me was when I killed Lidia. Almost a year ago now.

By the time I got to Lidia, I was getting better, smarter and darker. My face lit up with pleasure the first time I saw her. She was in first class on a flight to New York, and had a small, white dog tucked under her seat in a Louis Vuitton patterned pet carrier.

She was dressed in all black and an oversized pair of sunglasses were perched on her perfectly highlighted blonde head. She had dramatic fake lashes, and her lips were painted a striking shade of red. A perfect ski-jump nose was the result of exceptionally good genes or an exceptionally good plastic surgeon.

She reeked of money and expensive perfume. I watched her from the front of the plane and imagined dragging a knife across her well-defined collarbone.

The opportunity to connect with her after the flight fell into my lap, almost literally, when I discovered that she had left behind a two-carat diamond earring on her seat after everyone had deplaned.

My mouth curled into a smile as I pulled up her contact information and called to let her know that I would personally bring her earring to her, to ensure that something so valuable wasn't misplaced again.

I got out of the taxi at Park Avenue and tried not to be dazzled by the stately buildings and the innuendo of money everywhere I looked. Suited businessmen ducked into luxury cars and polished, well-dressed women stalked down the sidewalks in designer shoes.

I had followed Lidia's lead and changed into a black structured dress and slicked my hair back into a neat bun. Large, newly purchased sunglasses from an airport gift shop were perched delicately on my nose.

I studied the hurried, wealthy and important-seeming people pushing past me and concluded that I sufficiently blended. I had to move quickly, for fear that a pack of them might sniff out my outlet mall dress and heels.

What would it be like to live a life where money was inconsequential? Where everything and everyone you desired could be bought, it was just a matter of naming the right price.

On the taxi from LaGuardia, I had quickly pieced together the details of Lidia Paulson's life. She was originally from Poland and immigrated to New York in the 90's after her modelling career took off. As part of a model's code of conduct she married rich, very rich, and became the third wife of software billionaire, Michael Paulson, at the age of 25.

She was a regular fixture on the New York social scene, throwing money around like rice at a wedding. She was divorced from Michael by her early thirties after a very public cheating scandal, him not her, and never remarried.

She seemed to devote most of her time now to charity galas and fundraising events. She was recently featured in People magazine on the arm of a former Survivor contestant.

My heels echoed on the marble floor in the entrance to her building and the doorman smiled at me. He wore a conservative uniform and a dark grey hat and buzzed to Lidia to confirm my visit before showing me to the elevator and punching in the security code for the penthouse. I kept my sunglasses on and my head down and tried to be unmemorable.

I rapped the oversize gold ring knocker on a large door just off the elevator and Lidia opened it, the little white dog tucked under her arm like an expensive clutch. I noticed how strikingly beautiful she really was. Her skin was flawless and her eyes glittered a rich shade of blue, like the deep part of the ocean.

"Charlotte—yes!" she exclaimed. A thin diamond tennis bracelet dangled from her slender wrist and a long Cartier Love necklace hung off her neck and dipped into her bronzed cleavage. Her casual everyday jewelry was worth more than my house.

"Thank you so much for bringing this to me. I did not even notice it was lost yet," she continued in a thick, clipped accent that made her "s" sound more like "z".

"Oh, it's not a problem at all. We wanted to make sure that it made it back to you safely."

"You will come in for a drink. It is the least I can do for your troubles," she said venturing back into the depths of the penthouse. I followed obediently, mesmerized by the wiggle of her curvy hips that swung from side to side like a pendulum. Her waist was tiny and toned in comparison and her legs were abnormally long for her height. I was beginning to see what attracted her billionaire ex-husband.

The sprawling penthouse was elegantly decorated in designer shades of beige, white and gold. Tasteful original paintings and framed magazine covers and photoshoots of Lidia in various stages of undress adorned the walls. I didn't fault her, If I had a body like hers, I would commission a full nude to hang over my fireplace.

She led me through the living area, past large white sofas and a baroque fireplace, and out glass doors onto the patio. The patio area was as opulent as the inside, with a white marble fireplace, cushioned sectionals and a long, white dining table that seated twenty. The only thing more incredible than the view of the Manhattan skyline was the white pergola beside the immaculate rooftop plunge pool, covered in fuchsia clematis and string lights.

"Wow," I breathed, looking out over the rooftops, while she pulled two champagne flutes from a nearby cupboard and expertly uncorked a bottle. The bottle puffed a few wisps of smoke and the champagne looked like liquid sunshine as she poured it into the glasses.

She gestured for me to sit on one of the couches and sat down across from me with the little dog on her lap.

"So, you work for airline as manager?" she said, in that direct Eastern European way of making it sound more like a statement than a question.

"Yes, I've worked with them several years now. I love the opportunity to travel and meet new people." I sounded like I was interviewing for a job. I'm not sure why she made me feel so nervous. Beauty, intelligence and confidence can be a dangerous combination.

"Pretty girl like you should be model. Not stuck in airplane."

"Oh, I don't mind, I like being up there in the sky. Trust me, I would be a total basket case as a model. My sister was the one with all the grace."

"Your sister is older or younger?"

"Older, but only by a few minutes. We are twins. Well, we were twins. She passed away."

Her gaze felt suddenly more intense than the late afternoon New York sun beating down on us. How did they stand it, always wearing black, I wondered as I felt droplets of sweat slide down the small of my back.

"So, are you good one or evil one?"

"Excuse me?" I sputtered, feeling the bubbles of champagne rise into my nasal passage.

"It is joke. How you say, one twin is bad and one twin is good, no?" She smiled halfway so just the tips of her teeth showed. Something was off about her.

I laughed politely and made a show of looking at my watch. "Well, thank you so much for the drink but I really must be getting back to the hotel now," I said setting down my crystal flute on the quartz coffee table with a delicate tink. "Do you mind if I use your washroom before I go?"

"Through the doors to the left is one." She gestured.

Relived to escape the muggy, hot, outside air I followed her directions to the bathroom. Through the windows I could see her absorbed in something on her phone. I crept quickly down the hallway to scout out where the master bedroom was and then hurried back into the bathroom and shut the door.

The bathroom was finished entirely in white and grey marble and a bouquet of white roses on the vanity filled the room with their thick, perfumed scent. Did Lidia purchase fresh flowers or did a service exist that periodically arrived with armfuls of bouquets? I grabbed a bar of luxurious looking French soap and lathered my hands with it under cold tap water to try and lower my internal body temperature. I dried my hands on a white hand towel, careful not to leave any dirty fingerprints, and returned to the patio to say goodbye to Lidia.

"Lidia, thank you again for the drink. This place is amazing and I'm glad your earring made it back to you safely."

"Yes—anytime you are in New York, you let me know." She kissed the air in front of both my cheeks.

I hurried past the doorman and into the wilds of New York. I walked for a block before finding a small deli that reminded me of a place the Seinfeld characters might frequent. The checkerboard floors were scuffed but the counters were clean, and the pastry case was teeming with baked goods.

I sat at a table to review the menu and tried to choose something an authentic New Yorker might order. I ordered a grilled cheese and fries and chided myself for lack of inspiration. I joyfully chewed on the crusty, gooey sandwich as I casually searched on my phone for nearby sex shops. The nearest one was quite far away but I had time to kill while I was waiting to kill.

I arrived back at Park Avenue shortly after midnight. I had found what I was looking for at the sex shop and walked aimlessly around the city streets for a couple of hours. It wasn't hard to see how people fell in love with this city that seemed to have a life of its own. The constant throb and hum of people, sights and sounds was exhilarating.

I watched from across the street of Lidia's building as a pizza delivery car pulled up in front. Unbeknownst to him, the tall, freckled, pizza delivery guy that exited the car was headed to make a delivery to a condo on a floor that didn't exist. I waited for him to disappear through the front doors before following him. I strode confidently across the lobby toward the elevator.

If anyone looked twice at the security footage, they would notice a woman with long blonde hair, thanks to the sex shop wig, dressed all in black obviously, with a large, black floppy hat obscuring her face from view. The long, satin gloves, also from the sex shop, would be regarded as nothing more than a glamourous accessory of a wealthy New Yorker.

The security guard and the pizza delivery guy were both absorbed in trying to figure out where the mystery pizza was to be delivered. The guard didn't notice me enter the elevator and punch in the penthouse code I had previously watched him key in.

I stepped quietly out of the elevator and stood outside Lidia's door for a second, listening for any movement. The lights were off and I couldn't hear any noise except for the gentle hum of the appliances.

I love old buildings. Their walls are filled with history

and they seem to embody the souls of everyone who has lived within them. Developers and architects do their best to maintain the buildings' character and honor their historical features. They leave the crown molding; maybe the stain glassed windows, and the heavy, beveled doors, with their brass knobs and archaic locks.

I was thankful for preservationists as I pulled a bobby pin from my platinum blonde hair, stuck it into the keyhole of Lidia's door, and wiggled it around until I heard a familiar click. During my afternoon visit I hadn't noticed signs of an alarm system but I still held my breath as I slowly edged the door open.

The penthouse was dark and quiet and I began to wonder if Lidia was even home. I crept out the glass doors to the patio and let my eyes adjust to the evening glow of the city. I supposed people in cities like New York would never experience nights like I had in Sunshine. The light pollution, smog and tall buildings would obstruct the view of the stars. How sad that would be to a live in a world where the stars you are more likely to see are celebrities rather than constellations.

I stepped around the patio furniture to the trellis and inhaled the honey sweet smell of the Clematis as I carefully unplugged the patio lights intertwined in it. The pool glowed topaz in contrast with the night sky. The silence was interrupted by the yapping of Lidia's rat-dog, who bolted through the glass patio doors and ran over to me. All five pounds of it stood growling and yapping incessantly as I tried to make him stop.

Lidia appeared in the open doors, her eyes adjusting to

the darkness. "Is somebody there? Jacque?" she questioned. I ducked behind the fireplace as she walked out onto the patio to fetch the dog. It had lost interest in me and was sniffing around the outdoor sofa.

Lidia wore a silk nightgown, almost the exact shade of her skin, and the way her hair glowed in the moonlight gave her a goddess-like appearance. She could have posed for a magazine spread with a moment's notice.

She bent to scoop up the dog and noticed the cords astray by the pool. She picked up a cord in her hand and examined it, her gaze drifting to the water. I took advantage of the opportunity, came up behind her, and pushed her hard into the pool.

She sank like a rock and hit the shallow pool bottom hard before surfacing again and choking back water. Her long hair hung like a heavy curtain over her face and she struggled to brush it out of her eyes.

The patio light control was smooth and cool in my hand and, without hesitation, I flipped the switch and turned them on. The speakers automatically turned on as well and began playing the ill-timed *Wake me Up* by Avicii.

I had rerouted the cords so that the active ends of them ran directly into the pool. When I turned the switch on it sent volts of electricity into the pool water and subsequently through Lidia. She startled and gasped and her body moved in an unnatural way. The cords sparked and spit flames and started to smoke.

Lidia's entire body seemed to hiss and flail before finally becoming still and sinking into the water. I stood over the pool, careful not to touch the water, and studied her body at the bottom of the pool. With her silk nightgown and golden hair billowing around her, she reminded me of a penny at the bottom of a wishing well. Avicii continued in the background, turning the atmosphere from crime scene to potential dance party.

 A movement behind me startled me and I remembered the small, annoying dog. It looked at me nervously and I coaxed it safely back inside the penthouse and away from the water. I found the boarding pass in her toffee-colored Hermès handbag in the kitchen and exhaled deeply. The weight on my chest had been temporarily lifted, and I felt a semblance of relief and the connection to Cara that I needed.

Monday, November 2nd

The sound of birds wakes me up just after the sun rises. It's not an entirely unpleasant alarm clock. Abel is still sleeping soundly beside me and I try not to wake him as I get out of bed and pull on a scratchy sweater, jacket, toque and pair of jeans. My hypnogogic dreams are happening more frequently and my head is foggy with fatigue from living an alternate life in my dreams.

 The front door shuts softly behind me and in the pen, Stanley is wide awake and demanding breakfast. He greets me with an impatient whinny and his breath forms clouds of condensation in the cold air. I offer him an appetizer of hay so that he won't be too full and lazy for a morning ride.

 He finishes his snack and I hoist myself onto his bare back, tossing the reins back over his head. I want Stanley all to myself for a bit before Abel, or the rest of the world, wakes up. I lead him toward the access road we came in on, enjoying the sound of his hooves clicking rhythmically against the ground. I like to ride him without the barrier of a saddle, saddle pad and blanket between us. Our movements become one and I feel closer to him.

Everything is very still out here. The waves, the trees, the grass. It all feels very small and very big at the same time. Like I'm in the middle of nowhere and the middle of everywhere all at once.

I notice a trail off the main road and turn into it to see where it leads. It's just barely big enough to fit Stanley through. It could be an old deer trail that the animals use to move through the forest or it could be man-made and just neglected. As we ride deeper into the forest the canopies of the trees block out the morning sun and shadows consume the path in front of us. Stanley begins to act nervous, he twitches his ears, shakes his head and snorts.

"Fine, you wimp. We'll head back. Where's your sense of adventures?" I ask him, pulling the reins slightly to turn us back around. Stanley suddenly stops short and refuses to move forward. Now it makes sense why he was acting strangely. Blocking the path in front of us is a menacing looking timber wolf.

I think I'm a reasonable person, and, logistically, I know that there's a very slim chance that the wolf standing in front of us is the same wolf that Cara and I saw all those years ago at Riding Mountain Park. It's unlikely the wolf would have travelled over 500km between the two areas or exceeded the average life span of his species by this many years. But despite these hard facts, I can't shake the feeling that those haunting yellow eyes that are watching me so intently, are familiar.

We lock gazes for what feels like hours, but is only a few seconds, before the wolf disappears back into the bushes. I'm not scared because I know he wasn't meant to hurt me. He was here as a reminder. From Cara.

When I return to the cabin Abel is cheerfully cooking bacon with his shirt off. He really lives on the edge. I admire his broad, muscular shoulders, narrow waist and vibrant tattoo that snakes the length of his body. He notices me noticing him and grins, jumping as a spit of bacon fat hits his bare stomach, I'm so entranced with him I almost forget to breathe.

Over breakfast I suggest we try our luck at one of the hiking trails. We leave the dishes in the sink and prepare for our hike. I dress in every layer possible and Abel pulls on an insulated jacket I had recommended he bring. I fill a backpack with food and supplies and we grab a paper map that Carol gave us off the table. No cell service up here, not that the internet would be much help in navigating the uncharted trails.

According to Carol there's an old logging road that will take us along the lake to a cool limestone cave. Back when the forestry industry was booming and environmentalism was nothing but a word hippies tossed around between puffs of joints, forests were being decimated across the country. Paper mills and forestry-based companies were the livelihood of small towns across Canada, providing jobs to people at every step of the supply chain. Roads were created that led deep into the heart of the forests, providing greater access to the companies destroying them. When the industry started to decline in the early 2000's many plants were shut down and logging roads were abandoned, never to be used again.

In Manitoba you don't come across too many logging roads until you head farther North. There's something eerie about these endless paths that lead to the middle of nowhere. We walk a few hundred meters from the cabin and successfully find the orange tape denoting the start of the trail. It looks like it hasn't been used in a while and wild grasses cover what appears to have once been a path. I look back at Abel.

"What, are you scared of a little bit of bush, prairie girl?" he smirks.

"Not at all," I lie, stepping forward and up to my waist in grass.

The sun is shining and the air is crisp. Only a few remaining leaves cling to the tree branches. The first big snowfall could come any day now. As we walk along the trail, I catch glimpses of the bright turquoise lake glimmering through the trees.

"What are your parents like?" Abel asks as we walk.

"They're both really good people. They couldn't look more different; my dad is big and dark and burly while my mom is small and fair and dainty. They seem to make it work, though, they balance each other out. My mom's been a little obsessed with church since Cara died, but I guess it's her way of coping."

"You don't go with her?"

"No, not really. I mean once in a while at Easter or

Christmas Mags and I feel obligated to go with her but otherwise it's not really my thing."

"Church isn't your thing?" he asks.

"Church isn't, God isn't."

He's quiet for a few moments and the only sound is our boots crunching through the leaves. "Do you not believe in God because of what happened to your sister?"

"I just think that if there was a God, if there was this all-seeing, all-knowing being, then how could he let her die? How could he take a life away from someone that's just beginning it? It doesn't make sense to me." I bite my lip to redirect the surge of pain I'm feeling.

We walk in silence for a few minutes and I focus intently on the song of the chickadees. "What are your parents like?" I clear my throat, changing the subject.

"Good people. My old man is a little rough around the edges, he spends a lot of time at the Italian Club. My mom is a typical housewife, dotes on my dad, and has dinner waiting for him every night. Just like I'd want you to." He winks.

The bushes rustle in front of us and before we can react a hare bounds out of them. It looks at us for a second, twitches its nose and leaps back into the trees. We both laugh. The hare takes the tension that had formed between us with it and we walk for another couple of kilometers in easy camaraderie. As we make it further down the trail, the clear sky begins to turn overcast and dark clouds form on the horizon.

"That storm looks to be moving in fast and I doubt we can beat it back to the cabin. If the map Carol gave us is right then the cave should be coming up pretty soon and it might be best to wait it out there," Abel suggests.

Although I'm not crazy about sitting in a cave for a prolonged period of time, it doesn't really seem like I have an alternative at this point. At least I've brought a blanket, materials to start a fire with and food for lunch. We'll be decently comfortable in the cave while we wait for the storm to pass. The gentle wind is starting to turn violent and I struggle to keep my hair out of my eyes as it whips around my head. The trail leads us around a bend, narrows, and then stops abruptly at the edge of an embankment. We walk to the edge and look down the incline of rocks to a small strip of white, rocky beach and the mouth of a cave located just off the shoreline.

"Well, I guess the only place to go is down." Abel whistles. He opens up his backpack, takes out a length of rope and ties it tightly around a nearby tree. He pulls on it roughly to test its strength and is satisfied that the trunk of the jack pine seems to be up to the challenge. He slips his backpack back on and throws the other end of the rope into the air, letting it disappear off the edge of the embankment.

"I'll go first and help you down." He smiles.

I'm in no position to argue so I grudgingly agree and watch as he scrambles down the face of the rocks like a mountain goat. Heights, hills or cliffs are not really a common site in most of Manitoba and I feel ill prepared. The black clouds are catching up and everything's gone unnaturally silent. Even the birds have stopped singing; they've sensed the change in atmospheric pressure and taken refuge.

I look down at Abel nervously, estimating that it's about fifty feet from top to bottom. I grab hold of the rope and step backward off the edge, slowly rappelling down and strategically trying to place my feet onto jutting rocks or tree roots. Halfway down I misplace my foot and a piece of rock comes loose making me lose my footing. I yelp and try not to panic as I frantically try to catch my foot into some sort of crevice.

"Calm down," Abel yells up at me. "You need to shimmy down the rope about a foot and you'll find a piece of rock on your right that you can stand on."

I get the weird sensation of wanting to let go of the rope. The weight of everything seems to be pressing down on me as if hundred-pound boulders are balanced on my shoulders. What a relief it would be just to be weightless.! I close my eyes and everything is white.

A drop of rain hits my forehead and pulls me back to reality. I look up just in time to see a crack of lightning light up the sky. My survival instinct kicks in and I slide down the rope, letting it burn into my palms until I feel my feet connect with a shelf of rock below. From there I quickly rappel down the rest of the rock face and breathe a sigh of relief when Abel grabs me by the waist and pulls me safely to the sand below. The rain drops are turning fierce and we still have a few hundred meters to get to the cave. Abel grabs my hand and we run as the rain becomes so intense it's almost blinding.

We duck under the overhang of the cave and collapse to the ground trying to catch our breath. We're soaked and the rain is falling in a dazzling sheet over the mouth of the cave. Abel flicks on a flashlight and illuminates the interior. I survey the surroundings and shiver from the dampness of the cave and my soaking wet clothes and also from the unearthly atmosphere.

The cave looks like the inside of an Anglerfish's mouth; those otherworldly looking fish that thrive in the deepest darkest parts of the ocean. Stalactites hang from the ceiling like stone daggers and stalagmites protrude from the cave floor like a particularly dangerous type of fence. The cave is mostly dry, except for a few small pools of bright blue water, but the air is damp. I hear the rustle of wings and see clusters of bats huddled in the shadows. I remind myself that most bats only eat insects and fruits, except for Vampire Bats.

At our old brick schoolhouse there was a dark corner above the gym doors where bats would commonly nest. If the boys found them, they'd chuck rocks and sticks and try to scare or kill them. Cara became their unofficial protector and stayed late after school until she was sure everyone had left to ward off anyone intending to inflict harm on her newfound charges. She would plead with me to stay with her and play hopscotch to kill time.

"Bats are an invaluable part of the food chain, and they can eat over a thousand mosquitoes an hour!" She would exclaim, regurgitating facts from a book on them that she'd taken out of the library. "And they're also the only mammal able to fly."

I didn't trust the creepy creatures, with their beady eyes and fleshy wings, and I made sure to never turn my back to them. I couldn't understand the fondness she had developed for them. That was Cara for you, always giving the benefit of the doubt.

Abel gathers up dried driftwood scattered around in the sand and attempts to start a fire. He shoves bits of newspaper that we'd brought in between the makeshift teepee of driftwood and holds the flame of his lighter to it, letting the fire consume it. He flicks off the flashlight to conserve the battery and the shadows from the fire cinch up the sides of the cave.

"Take your clothes off," he orders, and strips his jacket and shirt off, leaving only his underwear on.

"What?" My hair is dripping wet and my entire body feels soaked to the bone by the cold autumn rain.

"You're never going to warm up with those clothes on. We'll take all our clothes off and dry them by the fire. We can wrap ourselves in the blanket and use body heat to keep warm."

"Well, aren't you just Bear Grylls," I say, referring to the survival expert and host of *Man vs. Wild*. I peel off my soaked layers of clothing to give them to him and he drapes them over the stalagmites closest to the fire. He hands me the large flannel blanket I'd brought to sit on and I wrap it around my shoulders, shivering. He arranges the last bit of his clothes next to mine and I offer him the other half of the blanket.

My skin feels cold and clammy like a fish but Abel is already heating up like a furnace and I eagerly snuggle into him. His hair is drying in dark waves and he pushes it off his face as he watches the dancing flames of the fire. I watch him watching the fire and wonder how long we're going to be stuck in this cave.

"When we were teenagers, my parents took my sister and me to see this cave a few hours outside of Seattle. It's called Ape Cave, and it's this crazy tube cave made out of lava, the longest in America or something. They were trying to make it into a family trip but by the time we got there it was raining and the fog was pretty thick. We decided to hike anyways, and my sister and I split off from my parents and walked ahead on our own," Abel began.

"Near Ape Cave was the sight of a famous Sasquatch sighting in the 1920s where some miners said they ran into a whole family of Sasquatch. Apparently, the cave was named after the scout troops that discovered it, but still it made you wonder what could be hiding in there. The deeper I hiked into the cave the narrower and darker it got. My sister fell behind me somewhere and I got turned around and my flashlight battery started to go.

"I called her name and she didn't answer, I could just hear my voice echoing off the walls. There was this slime all over the walls of the cave and I could hear water dripping off in the distance. Suddenly, everything became very still and while I didn't hear anything to suggest it, I could tell that something was in there with me. You know how you can feel someone's presence sometimes, before you even know they're there?" he asks.

"Yes. Always," I reply, thinking of Cara.

"My flashlight flickered out and I stood there in the darkness, terrified, very still, waiting."

"And?" I question, looking nervously around the cave we were currently trapped inside.

"And then nothing. The flashlight flickered back on finally and I heard my sister calling to me. I know there was someone or something in there with me."

I snuggled in closer to him and shivered again—this time not from the cold.

"Let's talk about anything other than creepy cave stories. Have you ever been in love?" I ask, unsure where I'm going with this line of questioning.

"It's hard to say. The line between love and lust gets blurry at times. There were a few girls I really cared about but I'm not sure if love is what I would have labeled it. What about you?"

"Umm same." My body temperature is finally starting to rise but I can't shake the feeling of malaise that has set in.

"Why do I get the feeling there is something you're not saying?" he says quietly.

I turn to face him and the eerie blue of his eye mixed with the hazel reminds me of the marl lake, constantly shifting in color.

"What do you want to know?"

"Well, for starters, are you as serious about me as I am about you? You know, Charlie, I don't make a habit of falling in love with someone I meet on an airplane. I came to see you because I can't get you out of my head and I want to make something of this. Whatever this is."

"I thought you did that for all the girls." I smirk.

"I've never felt this way about someone before." He puts

his hand up against mine, palm to palm, and intertwines our fingers.

"Me neither," I whisper. "Abel…I…"

A flash of lightning interrupts followed by the crack of thunder, lighting up the little bit of sky that we can see from the inside of the cave like a runway. The air is heavy with humidity and charged with that metallic smell, almost like pennies, that comes with a thunderstorm.

Reflexively, I count the seconds in between lightning and thunder, the way that they teach you as a kid, so you can tell how close a storm is.

One Mississippi, two Mississippi, three Mississippi, and the thunder booms. The blanket falls off my shoulder and the next flash of lightning bathes the cave in white light. It illuminates my naked body and the contrasting jagged red scar that runs four inches long, from my hip bone down the right side of my outer thigh. We both look at it and Abel traces it with his fingertip.

"I got it the day that she died," I say, answering the unasked question that's hanging in the air between us.

I count in my head, one Mississippi, two Mississippi, three Mississippi, and then with a deep breath I tell him how Cara died.

Chapter 31

I listened to the *Serial* podcast when it first came out. Industry research. It follows the pursuit of an investigative journalist as she tries to determine if a man, who has spent most of his life behind bars since being convicted of killing his teenage girlfriend, is actually guilty. At the beginning of the podcast the journalist, Sarah Koenig, tries to uncover why we remember certain days better than others. Why the details of some days stay so fresh in our mind that years later we can remember every smell, sight and sound, and why other days blur into one another like a blank stack of copy paper.

Koenig concludes that, *If some significant event happened that day, you remember that, plus you remember the entire day much better. If nothing significant happened, then the answers get very general.*

Every detail of the day that Cara died is committed to my memory and I play it repeatedly on a loop in my head, like a tragic version of *Groundhog Day*. It was the day after our botched swimming escapade and I remember waking up and feeling angry. I noticed that Cara and Natalie's beds were already both neatly made up. I gathered that they were probably eating breakfast together and bonding over the dreadfulness of last night, in that weird sort of way that tragedy seems to bring people closer together.

I laid on my back and stared up at the log ceiling. A perfectly formed spider web hung in the corner and a small grey moth was frantically trying to escape the sinewy threads. It struggled for a few moments before finally becoming still. I wondered when the spider would appear to assess its latest victim. The faintest of breezes drifted in through a cracked window but did little to ease the thick humid air that hung in the cabin.

I rolled off the bunk and pulled on a pair of jean shorts that I had made myself out of an old pair of Magnolia's jeans and a T-shirt with a Little Miss Sunshine cartoon on it. My hair was particularly unruly that day from my midnight swim and I pulled it into a quick braid over my shoulder. I studied myself in the dirty mirror by the door and my complexion was pale and chalky despite my summer tan.

I found Cara and Natalie as I expected, eating breakfast and whispering conspiratorially. I sat across from them with a tray full of rubbery looking waffles, greasy sausage links and a bowl of sad looking fruit. They stopped talking and stared at me with what could have been pity in their eyes, waiting for me to say something.

"We're going to forget last night ever happened. I don't want to talk about it anymore. You guys can make it up to me by doing something that I want to do today."

"Whatever you want!" exclaimed Natalie, eager to diffuse the situation.

"I found a place I want to show you. We'll need to take

Stanley to get there though. Maybe we can grab Kaitlin's horse, Bella, to use too."

Cara agreed but looked unenthusiastic as she ate her last bit of gluey looking oatmeal. Natalie chattered on about how her parents wouldn't let her pierce her nose and I pretended to be engaged with the conversation as I chewed on a waffle. I kept trying to catch Cara's eye across the table but she was absorbed with scraping the dried crusts of oatmeal off the side of her bowl. We were only a foot away from each other but somehow it felt like we were miles apart.

After breakfast we headed to the stable to get the horses. Cara wore jean shorts and a plain white T-shirt, the morning sunlight highlighted her regal looking profile and the curve of her jawline. She was wearing mascara, probably to impress Natalie. She was growing up and leaving me behind. I swallowed hard to banish the nausea that had crept into my throat.

Natalie walked beside her, their footsteps in sync as if it had been rehearsed. Her glossy hair was threaded through a baseball cap. The way it swung back and forth like a pendulum reminded me of the horses' tails as they swished away the flies. A crop top showed off her tanned stomach and white shorts emphasized her long legs. Her beauty was so effortless I burned with envy. I felt like a misplaced child next to the both of them.

I thought the barn could be something that would unite us. A special place that we could share, a secret just for us. Cara loved exploring and I thought by including Natalie it would show that I was willing to accept her. After all, it was better than being left out.

At the barn, I saddled Stanley while Natalie and Cara did the same to Bella. Bella was a lazy, calm, grey Appaloosa that was friendly and easy to ride. I gave her a pat on her big, warm, velvet head as they tightened the saddle straps. We mounted the horses and headed down the trail, eager to avoid the camp counsellors. We were hoping our absence wouldn't be noticed at the pottery-making class we had skipped out on.

The horses lumbered down the path in the heat like camels in the desert. Cara and Natalie rode together on Bella and I rode Stanley. It wasn't yet noon and the sun was already beating down on our heads through the tree tops. The horses' hooves plodded down the dirt path, crunching over twigs and stray brush on the trail. Somewhere from within the treetops came the short staccato of a woodpecker drilling into a tree. "So, what is this place?" asked Cara.

"You'll see when we get there." I knew I was being obnoxious but didn't care.

I tried to tell myself that everything would go back to normal after camp was over but I knew that it wouldn't. Natalie was here to stay and something had shifted in Cara, that I'm not sure was going to retract. We reached the fork in the road and Natalie questioned whether we should go down it. "It doesn't look like anyone's been down there in a while, Charlie, are you sure we should take the horses down here?"

"It's fine, don't be such a baby. I've been down it

already." I enjoyed being the boss and the fearless one for once.

She exchanged a glance with Cara who shrugged and urged Bella forward into the tall prairie grass. Grasshoppers chirped angrily and flew in and out of the grass as we disrupted their habitat. Soon the trees started to thin out and we reached the break in the tree line. The field shimmered like a golden lake as we led the horses toward the old barn. I jumped off Stanley and tied him loosely to a beat-up post.

"This is it?" asked Cara as she jumped down off Bella. I refused to acknowledge the sardonic tone that had crept into her voice.

"Wait till you see inside, we have the whole place to ourselves." I led them to the entrance and we all sucked in and slid sideways through the crack in the barn doors. Natalie and Cara walked around inspecting the rusting tools and empty stalls.

"So, you just come out here by yourself?" Cara asked me, throwing a sideways smirk to Natalie.

"Yeah, well, you guys are too busy with each other to pay me any attention," I said, feeling anger rise in me like a fever. The previous appeal of the old barn faded, and as I looked around, I saw it through my sister's eyes: a worthless, dirty, abandoned shack. I blinked back tears and tried to quell my disappointment.

Cara ignored my last comment while Natalie nervously shuffled her feet. "What's up there?" She pointed toward the hayloft.

"Nothing much, an old hayloft. Pretty good view of the

entire barn. We could climb up that ladder if you're not too scared," I taunted.

"I'm not a baby." She put her sneaker up on the first rung of the ladder and started to climb up to the loft.

"I'm not going up there," said Natalie, shaking her head.

I followed Cara up the ladder to the hayloft. The stale air inside the barn was thick with the smell of old hay. When I reached the top, she was studying the sinister looking hay pulley.

"Are you sure you're okay up here without your sidekick?" I sneered.

"Shut up, Charlie, you're just jealous and you know it." She turned to face me and I could see the darkness in her eyes. Her vivid green eyes had lost their brightness and dimmed to the color of the jungle when a cloud passes over it.

I snorted. "You think I'm jealous of you guys? That's hilarious, why would I be jealous of two brainless bimbos that only talk about makeup and boys?"

"Is everything okay up there? Why don't you guys come back down?" Natalie yelled to us in a shaky voice.

"You are jealous, Charlie, because you're still such a baby, you can't do anything without me and you have no life of your own." She spit the words out of her mouth like they were something bitter that she'd bit into.

My body reacted instinctively before my brain could chime in and I pushed her hard with both hands, sending her stumbling backward.

She fell onto the dirty loft floor and a cloud of dust and

dirt rose up around her. She sat back up with a surprised look on her face and disbelief that I'd pushed her. I couldn't believe it either. Cara and I rarely fought and when we did it had never gotten physical. She scrambled back to her feet and charged, tackling me.

I fell to the ground and instantly a sharp pain cut into my right side. I cried out and looked down to find that my leg had connected with the head of a rusty steel rake lying on the loft floor. Little droplets of blood appeared on my thigh and quickly turned into rivulets that trickled down my leg and pooled on the wooden planks.

My body turned to auto-pilot, my eyes glazed over, everything went fuzzy. My memory of the day that was so clear and sharp suddenly turned murky and it felt like I was back at the bottom of the lake trying to swim to the surface.

What I do remember is the screaming. I'm not sure if it was a combination of the three of us or just Natalie and Cara. The next scene I recall was Cara standing in front of me with a weird look on her face. Her eyes were so wide that I could see the whites all the way around her irises. She looked down at her chest and her white T-shirt was slowly turning red.

With her blood.

A prong of the hay pulley was pierced through her chest and the tip of it was protruding from her sternum in such an unnatural way that it was almost comical. It looked like something you'd see in a budget horror flick. She made a weird type of gasping sound and blood started to trickle out of her mouth and down her chin.

After that things get really blurry, like a camera on long

exposure. Only certain pieces come back to me in vivid detail.

Click.

A policeman picked me up off the floor of the loft. I could tell by the way he wouldn't look directly at me that it was bad. My hands, arms and shirt were covered in blood and I wasn't sure if it was Cara's or mine, because everything suddenly hurt.

Click.

Natalie sobbing hysterically and a group of camp counsellors trying to calm her down. When she spotted me being brought down from the loft, she became even more inconsolable. She pointed at me wild-eyed and screamed incomprehensibly.

Click.

Stanley picked up on the hysteria and bucked madly as a counsellor tried to calm him and Bella down.

Click.

Me alone in an empty white room and the sound of hurried whispers.

Click.

My mom wailing and clawing at my dad's chest while he tried to grab her arms and contain her.

Click.

White.

Chapter 32

Tears stream down my face and warm my cold cheeks. They dry into salty trails on my skin as they meet with the frigid air. Abel is watching me and although he still has his arms wrapped around me, his embrace has loosened. I can feel the weight of the unspoken words caught in his throat.

"How did she die?" his words echo through the cave and reverberate off the walls.

I bury my face in my hands and let my hair create a protective curtain around me.

"I mean, did the hay pulley fall?" he continues. I don't answer and he grabs my wrists and pulls my hands off my face, forcing me to look at him. He's staring at me intently and the fire reflects in his irises and turns them the color of lava.

I stare back at him. "What if it didn't?" I say evenly.

His pupils flicker, his mouth falls open slightly and he drops my hands.

Deep down I knew it would always end up like this. That it would culminate in this moment. That the tightly wound thread that we had bound each other together with would unravel.

I lean forward into the space that has opened up between us and softly touch my hand against the side of his cheek. He doesn't pull away and I reach for him. I've forgotten the cold and the damp and the only thing I'm conscious of is the feeling of my skin, heated like an electric charge.

He kisses me with such force and intensity that it almost knocks me over. I push him backward onto the blanket that's strewn on the ground and straddle him. We're both breathing so heavily that I barely make out the Iron Maiden ringtone coming from his cellphone inside the backpack. It must have picked up on a rogue signal. His hair is fanned beneath his head in wild tendrils that look like tree roots and the stubble on his chin resembles high grade sandpaper. The firelight flickers against his skin, casting shadows across his chest and abdominals, making them seem even more defined. He puts his hands around my hips and waits for my next move. Droplets of sweat bead off his hairline.

"I love you, Charlie," he whispers.

I commit every inch of him to memory because he is perfection.

"I love you too."

The thunder cracks outside. I lean forward as if to kiss him and instead grab a broken tip of a stalactite off the ground beside me. I raise it high above my head and bring it down forcefully, plunging it into the exact right spot to pierce his heart.

I close my eyes and my sister is right there with me. I had felt her presence all along.

Chapter 33
Now

White.

Bright white.

I'm alone in the small room, sitting cross-legged on an uncomfortable cot. I can feel the springs pressing into my thighs. Fluorescent lights buzz overhead. A cheap plastic alarm clock blinks *12:00* like it's been unplugged and not yet reset. Like an actor in a play, running through assigned motions, I reach for the family photo that should be beside the alarm clock.

My hand comes back empty.

I look around confused. Something else is missing too. The screaming.

I wait a few minutes and nothing but silence.

I get out of bed and look into a small wood framed mirror hanging on the wall. I recognize the reflection staring back at me but just barely. My usually lustrous hair hangs limp and dull and my skin is so pale it's almost translucent. My lips are chapped like I've been biting on them and my eyes looked glazed and hollow.

I'm wearing an unfamiliar fleece sweater and cheap feeling tights. I feel weak and tired. The sleeve of my sweater is rolled up and reveals a long, purple scar running up my wrist. I trace it with my fingers to gauge if it's healed. I hear the echo of footsteps clicking down the hallway. They stop outside my door and I hold my breath as the handle turns.

"Hi, you're up!" exclaims a thin, cheery, blonde woman dressed in brightly patterned scrubs. She walks past me into the room and picks up a chart at the end of my bed.

"Did you get breakfast yet or no?" She looks at me questioningly and I notice her cat-shaped indigo eyes, framed with long, curled, fake lashes. She's not as thin, and her hair lacks the usual style, but recognition washes over me like a wave.

"Becca?" I ask stunned.

She looks at me oddly and smiles tightly. "We've been through this, sweetie, I'm Kat, remember? Like the animal."

"I don't understand." I have a sinking feeling in my chest.

"Why don't I ask Dr. Naseck to check in with you? I'm sure he can answer any questions you have and maybe help you feel a bit more like yourself."

I'm confused by her answer and also by who the doctor is that she's referring to. Her casual tone seemed to imply that I'm supposed to know him. She leaves and I sit on the edge of the bed and stare at the wall, trying to will myself to wake up. This is just a nightmare, after all. It will be over soon.

I open the nightstand drawer and search for the family photo. I find a bottle of grapefruit hand lotion, a bible, and a half-used tube of my favorite red lipstick. I take off the cap and twist up the lipstick, admiring the contrast of the blood red color in the bleak white room. I shut it. I pull open a few of the dresser drawers and as I get to the last one I find the photo frame, sitting on top of a pile of clothes.

The frame is bent and the glass is cracked. The photo inside is a family photo we had taken the summer that Cara died. My mom arranged for one of her friend's cousins who was an aspiring photographer to take it. She took it all quite seriously and made us lay out and coordinate our outfits the night before. We drove out to a provincial park just outside of Sunshine to use the well-tended flower gardens as a backdrop.

My dad towers over all of us, wearing a crisp, short-sleeved, white shirt and dark slacks, his beard neatly trimmed. My mother stands to the right of him, her hands folded in front of her delicately printed floral dress. Her hair shone in the afternoon light like a flame. Magnolia stood beside my mother in a simple white dress with her head tilted slightly and her mane of hair hanging evenly over one shoulder.

Cara and I wore matching white lace dresses and stood in front of everyone. Our coal black hair was the exact same length and our green eyes glimmered for the camera. I have trouble remember who's who. I run my finger along the jagged little pieces of glass and notice tiny specks of blood on the photo where one of the bigger chunks is missing.

The door to my room opens and in walks a tall, dark-featured man that I instantly recognize.

I gasp. "Abel."

Chapter 34

It's Abel but it's not. The man's long dark hair is neatly cropped and styled close to his head and he's cleanly shaven. His eyes are hazel but the sectoral heterochromia, the slash of blue, is missing. He's wearing trousers with a starched button-up shirt tucked into them. I don't see any sign of a sprawling tattoo and I have a feeling I won't find it even if I were to look.

"Kat said you were feeling off today?" he questions with a warm smile.

"I'm just a bit confused, and I know this is a dream, and I'm just waiting to wake up."

He lets a moment of silence hang between us like a stratus cloud. "Charlie, we talked about this in our last session. If you can't accept your reality, it's really hard to change anything about it," he says calmly and slowly, like he's talking to a child or trying to convince a terrorist to release hostages.

"What is my reality?" I play along, studying his shoes. They look expensive like they're made of Italian leather.

"Your reality is what you make of it, but I think that establishing a few facts will help you put things in perspective." He sits down on a cheap metal chair in the corner of the room. He clears his throat, rests his elbows on his knees and looks at me. My heart flutters slightly at the memories of Abel that he's eliciting from me.

"Why are you in here, Charlie?"

"I don't know, if I did, I'm guessing we wouldn't be having this conversation."

"Okay, let's move on to another question and maybe it will refresh your memory. Do you know where you are?"

I look around the bleak room and a feeling of familiarity gnaws at me.

When I don't answer, Dr. Naseck continues, "You're at the Cedartree Center. We're a long-term residential care home for adults with mental health disorders."

"That doesn't explain why I'm here, I don't have a mental health disorder." I pace around the small room like a caged zoo animal.

"We're also an alternative to prison for youth who have committed violent crimes due to a mental health disorder."

I stop pacing and my heart thuds wildly in my chest. I'm about to say something when Magnolia appears in the hallway outside of my room and tentatively looks in.

"Oh, I'm sorry, I didn't know you were in here with her Dr. Naseck." She places one hand on the edge of the door frame as if she's unsure she wants to enter. I'm relieved that, at first glance, Magnolia is familiar and unchanged, with her trailing long hair and white form fitting sweater. She looks to Dr. Naseck and then back at me.

"Mags!" I rush over to her. "I don't know what's going on here but can you tell him this is some sort of crazy mistake?" I put my hand on her arm but she doesn't move and looks nervously again at Dr. Naseck. I withdraw my hand as if I've touched a hot element and been burned. The whole situation is ridiculous and starting to irritate me.

I push past Magnolia and stalk into the hallway, leaving her and Dr. Naseck to call after me. I run down a narrow hallway lined with pale green doors towards what looks like a common area. A radio somewhere plays Simon & Garfunkel.

As I pass by the doors, I catch glimpses and shadows of the people in the rooms. Their images blur together but details and familiarities jump out at me. A dazed, frail-looking elderly black woman; a pale, worryingly skinny teenage girl with hollow eyes. A large middle-aged man with long scraggly hair wearing a baseball cap. A middle-aged woman with high cheekbones in a velvet dressing gown.

I run past a large painting; red, white, black and grey blur together into a river of colors.

I round a corner and smash directly into someone, sending papers and a cup of coffee flying to the ground. They're bent over and temporarily confused. I scramble back to my feet and keep running but stop short when I hear my name called out in an all too familiar voice.

"Charlotte, stop."

It's Jake.

I'm so relieved to see him there that I stop and turn around and let him walk toward me. When he's close enough I wrap my arms around him and bury my face in his white coat.

"Jake, I don't know what's going on but I just want to wake up, or go home, or end whatever this is right now."

His chest is tense against my face and I feel his arms stiffen at his sides as if he's unsure how to react. I pull back to look at him and notice that he's let stubble grow in on his normally clean-shaven face. His dark blue eyes look back at me but the intimacy is gone. It takes me a second to notice the nametag pinned to his coat, *Jonas Lauer*.

"What the fuck is this?" I scream, pushing away from him. Magnolia and Dr. Naseck have caught up with me and are eyeing me warily like I'm a crazy person. Am I?

"Why am I here?" I demand, waiting for someone to answer.

"Charlie." Magnolia, takes a step toward me as if trying to coax a jumper down off of a ledge. She looks at Jake and Dr. Naseck for encouragement. I can smell her expensive French perfume and the jasmine shampoo she uses. She takes my hand in hers and looks me straight in the eye. "You're in here because you killed Cara."

The background noise disappears and I hear lyrics to *The Sounds of Silence*, echoing down the hallway.

Everything is suddenly hazy and out of focus like I'm looking through a tall glass.

Click.

I'm in the hayloft with Cara and she pushes me, but instead of getting up and going back toward her, I walk away from her, to the other end of the loft.

Click.

My hands are steady as they unwind the fraying old rope that's suspending the hay pulley in the air behind her.

Click.

It's too late before she realizes what's happening and

her mouth forms into a perfect "o". Her eyes fill with surprise and then shock as the pointed tips of the hay pulley prongs make their way toward her.

Click.

I close my eyes and let the darkness consume me, unsure whether I'm falling asleep or finally waking up.

About the Author

Jenna Boholij grew up in a small town in North-Western Ontario, on the shores of Lake Superior, and spent her summers in a small town in rural Manitoba, on the shores of Lake Winnipeg. She currently lives in Winnipeg, Manitoba. She is a published writer with more than a decade of experience in marketing and communications. She is of Ukrainian and Icelandic descent and very involved with the Icelandic-Canadian community. Her debut novel, a psychological thriller, *Lucid*, is published with Dreamsphere Books.

Instagram: @jbird_photos

Acknowledgements

As a writer it's an incredible and humbling process to see your work published. Thank you to everyone that supported me and was part of this process.

Thanks to my parents Nick and Debbie Boholij, for emphasizing the importance of reading and writing and encouraging me to keep at both. I hope to do the same for my kids, Lóa and Árni. To my husband Dave for tolerating the many late nights I stayed up writing and all my animal friends that sat with me while I did.

To my friends and family that encouraged me, my brother Brett, in-laws Mark and Linda Little, and my Hype Girls, Ashton Dewar, Mackenzie Dewar, and Laura Wittig.

Thank you to Amy Kroeker, Cheylynn Plese, and Hilary Lisi, my early readers who suffered through my first draft PDF and made me believe that Lucid was worth sharing. I'm grateful to Norma Bailey, Lorna Tergesen, and my pen-pal and fellow author, Bob Lower, for all their help and advice along the way.

Thank you to the amazing team at Dreamsphere Books for making this possible, Margaret Larson, Ave Basilio, Sanford Larson, Cali Kitsu, John Robin, and especially my publisher Craig Gibb for his patience and expertise.

The town of Sunshine is inspired by my favorite small town on the shores of Lake Winnipeg, where I was fortunate to spend my summers growing up. The characters in the book are fictional but Stanley the horse is real, and I still think of him fondly.

The book is dedicated to my Afi, J.T. (Joey) Arnason, maybe the first great writer in the family, who inspired me to keep writing.

More From Dreamsphere Books

Gearteeth
Timothy Black

On the brink of humanity's extinction, Nikola Tesla and a mysterious order of scientists known as the Tellurians revealed a bold plan to save a world ravaged by a disease that turned sane men into ravenous werewolves: the uninfected would abandon the Earth's surface by rising up in floating salvation cities, iron and steel metropolises that carried tens of thousands of refugees above the savage apocalypse.

Twenty years later, only one salvation city remains aloft, while the beasts still rule the world below. Time has taken its toll on the miraculous machinery of the city, and soon the last of the survivors will plummet to their doom. But when Elijah Kelly, a brakeman aboard the largest of the city's Thunder Trains, is infected by the werewolf virus, he discovers a secret world of lies and horrific experiments that hide the disturbing truth about the Tellurians.

When the beast in his blood surges forth, Elijah must choose between the lives of those he loves, and the city that is humanity's last hope of survival.

Available in paperback and ebook

More From Dreamsphere Books

The Crossing at Farrenhall
Andrew Wood

Haegar Ruthborne is a Vruskman of the Winterwood, fiercely proud of the forest that has provided his family with shelter and sustenance for generations.

But evil has awoken in its dark heart and a malevolent force is animating corpses with murderous intent. Forced to accept an unspeakable reality, Haegar reluctantly abandons his home. With his family and a small band of villagers, he heads westward to seek protection from the Old King.

Their road leads to the turbulent Tagalfr, the River of Rushing Ice. The only way across is the Gated Bridge of Farrenhall, but its Lord, Kalivaz Varkoth, has sealed the gates and set the Myrmidons, a cadre of elite zealot-warriors, to guard them.

Kasara, daughter of the Lord of the Bridge, is stunned and ashamed by her father's abandonment of his people. She vows to save them, no matter the cost.

With their escape route blocked, Haegar and the other Vruskmen are at the mercy of a menacing army of undead men and beasts. As night inexorably approaches, Kasara and Haegar make increasingly desperate plans.

In a battle where death is not the end but a horrific beginning, they must cross the River of Rushing Ice or become forever enslaved by the darkness haunting the Winterwood.

Available in paperback and ebook

Manufactured by Amazon.ca
Acheson, AB